RHODIUM

Elise Noble

Published by Undercover Publishing Limited

ISBN: 978-1-910954-75-1

Edited by Amanda Ann Larson, Dream Raven Editing and Nikki Mentges, NAM Editorial

Cover art by Abigail Sins

www.undercover-publishing.com

www.elise-noble.com

Never trust a shiny surface.
They hide a multitude of flaws.

Chapter 1

DEGRADED. MORTIFIED. EMBARRASSED. That was how I felt as I slammed the door of Rhodes, Holden and Maxwell and stepped out onto the busy street. All around me, life carried on as usual. Businessmen walked past on their way home, couples strolled towards nearby restaurants in search of dinner, and joggers dodged puddles in their quest for fitness. Normal activities on a normal day at the beginning of September.

For me, life would never be normal again. And now, to cap it all, I'd been utterly humiliated by Oliver Rhodes. I'd never felt so ashamed in my life, and considering I used to sleep with men for money, that was an achievement. The man was a massive cock.

In every way.

I reached the bus stop and sank onto one of the cold metal seats with a low groan. Oliver Rhodes, the man who took the worst night of my life and turned it into the best. I still clenched my thighs together every time I thought about it.

Except now I clenched my fists. Oliver was an asshole. An arrogant, rude, condescending asshole, who wore made-to-measure suits and a Patek Philippe watch that cost more than my parents' first home, and whose smooth hands I hadn't just spent the past hour glancing at as he twirled a Montblanc fountain pen around his fingers.

Dammit, Stef! Don't think about the hands. The trouble was, I knew what they were capable of. How they could make a woman come so hard she forgot her own name.

No. NO! I shook my head to clear my wayward thoughts. Oliver Rhodes was bad news from the ends of his dark-grey hair to the toes of his Italian leather wingtips.

And where was the damn bus?

Probably I should start at the beginning. What bizarre twist of fate led me to be sitting here at a shabby bus stop in downtown Richmond, wishing I had the courage to jump off a bridge or hurl myself under a passing semi? Well, it started with my ex-roommate, Christina; a faux-fur jacket; and a man old enough to be my grandfather...

"It can't be the fifth. The fifth is tomorrow."

Chrissie rummaged through her purse, tossing aside lipstick, tissues, condoms, and mascara as she dug deeper and deeper.

"Are you looking for your phone?"

"Yes."

"It's here."

I picked it up off her nightstand and passed it over, then took another sip of my strawberry milkshake. I preferred chocolate, but it was important to stay healthy.

Chrissie scrolled through her calendar then flopped

back on the bed with a huff. "Shit. It *is* the fifth. I could have sworn it was only the fourth."

"Why does it matter?"

"Because my mom's flying in for a layover on the fifth, and I have a date tonight." She used her fingers to form air quotes around the word "date."

"Oh. One of *those* dates?"

Chrissie was a girl who'd tried every job going. She got fired from her waitressing job because she kept dropping things. Mild dyslexia meant her two weeks as a filing assistant were a disaster, and she walked away from a stint as a receptionist after her boss propositioned her. Now she'd decided to give something new a go.

"Hey, don't knock it till you've tried it."

I suppressed a shudder. "Doesn't it creep you out? Having to do...*things* with men like that?"

Her tinkling laugh exploded. "Stef, don't be such a prude! It's perfectly normal nowadays, and I don't sleep with all of them. Some just want a nice girl on their arm to avoid unwanted attention. Last week, a client gave me an obscenely expensive dress and took me to a charity gala, and all I got at the end of the evening was a wad of cash and a kiss on the cheek..." She grinned as she glanced over at the turquoise box on her dressing table. "And that bought me a necklace from Tiffany's."

Expensive jewellery was something I only dreamed about. Right now, I couldn't even afford the textbooks I needed. Or my half of this month's rent. My credit card was maxed out, and every time I got a collection letter, I shed a tear and buried it in the pile with all the others. I tried to laugh.

"At least Julio gives me as much coffee as I can drink."

"You can't wear coffee."

Couldn't you? Julio, my persnickety boss at The Daily Grind, the coffee place I worked at after class on Mondays, Tuesdays, and Fridays, would disagree. Most of the time we got on well, but some days, like today, I wanted to smack my head on the counter. Or better still, *his* head. He'd insisted I dress up as a giant coffee bean and hand out coupons on the street, and I'd nearly frozen to death. He could have at least warned me so I wore appropriate shoes.

"I need a new job."

I also needed to stop chewing my hair. I pulled the ends out of my mouth and chided myself. It was a habit I wished I could break.

"Meanwhile, I need to work out what to do with Sanderson Everett."

"Sanderson Everett? You mean *the* Sanderson Everett? The guy who franchised himself across America?"

I'd done a case study on him last month for my business degree—he'd spot an opening in the market and set up chains ranging from phone stores to pet-grooming parlours to burger restaurants, making a fortune in the process. Every biography said he was married to his job.

"If that's the same Sanderson Everett who likes me to strip down to my underwear and serve him dinner every couple of weeks, then yes. All the girls love him. Easy money." She rubbed her thumb and fingers together. "He's got a massive house, but I'm not sure the rest of him measures up."

I nearly choked, and strawberry milk dribbled down my chin. “I can’t believe that. The man’s a genius, and he hires escorts from Rubies?”

Chrissie had started plying her trade through Rubies are a Man’s Best Friend a few months back. Clients booked via the website, and the owner forwarded the details on to her. She went out most nights now. Each girl got rated from one to five rubies, and as they gathered those gems, their pay grade went up accordingly. Chrissie had reached level three and had that fourth ruby firmly in her sight.

Now she carefully outlined her lips in a deep red. “Guess he can afford it. I mean, who needs a normal maid when you can have one with double D cups and a thong?”

“Well, you’re lucky to meet him. He doesn’t even give interviews anymore.”

She turned to me with a worrying look in her eyes—the wicked gleam she got when she had a great idea she knew I wouldn’t like. “If you want to meet him so much, why don’t you go tonight instead of me? Then I could see my mom.”

“Oh, no. No way.”

“Why not? You said you were short of money.”

“I am, but there’s no way I could sleep with a stranger. Or even Sanderson Everett.”

Or, in fact, anyone. A quick fumble in the back of a car with the guy I dated in high school was as far as I’d got. Since I arrived in Richmond, I’d put all my efforts into work and college because I didn’t want to graduate with a millstone of debt around my neck.

Chrissie burst out laughing. “The guy’s a hundred years old. I bet he can’t even get it up anymore. He hires a girl nearly every night, and not one of us has ever had sex with him."

"Really?"

"Really. And he pays three hundred dollars. Still cheaper than a wife, he told my boss."

Three hundred dollars was an awful lot of cups of coffee. "And all you do is serve him dinner?"

"Serve him dinner then stand by the table while he eats. And afterwards, we bring dessert and coffee." She gave me a full-on smile. "You're good at coffee."

"I can't. I mean, not in my underwear."

"Oh, come on. You're miles prettier than me, and it's no worse than wearing a bikini on the beach."

I considered it. My last vacation had been three years ago when I was eighteen. Mom and Chester, my stepfather, treated me to a week in Florida, a final goodbye before I went off to college. I remembered walking around the marina, thinking how much fun those girls sunning themselves on the big yachts must have. No work, no studying, just days of relaxing in the warm weather. And most probably sleeping with the owners. I'd be kidding myself if I thought they were there with anything else in mind. But still...

"I don't know... Isn't he expecting you?"

"It won't be a problem to sub in. He likes variety. Just tell him I'm not feeling well. Please? I'll clean the whole apartment this weekend."

Three hundred dollars, a clean apartment, and the chance to meet one of my business idols?

"And you're absolutely sure he won't want sex?" I whispered the last word. The very idea of it scared me.

"No, he definitely won't. I promise."

"You'll need to tell me what to wear."

"Easy. Oh, and you'll need a name."

"A name? I have a name."

"Stefanie's hardly worthy of a Ruby."

"Gee, thanks."

"Don't look at me like that. It's nothing personal. Hey, I call myself Crystal."

"So what do you suggest?"

She gave me her lopsided little smile, the one that made every man within a ten-block radius go nuts over her, and then her gaze drifted past me to the faux-fur coat hanging on the back of her door.

"Sable. We'll call you Sable."

And that was how I ended up parading around a mansion in black lace panties, carrying a roast dinner on a plain white china plate. I lost a little bit of respect for myself that night, and a lot for Sanderson Everett. It was hard to admire a man when he ordered you to "sit" and "stay" like a dog. Thankfully he didn't try "come," because at that point I had no idea how to. No, it took Oliver fucking Rhodes to teach me that trick.

But three hundred dollars was three hundred dollars, and how much worse was it than the coffee outfit? At least I was making a fool out of myself in private, and I didn't have to invite Sanderson Everett to "come and grind with me."

"So, how did it go?" Chrissie asked the next morning.

"I served up veal piccata. Everett read the business pages. Then he ate half a custard tart and asked me to close the drapes, tucked a hundred-dollar bill in the side of my panties, patted my bottom, pointed at the door, and said, 'Go.'"

"Wow, he must have really liked you. He only gives me fifty." She glanced at her watch and took another bite of toast. "Shit, I'm running late."

"You don't think that's utterly crazy?"

"Yeah, it is, but it's also normal. Last week, an octogenarian asked Maggie to dress up like a horse, and get this, the tail came on a butt plug."

I spat my orange juice across the table. "Are you serious?"

She looked down at the sticky mess and made a face. "Yeuch. Yeah, totally. But you should consider signing up. I mean, where else can you earn that much cash in a night?"

"Are you insane? You just told me a story about a butt plug."

She waved a hand dismissively. "Oh, don't worry about that. Maggie's got five rubies. She'll do anything. A-ny-thing. If you start off at one ruby, that's, like, holding hands. And sometimes you get taken out to really nice places."

"It's not for me."

"Think about it."

I did think about it. When I got up at six to catch the bus to The Daily Grind, I thought about Chrissie still asleep in bed. When a businessman snapped at me because I'd forgotten his shot of caramel syrup, I realised he was even ruder than Sanderson Everett. When I put on the damn coffee-bean costume once more, I recalled that although I'd been in my underwear at Everett's house, his heating system had made it the perfect temperature. And when I counted my cash and found I was a hundred and thirty dollars short on the rent—again—I began to wonder if being a Ruby mightn't be so bad after all.

Chapter 2

MY FIRST OFFICIAL date as a lowly one-ruby saw me accompany a businessman to a charity gala. You'll notice I called it a date? Well, that's because I didn't want to admit the truth—that I'd become a man's plaything and got paid three hundred dollars for the privilege.

Not much of that first paycheck went on the rent, though. When Chrissie saw what I'd put on to go out—a knee-length black number left over from a failed real date—she dragged me into her room and sat me on the bed.

Hands on hips, she stared down at me. "Stefanie Amor, I swear you've got more looks than sense."

"What are you talking about?"

"Have you even glanced in the mirror?"

At least twice. "Of course I have."

"Then why on earth are you dressed as if you're going for a job interview? The Benford Association's gala will be full of leggy models in slinky dresses. You can't go like that."

"I don't have a slinky dress."

She turned and threw open her closet doors. "It's a good thing I've been at this longer than you, isn't it?"

Not only did she fasten me into a bright-red halterneck, but she also insisted on redoing my make-up vamp-style and pinning my hair into an elegant updo. By then, I'd missed the bus and needed to leap into a cab to meet my client outside his office at the appointed hour. That was twenty dollars gone.

The rest of that evening's earnings went to lipstick, mascara, a handful of outfits, and a torture session, otherwise known as leg waxing. Chrissie came with me, and we had a small difference of opinion over some of my purchases.

"You've got no underwear," she pointed out.

"I don't need any new stuff."

"Oh, please. Everything you own is white cotton. You look like a Catholic schoolgirl."

"What does it matter? I'll be the only one seeing it."

"You'll never earn the big bucks thinking that way."

"Fine by me."

Small bucks suited me just fine. I took a couple of bookings a week, and that allowed me to quit The Daily Grind and knuckle down to my studies. My grades crept up slowly but surely since I had more free time to dedicate to my assignments.

Every couple of weeks, I'd have a crisis of confidence, usually before a date with a new client or if I happened to glimpse someone I knew while I was out working—more than once I'd seen a fellow student waiting tables in one of the high-end establishments we visited. But the job itself wasn't as bad as I feared it would be. Occasionally, I got a man who thought he could help himself to more than he'd paid for, but a few hints from Chrissie on how to say no plus the canister of pepper spray I'd taken to carrying in my purse gave me the confidence to deal with them.

Octavia, the owner of Rubies, wasn't at all what I'd

imagined. A dark-haired lady who dressed like a star from old movies, she acted as a bizarre cross between a pimp and a mom, checking up on us personally to ensure we were happy and also that we looked tidy. She took pride in her services. One weekend when she was in Richmond, we met up for coffee—her, me, and Chrissie.

Of all the things I'd expected to be doing that Saturday, it was safe to say having a conversation about breast implants and kink in the local branch of Starbucks didn't make the list. At least we weren't at The Daily Grind. My old boss would have had a field day eavesdropping on that one.

As we moved on to our second cups, it dawned on me this wasn't so much a check-up as a sales visit, although Chrissie didn't need much persuading. For weeks, she'd been talking about getting her fourth ruby, and when Octavia finished describing the extra services she'd have to offer, she nodded enthusiastically.

"Count me in. As long as they're not allowed to leave a mark on me, I'll do it."

All the talk of spanking made me cringe. Hands, rulers, paddles. Who would want to do that?

Then Octavia turned to me. "So, Stefanie. Have you thought about moving up to two rubies?"

I swallowed a chunk of chocolate muffin, and it went down the wrong way. Chrissie thumped me on the back as I took a gulp of coffee to ease the tickle.

"That's when the sex starts, isn't it?" I whispered.

"Yes and no." Octavia sounded so matter of fact, as if we were discussing a sandwich menu. "Straight sex or minor fetishes."

I dreaded even thinking about it, but at the same

time, I felt compelled to ask. “Minor fetishes?”

“Some men like the girls to dress up or speak to them in a certain way. There’s no sex involved, but due to the unusual nature of some of the requests, the money’s better.”

“Like what?”

Over a low-fat lemon slice, she described the proclivities of the men who could afford to indulge themselves. The banker who liked girls to walk all over him in high heels. The elderly gent who got his kicks from having a life-sized teddy bear watch TV with him every Saturday night. Apparently, he whacked off by himself, no contact necessary. Then there was the millionaire who enjoyed dressing girls up like Barbie and having them ride around his house in a tiny electric car.

“And they pay for this? Why?”

“Yes, they do. Because we offer complete confidentiality. Many of these men have wives and families who wouldn’t take too kindly to their extracurricular activities.”

“Go on, give it a try,” Chrissie said.

“We’re actually a bit short of two-ruby girls at the moment. They either move up to three or leave when they graduate.”

The teddy bear couldn’t be worse than the coffee bean, could it? “Okay, I’ll try it. No sex, though.”

So how did I go from feeding fruit to old men while wearing a bunny outfit to Oliver Rhodes? Desperation. And some really awful luck. They say disasters happen in threes. Well, Oliver was my fourth.

Chapter 3

IT WAS A Wednesday afternoon when my world fell out from under me. Quite literally. Disaster number one.

The rain fell faster than the stock market on Black Monday as I ran out of college, already late for my date with a man who liked me to wear an adult-sized onesie covered with teddy bears. And I'd forgotten my umbrella. Typical. I paused in the doorway before muttering to the heavens, "Anything else want to go wrong?"

Yes. Yes, it did.

I slipped on a candy wrapper and tumbled to the bottom of the steps. I knew I'd done major damage the instant I landed—the *crack* from my arm was a dead giveaway, as was the bolt of pain that burned all the way to my shoulder.

Do you know how much it costs to pin a broken arm? I didn't then, but I do now. Thousands. Thousands I didn't have, not least because I needed to take six weeks off from Rubies while it healed. Not many men had fetishes for being stroked with a cast. Believe me, when the rent came due, I checked with Octavia.

Then my little brother phoned. I called him little, and I called him my brother, but in reality, he was sixteen, my stepbrother, and at five feet nine, three inches taller than me. Mom married his father when I was ten, a year after my daddy died. At first, the speed with which she moved on upset me, and for a couple of years, our relationship stumbled as I came to terms with it. But now I saw what I couldn't back then, and what she would never admit. She needed a man to complete her. Alone, she'd been a shell, a half-woman. The big wide world and Maxine Amor did not mix. And I swore I'd never become her.

Ten-year-old me forgave her perhaps faster than I would have, because with Chester, her new husband, came my new brother. All too often Mason used to steal my candy and borrow my dolls to become victims of his action men, but he was so damn cute while he did it I forgave him every time.

And now he had a problem. I'll call it disaster one point five because, in the grand scheme of things, it didn't warrant a whole number of its own, not when compared to the rest of my life.

"Stef, I had an accident."

"What happened? Are you okay?"

"I'm fine, but Pop's new truck's got a bit of a dent."

"Bit of a dent?"

"It needs a new fender."

I couldn't keep my groan in. "What did you hit?"

"The gatepost at Reggie's place."

"Oh, Mason! What were you doing there? Reggie's always getting into trouble, and he'll take you with him."

"Just hanging out. But Pop's gonna kill me for the truck. He told me not to drive it."

"You should have listened."

"I know, I know. But you gotta help me. If I don't get rid of this dent before him and Mom come back from vacation, I can kiss my trip with the band goodbye."

Mason played the tuba, and he'd been invited over to England to play in a parade along with the other students in his school's marching band. He'd talked about little else for months, and knowing Chester, who was big on discipline, Mason's fear of being grounded was justified.

Shit. I cursed silently in my head because Mason and his potty mouth didn't need any more encouragement. "They're due back next Tuesday?"

"Yeah. Joey's dad can fix it at the shop, but it'll cost six hundred dollars. Can you lend it to me? I'll pay you back, I swear."

He wouldn't. He never did. And six hundred dollars was my emergency fund. But Mason was Mason, and when I used to sneak out at night to see my boyfriend back in high school, he'd covered for me every time. I owed him one.

"I'll wire it over. Just promise me you won't drive the truck again."

"Cross my heart."

The combined total of disasters one and one point five, plus the bill that landed for my tuition, led me to the most shameful night of my life, at least pre-Oliver Rhodes. The night Octavia, who may have been lovely but would always be a businesswoman first and foremost, auctioned off my virginity. It was the only thing I had left of any value.

As the bids rolled in, each one from a man with more money than morals, I thought time and time again about giving up and going home. Mom would have welcomed me back, but I knew if I did return to Hartscross, I'd be stuck there. Stuck with the I-told-you-sos and the whispers of "poor girl, she never was cut out for the city."

Chrissie did her best to help by preparing me for what was to come. Luckily, she had no inhibitions when it came to talking about sex–in fact, it was her favourite topic of conversation.

"Will it hurt?" I whispered one night over a glass of wine.

"Maybe a little. A sharp pain, but it'll be over quickly."

I closed my eyes and took another slug of wine. I felt ill at the thought of it, but how else could I pay off the bills? So many times I nearly pulled out of the deal, quit college, and ran back home, but the prospect of my stepfather's disappointment stopped me. He was the one who'd convinced Mom I could do this, and if I returned to Georgia with my tail between my legs, he'd lose face as well as me.

No, I needed to go through with it.

And, to be honest, it could have been worse. The auction winner, a wealthy businessman, prided himself on the number of V-cards he'd collected. If his brags over dinner were to be believed, he'd moved into triple figures. So I lay there, half-drunk, while he lubed me up and eased himself into me. Chrissie assured me sex could be pleasurable, but I just felt dirty, and not in a good way. I counted the seconds as he pounded away, trying not to wince at the scratch of his beard against my chin and, worse, the burning ache between my legs.

But he paid, and he paid well. Half of my medical

bills were gone in just one night. And after him, the floodgates were opened. Only metaphorically, of course. Getting wet for a man wasn't something I'd ever experienced. A month later, after some tuition from Chrissie involving a large black dildo that scared the crap out of me, I learned how to use my hands and mouth and moved up to the lofty position of three rubies.

I hated myself, but I survived. Mason sent me a calendar every Christmas, and I used it to count down the days until I could escape the lifestyle I'd fallen into, graduate, and get a job that didn't involve spreading my legs for any man who cared to pay my hourly rate.

One hundred and sixty-nine days. That was how many I'd had left when disaster number two happened. And as disasters go, it would take some beating.

Chapter 4

LOUD HAMMERING ON the apartment door woke me up, and I groaned. My phone informed me it was almost lunchtime, but it was Saturday, and I'd been out working until three in the morning. I needed a sleep-in. Hell, after the night I'd had, I *deserved* a sleep-in.

My client, a British fashion model who had two loves in life—money and himself—had decided on a little food-play. He'd covered me in honey, which wouldn't have been so bad in itself had he not then attempted to stick a banana into the back door. Judging by the whipped cream on the nightstand, I think he was trying to create some weird version of banoffee pie.

I'd practically stuck to the sheets as I attempted to roll off the bed.

"Get the hell away from there!"

"Oh, come on. Ease up on the attitude."

"No way. I don't do that stuff."

"I'll pay you extra."

And that was them. The four words that made me feel worse than any others. Every so often, I'd go on a date with a client who made me feel worth something, one who took me for dinner, had an actual conversation, and, when he fucked me at the end of the evening, almost made me forget his pickup line consisted of a sixteen-digit credit card number. But those were few and far between. Most men made me feel like trash.

"It's not about the money."

"With your type of girl, it's always about the money."

He lay there laughing as I pulled on my dress—easier said than done, as it kept sticking to my skin. Then I'd had to ride the bus home smelling like a beehive, with freaks and weirdos buzzing around me like they thought they could get a freebie.

So, screw the door. They could come back later or hope Chrissie answered it. It was probably for her, anyway. In my whole time in Richmond, my only visitors had been debt collectors, and I'd kept them away for over a year now.

"Go away," I mumbled into my pillow.

The knocking stopped, but ten minutes later, the visitor came back. "It's the police. Open up, please. Your neighbour said you were home."

The police? Oh, hell. Octavia had warned us about the risk of arrest for what we did, but she always made the chances sound so slim. The maximum punishment for prostitution in the state of Virginia was a year in jail or a twenty-five-hundred-dollar fine, but for a first offence, she assured us we'd only get a slap on the wrist. Chrissie swore she could spot an undercover cop a mile away, and all my recent clients apart from the model had been repeats. We always tried so hard to be careful. Had we been caught?

I tied my bathrobe around myself and pushed my hair back out of my eyes. Time to face the music.

"Hello?"

"Is this the residence of Christina Walker?"

"Yes?"

I willed myself to breathe slowly. So this wasn't about me. *Just keep calm.*

"Detectives Briggs and McConnell. Can we come in?"

I took the chain off the door and swung it open. Both cops looked tired with dark circles under their eyes. The fatter of the two—I didn't know whether it was Briggs or McConnell—had a rumpled look about him, as if he'd slept in his cheap suit.

"What's your name, ma'am?"

He'd called me "ma'am." That had to be a good sign, didn't it? If he was here to arrest me, he'd just have brought out the handcuffs.

"Stefanie Amor."

"And you're Ms. Walker's roommate?"

"That's right. Do you want to speak to her?"

They glanced at each other. What did that mean?

"She's here?" the skinny one asked.

"Well, I guess she's in her room."

I hadn't seen her for a couple of days, but that wasn't unusual. Our class schedules meant we often passed like ships in the dark. But she rarely stayed out, not unless someone paid her for the entire night, and most of our clients were too cheap for that.

"Could you check?"

"Sure."

I knocked gently, then a bit harder when she didn't answer. Still nothing. I cracked the door open and peered inside.

"Oh. She's not here."

"When did you last see her?"

I thought back. "Thursday evening. She was getting

ready to go out."

Another look passed between them.

"Are you close?" the thin one asked.

"Reasonably. We've been roommates for almost two years."

"Ma'am, I'm sorry to be the one to tell you this, but we have reason to believe Ms. Walker passed away."

It took a few seconds for me to process his words. Chrissie, dead? No way. There had to be a mistake. She was twenty-two, the same age as me. She had her whole damn life to live.

"Ma'am? Would you like to sit down?"

He didn't wait for my answer, just lowered me to the sofa as my legs gave way from under me.

Chrissie was dead.

My best friend was dead.

Disaster number two, and the path to my collision with Oliver Rhodes was set.

Chapter 5

IF I'D HAD half a brain, I would have left town after disaster number two, Chrissie's death. But common sense had deserted me when I got my first ruby.

No, it took disaster number four—an encounter with Mr. Rhodes himself—to send me running. After that, I gave up on the idea of the city, of making something of myself, and slunk back to Georgia to lick my wounds. And grieve.

Not only for Chrissie but for the victim of disaster number three. Another friend, dead. I'd always dreamed of meeting a man who loved me for who I was, in spite of what I'd been, and number three did. Lyle knew my history, and he still cared. It showed in the manner he spoke to me, the way he walked me back to my room at night in the temporary accommodation we both shared. The nervous smile that flickered when he asked me out on a date. A date we'd never got to go on.

What happened? Well, that's a whole other story.

Perhaps Lyle wasn't everyone's idea of a catch, but I'd have been proud to take him home to meet Mom and Chester. Even better, he wasn't a Rubies client. He'd had a heart, and he'd had a career. A lawyer, no less. Not the greatest one in the world, even he admitted that, but he was improving. A tadpole. One day he'd have become a frog, and who knows, maybe even a prince?

Not like Oliver Rhodes. Oliver Rhodes was a great white fucking shark.

But now I was done. Done with murder investigations. Done with Oliver. Done with Richmond. Done with all the disasters. Done with the big city and college and the illusion I could make something of myself.

Welcome to Hartscross, Georgia. Population: 1,523.

"Pippi, breakfast's ready."

That damn nickname. From ages six through eight, I'd been obsessed with Pippi Longstocking, refusing to wear my hair in any style but pigtails or answer to anything but a fictional name. Every birthday, I'd begged my parents for a horse and a monkey, or even a ship. Money never ran to the horse or the ship, and the closest I got to the monkey was a stuffed toy. When I arrived back in Hartscross, it was still sitting on the shelf in my bedroom, exactly where it had been for the last thirteen years.

And the nickname stayed too, if only in my mother's mind.

"Just coming," I called out.

I rolled out of bed and trailed down the hallway. Back in Richmond, I'd had the luxury of an en suite, but now I faced the daily struggle of finding a bathroom slot. For a teenage boy, Mason sure spent a lot of time in there.

"Will you hurry up?" I banged on the door, desperate to pee.

"Almost done."

Ten minutes later, I was crossing my legs as the

door swung open.

"What do you do in there?" I asked.

Mason's hair was half an inch long, he didn't shave his legs, and as far as I could work out, his tan was natural.

He shrugged and flashed his teeth. "Flossing's important."

I shoved past him and locked myself in before doing my business then attempting to wash my hair in the old claw-foot tub. It didn't have a proper shower, only one of those handheld attachments, and my hair was so thick it took forever to get the shampoo out. When I finally walked into the kitchen, Mom's pancakes were cold and so was her demeanour.

"Pippi, you need to start waking up earlier. Half of the day's gone by the time you get downstairs."

I'd always been a night owl while Mom got up with the larks, but it wasn't worth the argument. "I'll try."

"And if you're staying in town, you'll need to look for a job."

"I know."

Mainly because she'd said the exact same thing every morning for the last two weeks.

"I spoke to Mrs. Mackey at the store. She thinks Darly might have an opening for a shampoo girl at the salon while Patty has her baby. Think of that, Pippi—you'd get free haircuts."

"Okay, I'll think about it."

Mom bustled around the kitchen, reheating my pancakes and fetching a jug of maple syrup.

"Don't leave it too long. Jobs are hard to come by in this town."

Yeah, I knew that. Once a girl graduated from high

school, she had two options in Hartscross—work a dead-end job for minimum wage or start popping out babies. Neither appealed, not to mention the slight logistical challenge of the second option for a single girl.

Of course, that didn't deter my mom.

"And you'll need to keep your eyes open for a nice boy. How about Sheriff Bose's son? His girlfriend ran off to the city the way you did, and Randy's quite the catch."

She managed to make leaving for the city sound like a disease, something to be cured before the symptoms could take full effect. And since I went to high school with Randy Bose, I knew he was a nasty piece of work. Not a day had passed without him pulling a prank that crossed the boundary from funny to cruel.

"He's not my type."

"But, Pippi, you've never dated, so how would you know? Randy's got lovely manners."

That was Mom all over. She meant well, but her execution made me want to thunk my head on the table. The easiest thing to do in these situations was to change the subject and hope she forgot.

"These pancakes are delicious. Is it a new recipe?"

"Funny you should say that. Marnie at the diner was watching one of those cooking shows, and..."

Mom was off. I blocked out her chatter as best I could and concentrated on forking in my food. Only one question plagued my mind: what should I do now?

Chapter 6

"DO YOU USUALLY shampoo your hair once or twice?"

I'd run out of excuses and willpower, and Mom had taken it upon herself to speak to Darly. Monday to Friday, ten until four, I was the new shampoo girl. Of course, I didn't only shampoo. I got to sweep up hair clippings, take bookings, and make the coffee as well. And gossip. I'd forgotten how much small-town ladies liked to gossip.

"Just the once, honey. But did ya hear about Bobby down at the feed store? He got seen in Hartfield last week with a girl who didn't have his ring on her finger."

Oh, the scandal. Three years ago, I'd have been as interested as every other visitor to the shampoo chair, but I'd seen more of life now, the bad and the good. Mostly bad, being honest, and that meant Bobby cheating on his girl no longer held the fascination it once might have.

But for the folks of Hartscross, set in their ways and loyal to home, the next town over, Hartfield, was a world away.

"No, I didn't hear."

"He took her to a restaurant. No shame. None at all. And foolin' around while poor Betsy sat at home with their baby. Some men have no appreciation of a good woman."

Now that she'd got started, she happily rambled on about people I knew vaguely and cared about even less. What were they saying about me behind my back? *Poor little Stefanie, she tried to make it in the big city and couldn't cope*? Around here, people were sweet to your face then sour behind your back.

When I returned to Hartscross, I'd told Mom I felt homesick, and since she'd never understood why I wanted to leave in the first place, she'd taken it at face value. Chester knew something was up, though. Two days after I got home, he'd called me into the parlour while Mom baked cakes. The room always did have an air of loneliness. Mom insisted on having a formal room for the visitors she rarely got, and the family lived and ate in the kitchen with its old pine table and benches and squashy sofas, the air kept warm and fragrant by her constant cooking.

"Couldn't help noticing you came back here a bit sudden, Stef." His rich southern drawl sounded relaxed, but there was no mistaking the seriousness of his words.

I'd tried damn hard to lose my own accent while I was away, but every so often it popped out. Even though Virginia wasn't exactly northern, they still talked mighty different up there.

"I got homesick. Who wouldn't miss Mom's cooking?"

He shook his head and dropped onto the uncomfortable sofa. Blue-and-white flowers covered the fabric, clashing with the drapes, the carpet, and everything else in the room.

"She might believe that, but a girl doesn't turn her

back on her home of three years then come crawling back to Hartscross because she misses her mom's sweet potato pie."

I couldn't look at him. Instead, I headed for the window and stared out across the dusty yard. "I had a couple of problems."

"What kind of problems? Man problems? Money problems? Trouble at school?"

Try all of the above. "Man problems." Everything could be traced back to a man in one way or another.

"Do I need to do anything about him?"

Aw, Chester. I missed my real daddy, but in the years since he passed, Chester had made a reasonable replacement.

"No, it's over. I just want to forget what happened, heal up, and carry on."

He stood, walked over, and squeezed my shoulder. "Well, if that changes, you let me know."

"It's over," I repeated. "It's over."

"Pippi!" Mom yelled up the stairs. I'd gotten used to hearing her every morning, only today she broke from the norm. "You've got mail."

Great. That meant a credit card bill or a grumpy letter from the bank. They were the only two places I'd notified of my new address. And during my last few months in Richmond, I'd had to pay Chrissie's share of the rent as well as my own, even for the weeks I wasn't living there. My credit card hated me.

"Be down in a minute."

"It looks important."

Mom thought everything printed looked important. But today she was right. As soon as I flipped over the heavyweight cream envelope, I bit back a curse, because embossed on the back were the words "Rhodes, Holden and Maxwell."

What the hell did *he* want?

Mom looked at me expectantly, her lacquered hair unmoving as she tilted her head to one side.

"It's nothing. Just an old friend from Richmond. Probably catching me up on the news." I stuffed the envelope into my pocket, nauseated at the thought of calling Oliver Rhodes a friend. "I'll open it after breakfast. Did you make pancakes again?"

She took hold of my arm and led me to the kitchen. "Always do, Pippi. They're your favourite."

The letter burned away in my pocket through every mouthful, but I forced half of my food down, even though I'd lost my appetite.

"Not feeling so good?" Mom asked, gesturing at my leftovers. "I don't want you wasting away."

"I just have a bit of a headache. Best I rest for a minute before work."

I headed for the stairs, slowly at first, then took the steps two at a time once I got out of sight, tearing at the envelope as I went. How dare he write to me here? This was supposed to be my safe place.

I slammed the door of my room, then muttered a silent apology to no one in particular for the noise, spread the letter out on my desk, and began to read. The page was typewritten and informed me that the commonwealth attorney's office requested my presence as a prosecution witness. They'd helpfully put a number at the bottom for me to call and arrange an appointment.

Witness to what? I'd only been on the periphery of the mess, the murder case involving the high-profile music producer whose bed Chrissie's body was found in. The detectives investigating the case had promised an easy win. Electronic evidence, they said. A confession on tape.

And it got worse.

Before I left Richmond, I'd watched TV and read the papers. Both were full of news about superstar defence attorney Oliver Rhodes switching sides to prosecute Chrissie's killer. He'd done interviews, smooth-talking in his smart suit with his fan club hovering in the background. Go figure. What kind of lawyer had a freaking fan club?

Therefore, going back to the letter, the request came from Oliver, and it was bullshit. Men like Oliver didn't request. They ordered, and I'd been on the receiving end of that once already.

He could go screw himself.

Days melded into one. I got up, I ate breakfast, I shampooed, I ate dinner, I slept. Life became a production line, devoid of any excitement or variety.

Until one day two weeks later when Darly scurried into the break room, eyes shining.

"Stef, there's a man here to see you," she hissed. "And he's driving a fancy truck."

My first thought was Oliver, but then I gave myself a mental kick. Oliver didn't drive a truck. Oliver drove a big-ass Mercedes to go with his big-ass ego. So who the hell was it?

The stranger hovered near the door, eyeing up the half-coiffed ladies with some trepidation.

"My name's Barrett."

He removed his cowboy hat and held out a hand for me to shake.

"Stefanie."

"I know."

Of course. Silly me.

"So who are you?" I closed the door behind me so we were both outside. No need for half of Hartscross to hear about my business. "Why are you here?"

Barrett shuffled from foot to foot. "Uh, I need to give you a message."

"What is it?"

"Well, this is a little awkward."

"Would you tell me already?"

"See, I'm supposed to give you two choices."

I got a bad feeling about this. His words and his accent were Virginia all the way. I peered closer at his jacket, and the shield embroidered on the breast with its keyhole and its halo told me exactly where he'd come from. Blackwood Security.

"And what choices are they?"

"You can come back to Richmond with me, or you can wait for a subpoena via the sheriff's office."

"You mean I'm supposed to walk out of my job and get into your car, then travel across three states to a city where I no longer have a home, and all because your boss is an asshole?"

A glimmer of a smile flickered then disappeared. "That's about it, yeah. Except there's a plane waiting at the airport."

Oh boy, they were really sure of this, weren't they?

I snatched my phone from my pocket and thumbed through to the Os. Back in better times, Oliver had programmed his number into my contacts, and although I'd come close to deleting it a hundred times, I'd never quite brought myself to push the button. Now I hit dial.

One ring. Two.

"Oliver Rhodes."

"You bastard."

"Good morning to you too, Miss Amor."

So formal. It was almost as if the night we spent together had never happened.

"How can you do this? All I wanted was a fresh start, and now you're trying to drag me back again. What is this? Some sort of game?"

"As I wrote in the letter you decided to ignore, I need you as a witness."

"Witness to what? So I nearly got run down by a car. I didn't see who was driving it. And Carter confessed to Chrissie's murder, anyway."

A heavy sigh drifted along the line. "That's not why I need you."

"Then why?"

"Steffie, I'd rather do this in person."

"Don't you 'Steffie' me."

"Fine. Miss Amor, I'd rather speak to you in person."

"I don't want to see you. And threatening to set the sheriff on me is a low blow."

I closed my eyes as the words left my lips. I'd been the one getting the low blow last time, and it had nothing to do with a subpoena.

"So you insist on doing this the hard way?"

No, never again. "From my position, there's no easy way."

"In that case, I'll be blunt. Carter killed other women as well as Christina. We've just found one body, and there will be more. The fun part is he's going for an insanity defence. He claims that after having sex, he gets an uncontrollable urge to murder his partner, and as you're the only living person I can find who'll admit to sleeping with him, I need you on the stand to explain to the jury that he's talking shit."

I sat on the kerb, trying to process Oliver's words. He wanted me to get up in front of a roomful of strangers and explain every painful detail of the night I spent with my best friend's killer? The press was all over this case. What if the townsfolk in Hartscross found out? Or worse, my family? The phone slid from my grasp, and Barrett crouched down beside me.

"You okay?"

I glared at him. "Do I look okay?"

Oliver's voice crackled out of the speaker. "Steffie?"

I snatched the phone up again. "I told you..."

"Miss Amor. I need you for the case. And whichever way we do this, you'll be in Richmond on that stand, because Carter's not getting away with what he did."

"I hate you."

Another sigh, this one longer. "I know, Steffie."

CHAPTER 7

THE JOURNEY BACK to Richmond took the rest of the day. Darly was furious with me for leaving, and Mom ended up in tears, even though I promised to come back by the weekend. I wasn't sure Mom totally believed my excuse about having to comfort a friend who'd just broken up with her boyfriend, either.

Chester stood with her on the front porch, looking unimpressed by my sudden announcement. Only Mason seemed ambivalent. He simply waved as he headed off up the street, no doubt going to visit Reggie and get into some sort of mischief.

Barrett did a reasonable job of playing my imaginary friend's brother, then drove me to the airport, carried my hastily packed suitcase into the terminal, and waited until I got on the plane. Business class, no less. It was a whole world of difference to the bus ride I'd taken the last time I travelled from Hartscross to Richmond. On any other day, I'd have been impressed by the fancy seats, but today, as I lifted off into a life I longed to leave behind, anger clouded every thought.

And guilt.

Guilt because I'd referred my client to Chrissie and he'd ended up killing her.

And guilt because the night I realised, the night I

should have been grieving for my friend, I ended up in bed with Oliver Rhodes instead.

I'd been fragile enough before I realised what I'd done with Carter. Two friends murdered would do that to any girl, and now that day, the day of disaster number four, was burned into my mind along with the worst of them.

My mind drifted back—what a way to find out I'd slept with a murderer.

I'd arrived at Riverley Hall, the luxury home belonging to one of Blackwood Security's owners, during a discussion about the case. I didn't mean to eavesdrop. Okay, I did, but nobody seemed to mind. Dan di Grassi, the lead investigator, was full of news as I'd listened in, curious and hopeful, desperate for justice. They'd identified a prime suspect. Then I'd recognised the description of the killer, and when she saw me standing there and showed me his photo, that confirmed everything.

First, I did the grown-up thing and fainted, and after I came around, I vomited everywhere. I'd been numb when Oliver wrapped me up in his arms and walked me to my room.

Until that point, he'd been nothing but nice to me. After disaster number three—Lyle—Oliver had lent me a sympathetic ear and a shoulder to cry on, and I'd needed both.

I closed my eyes and burrowed into the plush airplane seat, first trying not to remember the way he'd touched me that night, then praying I'd never forget.

He'd been wearing a suit when I arrived at Riverley. In fact, I couldn't remember seeing him in anything else. Except that night, he'd loosened the tie and his shirt had a few wrinkles.

"Elevator or stairs?" he'd asked, his voice low.

"Elevator." My legs were shaking so much I'd never have made it up two flights of stairs alone.

I curled into him as the doors closed, relishing his warmth. My fingers had turned icy along with my heart. Pressed against Oliver's chest, I felt his heartbeat, slow and steady, and it soothed me. As the elevator rose, he stroked my hair in the way my daddy used to when I was a little girl.

The room I'd been sleeping in came straight out of a fairy tale, complete with a four-poster canopy bed, only I was no princess. Oliver led me inside and lowered me onto the velvet couch in front of the window, then crouched next to me.

"What can I get you? Something to eat? Drink? I bet your mouth doesn't taste good."

I tried to speak but the words came out as a croak, so I swallowed and tried again. "A drink. Please."

"Alcoholic?"

I nodded. If any night called for alcohol, that was the one. He came back five minutes later with a bottle of red, one of white, and a couple of glasses.

"I don't know what you usually drink."

"Not much at all. Either's fine."

"Let's try the red, then. This one's a good vintage."

To me, a good vintage was the one in the bargain bin, but I nodded and accepted a glass. Either my taste buds weren't working or Oliver got it wrong, because the wine didn't taste of anything. I knocked back half a glass and hiccupped.

"Do you want to talk about it?" Oliver asked.

"Not really."

He laid a hand against my cheek. "You're freezing."

My teeth started chattering, and he shrugged out of his jacket and tucked it around me. It smelled of his cologne and more. Him. It smelled of him. Oliver had his own scent, a dark musk, and it only grew stronger when he got aroused. Now, on the airplane, I inhaled deeply as if I could still detect it, but all I got was the rich leather of the seats and a faint whiff of something floral. Air freshener, maybe?

But that fateful night, it was pure Oliver, and when I didn't stop shivering, he added his arms into the mix, wrapping them around me and holding me close. I surrendered to the feeling because, for the first time in ages, I felt safe. And I thought he cared. Why would a man do that if he didn't care?

"I slept with him," I whispered. "The man who killed Chrissie."

Oliver twirled a lock of my hair around his finger. "I heard that part downstairs."

"I sent him to her. It should have been me who died."

"It shouldn't have been either of you."

"But if... If I'd done the things he asked, she'd still be alive. How the hell do you get over that kind of guilt?"

Oliver closed his eyes and took a deep breath, then swirled his own wine in the glass and sipped. "I distract myself."

Many times since that night, I'd wondered what he meant. What guilt did he need to distract himself from? But in the depths of my own sorrow, I hadn't picked up on what he was telling me.

Instead, I simply asked, "How?"

Another sip and his eyes met mine. "Do you really want to know?"

He'd moved closer by then, almost without me realising, and his lips were mere inches from mine as I nodded.

He drew back a little, and his mouth twitched as if he was undergoing an internal struggle.

"Tell me," I pleaded. "Please."

He leaned over, slowly, deliberately, and put his wine glass on the side table.

"I can't tell you. I can only show you."

Stupid, stupid me. I fell for it. "Then show me."

His first kiss was barely there. Just a slight brush to the corner of my mouth. He drew back, waited.

"Yes or no, Steffie?"

Oliver was totally wrong for me. Older, more experienced, good looking in a way that would never age. And dangerous. Oh yes, he was lethal, because once I'd had a night with him, all other men seemed half-dead to me.

I nodded again, and this time, the kiss was deeper. A gentle nibble on my bottom lip before he licked along the seam and invited himself in. My mouth opened of its own accord, and suddenly I wasn't cold anymore. Heat fizzed through my veins as he peeled his jacket away and tossed it onto the floor.

I'd worn a simple checked shirt that day, perhaps unconsciously thinking of home, and Oliver untucked it from my jeans before snaking his hand underneath. I'd reverted to the white cotton underwear Chrissie disliked so much, and Oliver yanked my bra cups down before pinching my right nipple hard enough to make me gasp.

"Relax," he whispered. "Don't think, just feel."

Thinking was the last thing I wanted to do, and I slithered down the couch as Oliver gave my left nipple the same treatment. This time I anticipated the pain, and rather than making me jump, it shot through every nerve ending to my...

"How did you do that?"

"Do what?" he asked, but his smug smile told me he knew exactly what I was talking about. Then he nibbled my earlobe, and another bolt of pleasure shot between my legs.

I surrendered to his touch as he undid my buttons, taking his time. As each one popped loose, he caressed the skin revealed underneath with soft fingertips, leaving a trail of fire wherever he touched.

Once my shirt fell open, he paused for a second and met my eyes. "Okay?"

I nodded.

"I need you to tell me."

"I'm okay."

His answering smile seemed to be almost for his own benefit rather than mine, and he dropped his mouth to my breasts.

Perhaps I should have stopped things at that point, and no matter what he did to me that night, what I let him do to me, I couldn't accuse him of forcing me into it. Quite the opposite. While his tongue and fingers held me under their spell, I was a more than willing participant.

"You're exquisite, Steffie. You know that?"

My eyes had been hovering at half-mast, but now they sprang open to find him focused on my face.

"Nobody's ever made me feel that way," I

whispered.

"Then I'll change that tonight."

My shirt fell away as he picked me up bridal-style, his eyes never leaving mine. He laid me on the massive bed and knelt alongside, still fully clothed. I reached for his shirt, but he gently took my hands and raised them above my head.

"No, Steffie."

Nobody else called me Steffie. I'd always been Stef, or Stefanie if I was in trouble. Steffie sounded sweet coming from his lips.

Before he let me go, he'd released the back clasp of my bra, expertly—too expertly—and now he pulled the straps down my arms, one at a time, using his teeth. He let them graze my skin as he did so, each touch sending a jolt through me until he discarded the garment on the floor.

Oliver's fingers went to my belt, then to my top button, then to my zipper. With each movement, he teased my stomach with soft, fluttering kisses, and before he'd even got my pants off, my core began to throb in a way I'd never experienced before.

I wanted to scream at him to move faster, but I got the impression it wouldn't make a difference. I may have theoretically been the professional in that room, but I wasn't the one who knew what I was doing. Oliver, on the other hand... Every movement, every touch, was designed to stimulate parts of me I didn't know existed.

I tried to keep my eyes open, to watch his chiselled jaw working its way across my body, but he'd sent me into a stupor. What the hell was wrong with me? I'd had sex plenty of times, but it never felt like this. I felt...

I felt wanted.

And then he stopped. I lay there in my plain white panties, ruing my decision to go for comfort rather than style, when he got to his feet.

And he was still fully dressed. Even his tie remained knotted at his throat.

He strode to the side of the bed, leaned over, and kissed me hard on the mouth. "Don't move, princess."

I stared as he slipped out the door, leaving me wound up tighter than a banjo string. Where the heck had he gone?

I never did find out, but he came back a few minutes later, carrying a bundle of slinky material.

"What's that?" I twisted to look.

"Shh. Lie back. Don't think."

"Just feel, right?"

That got me a genuine smile, followed by a sweet kiss on the tip of my nose. "Now you've got it."

He carried on where he'd left off, making me squirm as his tongue trailed across a ticklish spot on my side. Then slowly, slowly, he slid my panties down my legs, taking all the time in the world.

As soon as the scrap of fabric had gone, his head moved between my legs. Now, I'd given enough blow jobs to hate them, so I grabbed at his arms to pull him up, but he shook his head.

"Lie still, Steffie. I want to taste you."

"But it's icky."

He swiped his tongue along my slit before circling my nub, and I almost fell off the bed.

"Never describe yourself as icky, princess." He crawled further up the bed. "I can see I'll need to do something about your errant limbs."

"Huh?"

You know that bundle he brought back with him? It was scarves. Silk scarves. And before I realised what he was up to, he'd looped one around my right wrist.

"What are you doing?"

I tried to snatch my hand away from him, but he laughed and kissed his way along my biceps.

"I promise you'll enjoy this. If you don't, just say the word and I'll stop."

"What word?" My voice rose. I'd read *Fifty Shades of Grey*, along with Chrissie and most of the rest of the female population. "Do I need a safe word?"

"If it makes you feel better, but I'm not planning to go that far with you tonight. Pick something."

"Red and yellow," I gasped out as he tied a scarf around my other wrist. Highly unoriginal, but my brain barely functioned at that point.

He chuckled, and I wondered if he'd read those books as well. "Fair enough. Red and yellow. And what does green mean, Steffie?"

"Get on with it."

"And what's your favourite colour?"

"Green. Please, green."

He tied my hands to the bedposts, not tightly, but not loose enough for me to wriggle around, then repeated the process with my legs. Spread wide open to him, I'd never felt so naked in my life.

"This isn't fair," I told him.

"What isn't?"

"You're still dressed. I don't want to look at your suit."

"I told you, Steffie. Tonight's about you. But since you've mentioned it..." He tugged at the end of his tie.

"I'll rectify the situation."

Blindfolding me wasn't quite what I'd expected.

Being unable to see heightened every other sense, and when he pressed his thumb over my nub and slowly circled, I arched up off the bed like a yoga pro, restrained only by the soft tug of silk.

I climbed higher, higher, and when he plunged a finger inside me, I gave in and clenched around it, moaning long and low in my first ever orgasm.

"Oh my..."

Oliver covered my mouth with his, and I tasted myself on his tongue. Another first. I wanted to be repulsed, but instead, my thighs clenched and I took a shaky step up the mountain again.

"Steffie, you look beautiful when you come," he whispered. "Uninhibited."

"It's your turn."

This was my job, after all, and I knew how it worked. The whole point of sex with a guy was so he could get his rocks off.

But Oliver didn't seem to understand that.

"Later. Lie still, Steffie, and stop pulling. You'll hurt your wrists."

Sweet sassy molassy, he'd gone there again. He licked, he sucked, and he stroked me from the inside out. My legs were sticky with my juices, which made me cringe a little, but when I attempted to writhe away, I only got a growl.

"Stay still or I'll spank you."

Was he serious? I couldn't tell, but I didn't want to find out. I tried my best to keep still, and he soon sent me over the summit for the second time.

By that point, my language skills had been reduced

to gibberish, but as he pressed himself against me to kiss my lips again, I felt his hardness against me and knew I wanted it.

"Please." I tried to rub against it. "Green. Fucking green."

He laughed and moved away again, but this time I heard the *snick* of a zipper followed by the rip of foil. I expected his cock straight away, but instead, he reached above my head.

"Raise your hips," he instructed, and I complied instantly.

He slid a pillow under my bottom, leaving me at a strange angle.

"Why did you do that?"

This time I felt him probing at my entrance, rubbing his cock through the moisture dripping out of me.

"Because then I'll hit the right spot and you'll come harder."

Harder? Was that even possible?

He pushed inside me with one smooth thrust, and I gasped at the size of him. I think I did more gasping that night than I'd done in the entire rest of my life. That was what the man reduced me to.

I wanted to touch him, to run my hands over his chest and tangle them in his hair, but he'd trapped me. I was helpless to relieve the pressure building inside me as he pistoned in and out, and he was damn right about that pillow. When I came down from that euphoria, it was like the aftermath of a high I'd spend the rest of my life chasing. With one final grunt, he came too, a delicious warmth that I felt even through the condom.

I couldn't move. Could. Not. Move. He untied my

legs and then my arms, but I simply lay there like a beached starfish as he reached over and undid the blindfold, peppering my cheeks with tiny kisses.

His face was flushed pink, but apart from that, he looked little different. How did men do it? I was paralysed, yet if Oliver knotted his tie again, he could go straight into a business meeting. And he'd zipped himself back in, which wasn't fair. I'd at least hoped for a quick glimpse.

He lifted me again so he could tuck me under the quilt, then arranged my hair over the pillow.

"You look tired, princess."

"Mmmm."

He leaned over and pressed a kiss to my forehead. "Sweet dreams."

A modicum of my brain came back. "You're leaving?"

He hesitated, halfway up from his seated position. A second passed. Two. Three. Four. "No, I'll stay."

Still fully clothed, he slid into the bed beside me and curled me into his chest. I fell asleep like that a minute or two later, listening to the sound of his heartbeat, his warmth seeping into my muscles and lending me strength.

For the first time since my daddy died, I felt content. Even after all the shit that had happened, I felt content.

Then I woke in the morning and Oliver had gone.

Chapter 8

BARRETT'S CLONE DROVE me to a nondescript apartment in central Richmond and pointed at an empty bedroom.

"Wait in there, please. I'll be out in the lounge if you need anything."

"What, all night?"

"All night. You're due at Rhodes, Holden and Maxwell at nine."

Thanks for telling me that, buddy. You just ensured I'll get no sleep. Well, maybe a couple of hours. I drifted off as the moon began its descent, having relived that night with Oliver at least twice more. I could still feel his hands roaming over me, just a whisper, and each time I nearly fell asleep, I came so hard I woke up again. Who needed a vibrator? Or even a man? The mere memory of Oliver sent me crazy.

And now I was about to face him again.

I'd brought a suit to wear for the meeting. Power dressing, if you like, even though I held none of it. Barrett had given me another reminder of that yesterday.

"Ready?" his clone asked. My hour of doom had arrived. "You want breakfast?"

I shook my head. I couldn't eat, not now.

It turned out the apartment was only ten minutes

from Oliver's law firm, and the car journey went far too quickly. Soon I was being shown into a medium-sized conference room, all light wood and glass. Not really what I expected, but then again, I'd never seen the inside of a real-life law firm before.

"Cup of coffee? Tea? Water?" the assistant who motioned me to my seat asked.

"Just water."

No "please." They didn't deserve manners today. Not when I'd been forced to come here. Right now, I should have been shampooing hair and catching up on gossip, not becoming the subject of it. What were they saying behind my back?

Then the door opened again, the temperature dropped a couple of degrees, and the lights flickered. Okay, that last part might have been my imagination, but if they didn't, they should have.

"Thank you for coming, Miss Amor."

Oliver kept his tone light, professional. Exactly the way he had ever since disaster four. *Exactly* the way. When I'd stumbled down to breakfast the next morning, he'd greeted me in that cool, detached way of his, as if he hadn't just spent hours exploring every naked inch of my body.

In the kitchen at Riverley, he'd glanced up from his laptop. "Good morning, Stefanie."

The first thing I'd noticed was that we were back to Stefanie. Not Steffie. That alone should have given me an indication of how the conversation would go.

I'd stood awkwardly in front of him while he finished typing an email. Then he raised an eyebrow.

Another member of the Blackwood team bustled around the coffee machine on the other side of the kitchen, so I kept my voice down.

"I thought you might like to eat breakfast with me?"

He waved at his coffee. "I already ate."

"Oh. Uh... About last night."

"Don't overthink it, Stefanie. You wanted a distraction and I gave you one. Nothing more, nothing less."

That was the moment my heart turned to ice, freezing tentacles spreading out through my veins. How could he not feel anything from...from that?

"So that's it? You fucked me, and now you'll forget me?"

"Forget's the wrong word."

"So what's the right word?"

He sighed. Or huffed. One or the other, it was hard to tell. "Stefanie, take last night for what it was. An enjoyable distraction, no strings." His phone rang. "You'll need to excuse me."

Just like that, I was dismissed. A distraction? *A freaking distraction?* I almost smacked him over the head with his coffee cup, but Dan walked in at that moment and helped herself to a glass of juice.

She looked at each of us in turn. "Everything all right?"

Oliver covered the mouthpiece of his phone. "Fine."

She turned to me.

"Fine. I need to shower."

And to pack. I couldn't stay near Oliver a moment longer.

Since that morning, our conversations had consisted of the odd awkward greeting while I found a new place to move into. Until now. Now, he met my eyes as he settled onto a leather seat directly opposite me. The assistant who followed sat next to him and busied herself setting up a digital recorder while I took off my suit jacket. The temperature in there was stifling.

He allowed us a minute, then took out his Montblanc pen and straightened his legal pad.

"Shall we begin?"

"I wasn't aware I had a choice?"

He sighed, a faint sound I interpreted as disappointment. "Let's try to make this as easy as possible, shall we?"

"Yeah, best not overthink it, eh?"

That got me a small frown.

"So, as I mentioned on the phone, Carter's decided to make our lives difficult, which means we need your testimony. I'd been hoping to avoid that."

"At least we've got something in common."

His gaze flicked to the girl sitting next to him, scratching away on her legal pad. Why was she there when the conversation was being recorded? So I wouldn't ask any difficult questions of my own? Well played, Mr. Rhodes. Well played.

Those questions burned away inside me. He'd mentioned they'd found another girl. So the rumours were true and there were more victims? I wanted to ask for the full story, but I kept my mouth shut because I didn't want this meeting to take a moment longer than it absolutely had to.

"Today, I'd like to go through the night you spent with Carter. He's claiming he couldn't help but act on his murderous impulses, so we need to understand whether he did anything during his time with you that signalled a darker purpose."

"It was over a year ago. I don't remember all the details."

"Yes, I appreciate that. We'll talk through what you do remember. Let's start at the beginning. I understand you offer certain services to men?"

"Used to. And you know damn well I did."

"I do. But the court doesn't, and that's what I'll need to ask you in front of the jury."

My heart began to hammer. Up until that point, I hadn't truly appreciated what testifying would mean, but now it sank in. "You mean I'll have to tell all this to a bunch of strangers?"

"The jury, the judge, the attorneys, the court staff, plus whoever happens to be in the public gallery. Maybe a few journalists."

I shoved my chair back. "I can't do this."

"Sit down, Stefanie. You can, and you will."

"I won't. I'll sit there and say nothing."

"Then you'll be held in contempt."

"I hate you."

"You already mentioned that yesterday. Now, answer the question. Please."

"Fine. I used to fuck men for money. Is that what you wanted to hear?"

"Perhaps a little less bluntly. Could you elaborate on exactly which services you mean?"

"I'd escort men to events and cater to their needs."

"Which needs, Stefanie?"

Why did he have to sound so damn condescending? He hadn't worried about my job when he wanted *his* needs catered to. Although who was I kidding? He'd spent more time looking after mine. Needs I didn't even know I had until that night.

"I offered sex, blow jobs, hand jobs. Other messed-up fetishes they might have."

"Thank you. And how did men book you?"

"Through a website."

"Called...?"

"Rubies are a Man's Best Friend."

He briefly cracked a smile. "I always thought that was dogs. So, Carter emailed you?"

Did Oliver just call me a dog? I didn't think it possible to hate him more than I did before, but he'd proved me wrong.

"Not directly. Each girl had a calendar with her available slots marked on it. Men booked the time they wanted, and then the website's owner emailed us."

He glanced at his notes. "Octavia Jackson?"

"Yes."

"And that was the only way of arranging a date with you?"

"I only worked through the one website, but sometimes Octavia would book us for other jobs directly. She said they came through associates of hers who didn't have what the client was looking for. But she promised they were all vetted."

"Okay, and what about Carter?"

"He came through the website."

"How do you know?"

"Those bookings appeared in a different colour on my calendar. I only had three or four regulars referred the other way."

"And Carter—did he request you specifically? Or did he just book any girl?"

"I don't know. You'd need to ask Octavia. As far as I remember, I just got the booking and went—that was it."

"Did the men use credit cards?"

"Yes, but not always. Rubies was one of the first escort sites to take Bitcoin—it was one of Octavia's selling points."

"Did any of the men pay cash?"

"About a third of them, roughly. Credit cards were the most popular. Octavia made the transactions show up as car repairs or something."

"Clever. Do you recall how Carter paid?"

"No."

Another murmur of disappointment. "And how would a man go about selecting which girl he wanted?"

Oliver made it sound so sordid, like picking out a side of meat at the supermarket. But no matter how much I tried to deny it, that was the truth.

"Once a man paid the membership fee for the website, he could access our photos and...well, Octavia called it a résumé, but it was all in code. So if a girl was resourceful, it meant she brought her own toys, and if it said she was hard-working, she'd do two men at once."

A résumé. A fucking résumé, quite literally.

"I can get the details from her. How far in advance did Carter book?"

Great. So now Oliver would know I'd do role-play, dress up in an outfit of the client's choice, and go down on a man for an extra two hundred dollars. Or in Octavia-speak, I was personable, well-presented, and had two years' experience in handling food.

I cringed with embarrassment as I answered Oliver's question. "I'm not sure."

He made a few notes, then looked up at me again. "Where did you meet him?"

"In a hotel. The Stanfield, I think."

"Do you remember which room?"

I shook my head. Most likely, I'd barely even remembered on the day. I stumbled into those places, did what I needed to do, then got out.

"For the tape, please."

"No."

"Was he there when you arrived?"

"I think so. A man rarely wasn't, but I don't remember specifically."

"Then what happened?"

"We had sex."

"That was it? No warm-up? No preamble?"

"When men pay by the hour, they rarely want to bother with that."

"Did you come?"

Did those words really just leave his lips? Even the girl beside him dropped her mouth open.

"What the hell kind of question is that?"

He leaned back in his seat and steepled his hands. "The kind the defence attorney will ask to rattle you. Answer the question, Miss Amor."

I looked him straight in the eye. "No, I did not come."

"And how do you remember that when the other details are a little hazy?"

Oh, shit. I'd walked right into that one. If only I could turn the clock back to yesterday morning. I'd have gathered my belongings, caught a bus to the airport, and got right on a plane. Any plane. No matter which country I might have ended up in, it couldn't have been worse than this room with its fancy lights and asshole of an occupant.

"Because only one man has ever made me come, okay? And it sure as hell wasn't Carter."

I thought I detected a faint twitch at the corner of Oliver's lips, but beyond that, his expression didn't change. The girl next to him turned the colour of a ripe tomato.

"Fair enough, Miss Amor. So you had sex, and there was nothing memorable about it, apart from the fact you did not come." He shook his head slightly, as if such things never happened in his world. Probably they didn't. "Yet I understand you passed the client on to Miss Walker?"

I nodded, and he looked pointedly at the recorder, its green light flashing as it recorded the most embarrassing moments of my life.

"Yes."

"Why was that?"

That was the only bit I did remember. "Because he wanted to carry on, and his request was one I didn't entertain."

"And what was that request?"

"He wanted to tie me up." I almost whispered it, the words sticking in my throat.

The idea of being incapacitated by a stranger, gagged so nobody could hear me scream, left me paralysed with fear. Only I hadn't felt like that with Oliver. Why not? I'd never taken the time to analyse it, and I didn't want to start now.

"I see. And Miss Walker did that sort of thing?"

"Yes."

"Why didn't you?"

"Because it scared me."

His mask slipped a fraction, then he swallowed and

it slammed back into place. "Why did it scare you?"

"Is the defence going to ask that as well?"

The assistant's head swivelled back and forth between us as if she were watching a tennis match. She'd long since given up pretending to write.

Oliver dropped his own pen and glanced at his watch. "I would hope not. Do you know if Miss Walker saw Carter?"

"I believe so. More than that, I think she liked him."

"What makes you say that?"

"Chrissie thanked me for the referral. And over the next few months, she mentioned a guy several times—not his name, but she got this look in her eyes. Like hope. I think she hoped he'd be her ticket away from the game." A tear ran down my cheek. "And he was, wasn't he?"

Oliver offered me his handkerchief, but I ignored it and used my sleeve instead. Of all the times to get emotional, why did I have to do it in front of him? Again?

The assistant spoke up. "Uh, should I get some water?"

"No thank you, Nancy. We're done here for today." He turned back to me. "Take a few minutes, and I'll show you out."

"I can find my own way."

"I'll show you out," he repeated.

I tried, and failed, to hold back the sniffles as I shoved my arms into my jacket. Would this nightmare ever end? I just wanted to get back home and find out if I still had a job shampooing hair.

"Don't leave town, Stefanie."

Except it seemed that wouldn't be happening

anytime soon. "Why not?"

"Because I have to go to the grand jury next Wednesday to get an indictment, and I might need you then. Let me know where you're staying."

"I don't know. It's not like I live here anymore. I didn't even bring enough clothes for a week."

"I'll arrange an apartment for you."

I put my hands on my hips. No way was I taking his charity. "Don't bother. Besides, I have a family dinner this weekend. I'm going home."

"Then I'll have my assistant book you a flight."

"I'll book it myself."

"As you wish."

He held the door open and motioned me through it, over to the elevator. I tried to head for the stairs instead, but a contractor with a fancy toolbox had them cordoned off with plastic tape. Did Oliver plan this?

I trailed behind him, making sure to keep my eyes above waist level. I wasn't about to give in to my impulses and admire his ass, even if it was a damn fine one. He called the elevator, and it arrived seconds later.

"After you."

Why did he have to act like such a gentleman when we both knew he was anything but? To save face with his staff, I bet. The doors whooshed shut, and I kept my gaze firmly fixed on them as the elevator descended. Please, let this one be the express.

We'd barely gone one floor when Oliver spoke.

"I'm sorry." It came out as a whisper, and he didn't look at me.

"Sorry?"

"I didn't mean to scare you."

Scare me? Oh, I got it. He meant with the scarves.

"You didn't. I... You just didn't, okay?"

"All the same."

The elevator stopped, and a man joined us. He rode down two floors before he exited, whistling like he didn't have a care in the world.

"If you want to be sorry about something, be sorry about the morning after. You were a complete dick."

We reached the first floor, and the doors opened. Three people stood aside to let me off before they got on.

Oliver didn't move.

"I don't know how to be anything but," he murmured, right before the elevator removed him from my life for the second time.

Chapter 9

OH, WHY DID I pick that moment to hop up on my high horse? I'd barely got fifty yards when I began to regret throwing Oliver's offer of a flight back in his face, but I'd eat snails before I set foot in that office again. No, I'd rather walk to Georgia than grovel, and my shoes already pinched.

"Damn asshole," I muttered as I dragged my case towards the bus station, mentally counting the dollars left in my purse.

Just a single bus ticket would be a stretch. A fine drizzle misted the air, and I tugged my overcoat around myself, grateful for its warmth, even if it had prevented me from flouncing out of Oliver's building in style. Having to wait for the receptionist to find my belongings and give them back had spoiled the effect somewhat.

My phone rang as I debated spending a couple of bucks on lunch. Unknown number. If this was Oliver...

"Hello?"

"Sable?"

I stiffened. "Who is this?"

"Octavia. You remember me?"

For a moment, I'd been worried about the press. They'd been sniffing around the case, seeing as it involved a celebrity, and I'd done my best to keep out of the papers. No doubt Octavia had been affected just as much.

"Of course I remember you."

"Good, good. I figured you'd be in town for this court thing next week, and I wondered if you wanted to get a coffee?"

I felt torn. Half of me wanted to run from Richmond and never look back, but the other half? There were few people I could talk to about the Carter mess, and Octavia was one of them. Daddy always told me a problem shared was a problem halved, so maybe it would be good to have a chat?

"Sure, I'm in town, but only for a few hours, and then I'm heading back home. Where do you want to meet?"

The coffee shop was tucked into a side street close by, a world away from the bustling atmosphere of The Daily Grind. While my old place of employment had attracted the student crowd with its daily offers and all-you-can-drink specials, Java catered to a different audience. A retro chalkboard displayed a hundred types of coffee, and the prices made my eyes water.

A bubbly blonde waitress sashayed up to the table, pad in hand. "What can I get ya?"

Yup, table service. In a coffee shop.

Octavia perused the board. "Flat white, Colombian roast, and one of those little cakes with the strawberries."

"Coming right up." She turned her pearly teeth in my direction. "And for you?"

I looked at the menu too, but not the descriptions, only the prices. "Espresso, please."

"Which blend?"

The cheapest one. "Uh, Kenyan."

"Anything to eat?"

"I'm on a diet."

The can't-afford-food diet. Worked a treat. I'd dropped a dress size before I went home, and only Mom's cooking had saved me from needing to wear a belt with everything.

"My treat," Octavia said.

She knew, didn't she? But I couldn't go back on my fib now. "That's kind of you, but I really am trying to lose a few pounds."

She shook her head as the waitress headed back to the counter. "You don't want to drop weight, honey. Men go for the curves every time."

"So? It doesn't matter anymore, does it?"

"That's what I want to talk to you about."

"What do you mean?"

"I'm starting up the business again, and I can always use good girls. The men loved you."

"I thought you got arrested?"

She shrugged. "Occupational hazard. I've been in this trade long enough to know how to avoid the pitfalls." She ticked off the points on her fingers. "Always have a long-term plan. Never put anything in writing—all the men understood what the résumés meant, but I never listed it in black and white. Oh, and get a good lawyer."

"He's not called Oliver Rhodes, is he?"

She threw her head back and laughed, a rasp you only got from smoking forty a day. "That man eats women like you and me for breakfast."

Well, it was more of a midnight snack in my case. "Did he ask you questions too?"

"Not many. He got one of his minions to take over, but I couldn't help much. Crystal took whatever relationship she had with Carter off the books. Shame, because that man deserves to burn."

The blonde came back with our coffees and set them on the table. "Enjoy."

The first sip of espresso scalded my tongue. Anything else want to go wrong today?

"So, how about it?" Octavia asked.

"How about what?"

"Do you want to be a sexy Sapphire?" She leaned back and sized me up. "Actually, no. You're more of a sweet Sapphire."

I should have known, shouldn't I? It was another sales visit. "I'm out of that game for good."

She didn't argue, merely nodded. "I suspected that might be the answer, but I had to ask. What are you doing instead?"

"I moved back home."

The laugh came again, and a man at the next table glanced over at her, then his eyes lingered. Not surprising. Octavia had to be at least fifty, but she'd looked after herself and still turned heads.

"What, to Hicksville?"

"It's not that bad. I got a job at the salon."

"Hairdressing?"

She eyed up my own locks, and I cringed. The rain had made them go all frizzy, and the ends I'd chewed hung ratty around my face. A salon poster girl I was not.

"Shampooing."

"I give you six months. You're not a country girl at heart, Sable."

"I'm not Sable either."

"Maybe not, but there is middle ground. Don't waste your life in a dead-end job. Didn't you do a business degree?"

"I didn't finish. I had six months to go when... everything happened."

"Then go back to school. Get your certificate."

"It costs money, and I don't have any."

"Then get another job. Don't give up." She waved the waitress over. "Honey, you got any jobs going here?"

The blonde bobbed her head, and perfect curls bounced around her chin. "Only part-time, Monday through Thursday mornings."

Octavia pointed in my direction. "See, there are jobs."

The girl turned to me. "Are you interested?"

"No. I mean, I don't know." Was I? "Maybe. I'll have to consider it."

The blonde giggled, the sweet sound that escaped her lips a contrast to Octavia's throaty cackle. "Suit yourself, hun."

As she walked off, Octavia lowered her voice. "She used to be you."

"What do you mean?"

"A Ruby. Now she's gone straight."

I took another look at the girl, my gaze lingering longer this time. A customer came in, and her face lit up as she smiled at him. I bet she got good tips.

"I'm not sure I could do it. Move back here and

start again."

Life with Mom and Chester was easy. Secure. Sure, it got a little dull, but I didn't have to worry about going hungry, or worse, lawyers out for blood.

Octavia reached over and patted my hand. I noticed she'd replaced her ruby ring with sapphires. They sparkled and twinkled as they caught the light, the treasure at the end of the rainbow.

"Honey, you can do anything you put your mind to."

The bus ride home took almost ten hours, and the thought of doing the reverse next Tuesday made my stomach sink. At least I had Mason's birthday lunch to look forward to on the weekend, even if he didn't. At seventeen, the last thing he wanted was to be fussed over by the entire female contingent of the Amor/Carlton family, but he loved Mom almost as much as I did, so he'd put up with it just like always. Plus she'd promised to make lemon meringue pie, and he'd never miss that.

Darly forgave me, grudgingly, so Friday found me back at the shampoo station, elbow-deep in suds as an elderly customer told me all about "that young girl who ran off to the city, then came back with her tail between her legs." I didn't know what was worse—having to listen to her tell me what a mess I'd made of my life, or the thought that she'd most probably discussed it with everyone in town.

But I got paid. Cash.

On Saturday, I spent a few dollars on Mason's gift.

If I'd been rich, I'd have bought him the car he'd always wanted, but he'd have to make do with a Corvette key ring and an IOU. And the pie. I helped Mom, and we went all out with his favourite lemon meringue, plus a coconut cream and a pecan to round things out.

"How many people did you invite?" I asked her. We could have fed the whole town with the spread on the table.

"Oh, just the usual. Your grandparents, Mason's grandparents, Auntie Beth, your cousins, some of Mason's friends, the Boses."

"The Boses? But they're not family."

"I think you and Randy would make a lovely couple."

"He's not my type. And he cheated on his last girlfriend."

I'd heard all about it at the salon. The story changed depending on who told it, but the key facts were always the same: Randy got caught with a high school senior in the bathroom at Marnie's Diner. She'd been on her knees, which was bad enough in itself, but in a public restroom? Thinking of the sticky state of that floor made me shudder.

"Give him a chance, Pippi. Everybody knows Mary Kate was a difficult girl."

A bit highly strung, perhaps, but she still didn't deserve to be humiliated like that. And did Mom really think that little of me that she'd set me up with a man who'd been voted "top horndog" in high school two years running?

To his credit, Randy made the effort to put on a tie, but he'd tied it too short and it hung halfway down his little pot belly like a clock pendulum. I watched it swing backwards and forwards every time he reached across the table for more food.

"So, how was your time in Virginia?" he asked in between shovelling fried chicken and grits into his mouth. And he chewed with his mouth open. I tried not to look, but the sound alone put me off my own dinner.

"It was an interesting experience."

"You didn't complete college, huh?"

Thanks for reminding me. "No, I still have half a year to go."

"Why'd you quit?"

"I missed home."

"I bet. What's not to like about Hartscross? Bet you don't get peach pie as good as your momma's in Richmond."

"Not unless I make it myself."

"Don't get why people want to go to college, anyway. I've done just fine without it."

Randy managed the local sports bar, or rather, he hung out there while his dickwad friends got drunk every time football was on. Or baseball. Or boxing. So most of the time, really. And everybody knew Randy's daddy bought him his truck.

"I wanted to learn."

"As long as a woman knows how to cook, that's plenty." His daddy nodded in agreement. Then Randy leaned in and lowered his voice. "And fuck. A woman's gotta know how to fuck."

He nearly ended up wearing his damn pie. I gritted my teeth so hard I thought they'd end up as dust, then lurched backwards over the wooden bench.

"If you'll excuse me, I'm feeling a little sick."

Mom's brows knitted together. "You need to lie

down?"

"I think that's for the best."

Because I couldn't kick Randy in the testicles if I was in my bedroom, could I? How dare he? I stormed up the stairs and slammed the door behind me. What a pig! And worse, half of the men in Hartscross belonged in the sty. Randy wasn't the only one to think a woman's place was in the home, either at the stove or on the bed with her legs spread. I'd rather become a lesbian than date any of them.

Stretched out on the bed, I fumed quietly as the sounds of the party drifted up from downstairs. I didn't even get a slice of coconut cream pie, and I bet by the time Randy left, the boys would have put away the lot.

Light footsteps sounded on the stairs, breaking me out of my funk, followed by a soft knock on the door. Tell me Mom had brought pie?

"Come in."

The door cracked, and Randy slipped inside, grinning.

"What are you doing here?"

"Thought I'd see how you were feeling."

"Like I'm gonna puke."

I wasn't lying. He had a glob of cream stuck to the side of his mouth, and I couldn't take my eyes off it.

"Looks as if my offer might have to wait."

"What offer?"

"I know cash is hard to come by in this town, especially for a girl like you. So I thought I'd become a client."

"What the hell are you talking about?"

He dropped down on the edge of my bed, and I shuffled to the far side. The way he looked at me didn't escape my notice, his slow appraisal as he scanned my body from neck to toe.

"I know what you do in Richmond. Overheard Pop whispering on the phone. Something about a lawyer wanting to subpoena you for your part in that murder case." He palmed himself through his pants. "So, what do you say? Why not earn a few bucks while you're back here?"

I suppose you could count that as disaster number five. The one place I felt safe, the one place I thought I could escape from my past, and Randy had just stolen that from me.

"I-I-I don't do that anymore."

"Maybe not as a job, but how about as a sideline?"

"Get out."

He sighed. "Why do women play so hard to get? Look, let's make a deal. You play with me, and I'll keep your little secret."

"You're blackmailing me? You... You..."

He leaned over and trailed a finger down my breast, and I shoved his hand away. Filthy swine.

But he only grinned. "Tell you what; I'll give you a couple of days to consider it. I know you'll see sense. After all, I'm sure your mom wouldn't want to hear about her precious Pippi's sordid past."

"I'll kill you, you bastard," I hissed.

"Not when my daddy's the sheriff, you won't." He lurched to his feet. "You and me, we're gonna enjoy getting to know each other."

Chapter 10

"WHY D'YA HAVE to go back to Richmond, Pippi? You only just came home."

Mom stood in my doorway, watching me pack. Every so often, she dabbed at her eyes with a handkerchief, all dainty like in the movies. A stickler for detail—the parlour excepted—she'd even coordinated it with the blue of the flowers on her dress.

"I got offered a job. And I want to finish college."

Of course, Randy could still spill my secret if I wasn't in Hartscross, but I didn't think he would. There was no fun for him if he couldn't witness the full effect of his cruelty.

"But you have a job here."

"Shampooing hair. I don't want to spend the rest of my life shampooing hair."

"But Darly's such a sweetie."

"I know, Mom." My case was full, and I flipped the lid shut. I had no idea whether I'd be away for a week or a month, so I needed to take enough clothes for an extended trip. "But I always wanted to run my own business, and I can't do that in Hartscross."

"Sure you can. Jaycee Colbertson set up a nail salon last year, and she's done real well."

Dammit, why did Mom have to make things so difficult? This was the side of her I vowed never to allow in myself—the neediness that would make my happiness dependent on another person. I wanted to find my own way in life, even if I hadn't done such a great job of it so far.

Meanwhile, all I could do was give my mom a hug. "I'll visit more often than before. I promise."

"But it's your birthday coming up in February. I had a big party planned."

"We can still have the party. I'm looking forward to it."

Only I hoped to have a little more control over the guest list.

She brightened a touch and gave me a quick half smile. "I thought we'd go with jewels as the theme. Marnie based her daughter's celebration on flowers, but I don't want to copy. We can have decorative centrepieces, and glasses to match, and..."

Jewels? Great. Rubies and sapphires.

Mom chattered away as I took one last look around my room. I'd once thought it was cute, the way she left it exactly as it had always been, but now I realised she lived in the past. She hated change, and in her head, I'd forever be a child.

Chester drove me to the bus station, his face serious. He'd made his feelings about me leaving yet again quite clear.

"You can't keep doing this to your mom," was his parting shot as he heaved my suitcase out of the trunk.

"I'm sorry," I whispered, but I was talking to empty air. He'd already driven off.

Ten hours seemed like twenty as the bus rumbled north overnight. All was in darkness as we meandered up through Georgia and the two Carolinas, and I'd lost the will to live by the time the bus pulled into Main Street Station.

The first time I made this trip, I'd been full of hope for the future. Apart from one week in Florida, I'd never spent more than a day away from Hartscross, and the bright lights beckoned. Now I knew their glare hid the dark side of society that most people didn't want to talk about, even the ones who secretly roamed there at night.

And now I'd exhausted my college fund and my dreams. I had six hundred dollars in my checking account, no home, and no job. And only one long shot of an idea.

The businessman sipping from a sleek black cup at the table next to the door looked down his nose at me as I wheeled my suitcase into Java. I knew what he was thinking: "that girl's lost."

And I was, just not in the way he thought.

The same blonde girl from last week stood behind the counter, watching curiously as I shuffled towards her.

"You want coffee?"

"Actually, I was hoping for a job," I blurted.

"You were with Octavia last week, weren't you?"

I nodded, holding my breath, both apprehensive about her response and hopeful because she'd been in my position and come out on the other side. Maybe she'd understand?

"You'd better come through. You can wait in the break room while I serve this lot." She jerked her head towards a gaggle of suits who'd just walked in. "Then we can have a chat."

She lifted the counter for me to go past, and I scurried through the doorway she indicated. The break room was little more than a cupboard with a couple of battered chairs wedged into the corners, shabby and mismatched. I perched on the edge of one, terrified of the situation I'd got myself into but at a loss over how to find a way out of it. Perhaps I should have stood up to Randy, but he'd always had a habit of spreading gossip in high school, and worse, he liked to see his victims squirm.

So, here I was, back in Hell, Virginia. Population: two hundred thousand perfectly nice citizens and one arrogant ass of a lawyer.

"I thought you could use a coffee. Espresso, right?"

The blonde squeezed past my suitcase and settled into the chair opposite, our knees just inches apart.

"Thanks."

I hadn't drunk anything since North Carolina, or eaten for that matter.

"Still on a diet?"

I shook my head no.

"Would you like a muffin? On the house?"

"Yes, please." My voice cracked a little. I wasn't used to that sort of kindness.

She wriggled out again and came back with a double chocolate, wrapped in a napkin.

"You look as if you need this."

I balanced it in my lap, careful not to take a layer of skin off my tongue this time as I sipped my drink.

"I'm Imogen," the girl offered. "Also known as Ginger."

"Ginger?"

"I used to dye my hair."

"Stefanie." I felt my cheeks heat. "Also known as Sable."

"You had the guy with the bunny fetish, right?"

"Yes."

"Octavia mentioned that. Like a Playboy bunny?"

"That's what I thought when I first got the booking, but it was more like the Easter bunny. I had to wear the outfit then feed him fruit out of a basket. Grapes, mainly, but he also liked pineapple. Crazy, huh?"

"Every Friday night, I had dinner with a man who enjoyed dressing in a rubber suit and having me lead him around like a dog. I say 'had dinner with,' but he didn't used to eat on account of the suit didn't have a mouth hole. Or eyeholes."

I couldn't help the giggle that escaped. "For real?"

"Yeah. And he was loaded. He had a Ferrari and a Bentley parked in the driveway."

"I also got the man who liked me to go to charity fundraisers with him. It all looked perfectly normal from the outside, but he insisted we wore each other's underwear."

"Didn't you get VPL?"

"I had to be real careful which dress I wore. Those parties were full of singers and movie stars."

"Ohmigosh. Proper A-list?"

"More like Z-list."

"I spent an evening with a movie star once. B-list but, like, ten years ago. He spent dinner referring to himself in the third person and then he couldn't get it up."

In my whole life, I'd never come across someone I

clicked with as easily as Imogen. Even Chrissie. I mean, we used to discuss work, but not all the details, not like this. Imogen was a hoot. We chatted about the ridiculousness of Rubies for ten minutes until we both had tears streaming.

"Hang on," she said. "I just need to let Lance know I won't be long. Technically we only get fifteen minutes for breaks, but he's flexible."

She poked her head out the door then sat down again. "So, you've turned up with a suitcase. That looks serious."

Before I could stop myself, I told her about the court case, home, and Randy Bose. Not Oliver, though. Somehow, what happened with *him* made me feel more stupid than all the rest put together.

"I heard about the court case. I'd quit by then, but us girls still talked."

"Why did you leave?"

"My old roommate had this boyfriend, and they used to curl up on the sofa every Sunday night and watch movies. She always looked so content. And I realised I'd never have that, not if I carried on being a Ruby."

"So you've met someone?"

"Not yet, but at least now I go on dates with relatively normal people."

"I struggled with money. Before Rubies, I used to work in a coffee place, but I got behind on all the bills."

"I won't kid you—it's tough going straight. I work here four mornings a week, plus vacation cover like today, and I waitress a couple of evenings at a restaurant too. And do manicures in my spare time."

"Is it worth it?"

She stared at the wall behind me for a few seconds. "Yes, I'd say it is."

I coughed nervously. "When I came in last week with Octavia, you mentioned there was a job opening. Is it still available?"

Her smile lit up her face again. How many rubies did she have? That grin alone was worth five. "Sure is. Mornings have been a nightmare since the last girl left, and the boss put hiring a replacement on my plate as well as everything else. He hates getting his hands dirty."

"Can I apply?"

"Better than that, you can start tomorrow. Octavia says you're reliable, and if you've served coffee before, this'll be a breeze."

I sagged back in the chair. "Oh, thank goodness." Then I remembered. "But I have court next Wednesday."

"You poor thing." Imogen was one of those touchy-feely people, and she reached out to squeeze my hand. "I can get Lance to cover for you that day. He doesn't mind doing the occasional extra shift."

"You're the kindest person I've ever met."

"Oh, I've got my own interests at heart. I need the help." Imogen clapped her hands then glanced over at the suitcase. "Do you have somewhere to live?"

"Not yet. I'll pick up a cheap hotel room tonight, then look for a place tomorrow." I stifled a yawn. "Sorry. I'm so tired."

"I only mention it because I'm looking for a roommate. The last one left on real short notice and left everything in a mess. I haven't finished clearing, and the only applicant I've had wanted to know if I'd have a problem with threesomes."

A bit of my coffee went down the wrong way, and I spluttered into my hand. "She wanted to hold threesomes in your apartment?"

"He. And he wanted me to join in."

"Oh my..." I had no words.

"So if you're interested and you'll help with the tidying, I could offer you half rent for the first month."

Never before had I felt the urge to kiss another girl, but today I wanted to fall at Imogen's feet and lick them. In some ways, she reminded me of Chrissie.

"That sounds perfect."

"Awesome! Let me finish my shift, and then I'll show you the apartment. You want another drink?"

"I'd love one. And I don't usually drink espresso."

She winked at me. "I know, sweetie."

Imogen lived a ten-minute walk from Java in a cute little fourth-floor apartment. Nothing flashy—just a tiny lounge with two bedrooms leading off it, a shared bathroom, and a kitchen with two stools at the counter. It may have been small, but she'd decorated it to be cosy, just the way I liked it.

And the room wasn't even that much of a mess. It would only take me a day to fix up, and I didn't need much more than what it contained: a bed and nightstand, a tiny closet, and a desk and chair. If I ever got back to college, that would be perfect for studying.

"I've got spare sheets you can borrow, and towels." Imogen poked her head around the doorjamb. "And we get as much free coffee as we can drink."

"At the moment, I think I need it."

"Take the day to rest. Tomorrow's Monday. A fresh week, a fresh start."

"What time do we need to be at work?"

She grimaced. "Six. That's the worst part of the job, especially as I don't wake up until six thirty."

"I'll cope with the mornings."

Mom had always been an early bird. All through my childhood, the smell of breakfast drifted up the stairs at five thirty, and Mason and I would race each other to the kitchen. It was only as I got older that I'd claimed the night as my own.

"We're gonna make a great team. I'd suggest going out to eat this evening, to get to know each other better, but I have to work."

"At the restaurant?"

She nodded.

"What kind of food?"

"All that fancy nouvelle cuisine. Big plates, tiny portions of weird stuff. I can't even pronounce half of the stuff on the menu. But the tips are good, and Jean-Luc, the pastry chef, always gives me the leftovers to bring home."

She blushed as she said that, and I wondered if I'd be hearing more about Jean-Luc and his goodies.

"You like him?"

"He's got a girlfriend."

The good ones were always taken, weren't they? And his kindness sure beat my waitressing experience.

"I worked at a diner once, and I was lucky if I got soggy cigarette ends or a piece of chewed-up gum at the end of the night."

She gave a tinkly little giggle. "Oh, sweetie, you sure

do pick 'em."

Yup. I sure did.

CHAPTER 11

WORKING AT JAVA turned out to be a lot better than The Daily Grind. There wasn't a coffee-bean outfit in sight, and the suited-and-booted clientele must not've been keen on coins rattling in their pockets, because they dumped them all straight into the tip jar.

Imogen and I got into a good rhythm, with me working the register while she made the coffee from six till twelve.

"Another day, done," she said on Tuesday when we got home and collapsed on the sofa.

"Do you have to work tonight?"

"Day off. You wanna go out?"

"I've got court tomorrow, maybe."

I still didn't know. One of Oliver's minions had telephoned to tell me my presence was required at Rhodes, Holden and Maxwell from eight, but he wasn't sure whether I'd need to take the stand. The uncertainty was worse than a definite "yes."

"I can't believe they're messing you around like this. It sucks."

As did Oliver, in more ways than one.

"The faster tomorrow comes, the faster it'll be over."

"And going out for dinner will make the time fly by. Come on; we won't be late back."

I hesitated. Honestly, I wasn't in much of a party mood.

But Imogen turned her smile on me. "And there was plenty in the tip jar today."

"Oh, go on. Just dinner, nothing else."

"Espresso?" Imogen asked.

I raised my head from the wall in the break room, and the pounding started again. "Quadruple."

"Coming right up."

I checked my watch. An hour and a half until I needed to be at Oliver's beck and freaking call. The good news was, I didn't lie awake last night like I thought I would. But that was only because after happy hour we'd gone to a burger place, and at the burger place we'd met a group of guys, and the group of guys took us to a club, and the club offered two-for-one cocktails, and I passed out rather than fell asleep at three o'clock this morning.

Imogen levered me out of bed at five thirty. I threw up once and brushed my teeth twice, then tried to crawl back under the duvet. She wouldn't let me.

"I thought you were my friend," I whined.

"I am. Which is why I'm going to make sure you get to where you need to be instead of leaving you here unconscious."

At the moment, sweet oblivion seemed like a far better option. I'd changed out of my party dress now, but the blouse and pencil skirt didn't do much to hide the fact I was trashed. By a quarter to eight, I wanted to puke again and caffeine had wired my eyelids open.

Imogen, my so-called friend, shoved me out the door of Java because my feet didn't want to go of their own accord.

"It'll be over before you know it."

Quite possibly. My brain didn't seem to be functioning properly right now. "I wish I didn't have to go."

"It'll help put Carter away, and that man's a monster."

I sighed. "Yes, I know. I'll see you this evening."

Head down, I shuffled off along the street. Rhodes, Holden and Maxwell was four blocks away in a high-rise office building that dominated the skyline. Unsurprisingly, they had the top three floors with a view out over the city.

The receptionist in the atrium handed me a visitor's pass, and her once-over didn't escape my notice. *No, lady, I'm not on drugs*. Not illegal ones, anyway.

The elevator rose smoothly to the twentieth floor, and when it dinged, I tripped over the edge and half-fell out. Right into Oliver Rhodes. Just when I thought my day couldn't get any worse.

His cool, assessing eyes scanned me up and down, and his mouth hardened into a thin line. "My office. Now."

"You're not my boss."

He raised one eyebrow, and I shuffled in the direction he pointed.

I'd never been in his office before, but the furnishings were exactly what I'd imagined. Wood panelling, leather seats, a huge penis-extension of a desk. Not that he needed one of those, but I guess he had plenty of cash to spend. The corner windows gave him a view over downtown Richmond in two directions, and me plenty of options if I decided to throw myself out. Paintings of crusty old men in suits glared down at me from the walls, adding another layer of disapproval to Oliver's radiating anger.

I pointed at the closest, a grey-haired man who looked as if he'd had a stick inserted up his rectum at birth. "One of your ancestors?"

"We're not here to talk about my décor. How in hell did you get into this state?"

"Did you know, when you're pissed, your accent sounds a tiny bit English?"

He clenched his jaw, and the edge of it ticced. "Stefanie, perhaps you don't understand. Today, I need to go to court and get an indictment against the man who killed your friend. If I don't, he walks. His lawyer's a demon, and he's got the advantage of a guilty client, so I need all the help I can get. Help that does not include you showing up at my office at eight in the morning still drunk."

"I'm stressed, okay?" And I also felt a tiny bit guilty for being difficult when justice for Chrissie was at stake. "Why is having a guilty client an advantage?"

"Because Carter knows every detail of the crimes he committed, so he can pre-empt my arguments," Oliver said. "Why are you stressed? I'm the one who's got to stand up in front of the judge."

"Because I have to stand up in front of you," I mumbled.

His eyes softened infinitesimally, and he took a step towards me.

"Leave me alone."

I opened up the distance between us again and

looked out the window instead. *Was* I still drunk? Maybe, just a little. A bird soared past, and I envied its freedom. Birds didn't need to worry about rent and bills and overbearing assholes.

Oliver's hand on my shoulder made me jump, and I swiped it away. "Don't touch me."

"Look, I'll only call you if I need to. Come and sit down. You can sleep this off on the couch."

Why was he being nice? I didn't know how to deal with him being nice. "I'd rather stand."

"Suit yourself."

I heard the sound of a cupboard door opening then closing again, and a few seconds later, Oliver's breath whispered over my ear.

"I have to go to court. There's a blanket on the couch, and my assistant's outside if you need anything. Do me a favour and don't vomit on my furniture."

"Why exactly am I here?"

"Because if I have additional questions, I need to be able to get hold of you in a recess, not spend my time worrying whether or not you'll answer the phone."

"What about the others? I'm not the only witness."

"Ethan and Caleb are in one of the conference rooms, and Dan, Emmy, and Bayani are already at the courthouse." He plucked his coat from an old-fashioned wooden stand and shrugged into it. "I'll see you later."

Great. I couldn't wait.

Despite what I'd told Oliver, I collapsed gratefully onto the sofa once he'd left. It was upholstered in a deep-chocolate leather, and when I leaned back on it, surprisingly comfortable. The blanket matched, a soft fleece, and I pulled it around myself for extra warmth, although I wasn't convinced my shivers were entirely down to the cold. More the man.

And the blanket smelled of him. When I inhaled deeply, his musk snuck into my brain and memories of that night assaulted me again. Exactly what I didn't need this morning. I threw the blanket to the side and curled up on the seat. I'd rather freeze to death than be wrapped up in Oliver Rhodes.

When I woke, the first thing I noticed was that the pounding in my head had eased a fraction. We'd gone from bass drums to maracas. The second thing I noticed was Oliver, or at least his scent. Was he here? I raised one heavy eyelid and realised I'd tucked that damn blanket around myself again. What was wrong with me?

The door clicked open as I began to unravel my limbs, and a dark shadow fell across my face.

"She wakes."

"Aren't you supposed to be in court?"

Oliver dropped his briefcase beside his desk and took off his coat. "I've been to court. You've been asleep for eight hours."

"All day?"

"Unless you're working on a different timescale to the rest of the planet."

I sat up fully, and my neck cricked. I worked it from side to side, trying to ease the pain. "The indictment—did you get it?"

"Yes."

"So you dragged me in here for no reason?"

"No, I invited you to sleep off your hangover on my couch as a precaution."

"Your couch sucks. My neck hurts."

"I'd offer you a massage, but I quite like my testicles where they are."

Of all the... I scrambled to my feet and looked around for my purse. Where did I leave it? Ah, yes, over there by the antique globe. Who needed one of those in their office? What did he use it for, planning his next vacation? I snatched the bag up and headed for the door.

"I'm going."

Oliver, playing the part of the gentleman, held it open. "I'm not stopping you."

"Good. And I'm not doing this again." If he wanted me to testify at the trial, he'd have to make good on his threat to subpoena me. "I could have stayed at home in bed today and slept properly. Or better still, gone to work and earned some money." I strode towards the elevator with Oliver following at my elbow, and when I reached it, I jabbed the button. "Hurry up," I muttered.

"You got a job?"

"Yes, Mr. Moneybags, I got a job. It's what mortals who aren't stacked with cash have to do."

"What kind of job?"

"None of your business. And I'm not wasting time in your office again or answering more of your shitty questions. Did you get a cheap thrill out of them?"

Oliver followed me into the elevator and the doors closed, trapping us together in a tiny metal box. I should have thought this through. Next time, I'd take the stairs.

Hang on. Not next time. There would be no next

time.

“No, Stefanie, I don’t get a thrill out of asking you questions like that.”

“They were so intrusive!”

He moved towards me, and I backed away until I hit the elevator wall. Even then he didn’t stop until we were an inch apart, him caging me in with his forearms on the mirror behind.

His voice dropped a notch. “If you can’t deal with those questions from me, the defence will slay you in the trial.”

Oliver was so damn close I could feel the heat radiating from him. I tried to look away but his eyes held mine. I’d never studied him up close before, and now I saw the gold flecks in his deep-brown irises, the way his pupils widened slightly as he got near. I wanted to push him away, but I couldn’t move. My arms stayed limp at my sides as our breath mingled. Tension rose, pulled skywards by an invisible thread.

To this day I don’t know why I did it. Desperation, perhaps. Anything to break that impassive mask he’d worn since the night he left my bed. And stupidity. There was certainly an element of that involved.

I reached out my tongue and touched his bottom lip.

His dark eyes widened, a true expression of surprise from Oliver. I thought he’d move away, but I’d underestimated him. He leaned forwards instead and pressed his lips to mine in a hard, closed-mouth kiss. Then, before I could process that and push him away or pull him closer or kick him in the groin or kiss him back, the elevator doors opened and he was gone.

I must have stood in the empty car for a full minute

before a bespectacled gentleman tapped me on the shoulder.

"Miss? Are you okay?"

No, I was far from okay. Say, if okay was in Chicago, then I was on the moon. Or Mars. Or in a whole different solar system. But I didn't think the nice man would like to hear that, so I nodded and smiled and stepped out into the icy sterility of the reception area with its perfect blonde receptionist and its fancy umbrella holder. Ahead, the door opened invitingly, hinting at the sanctuary of the street beyond.

I craved air.

"Miss? I need your pass."

The receptionist chased after me, heels clacking on the polished floor, and I ripped the damn badge off and threw it behind me. She could do whatever she liked with it and give me as many disapproving looks as she wanted. I didn't plan on coming back to the offices of Rhodes, Holden and Maxwell. If Oliver wanted my testimony, he could talk to me in court.

Chapter 12

WHAT THE HELL just happened?

I walked home in a daze, the touch of Oliver's lips still burning on mine. In fact, I walked further. I'd gone a block and a half past my new apartment before I realised where I was.

What on earth had I been thinking? I'd licked Oliver. Freaking licked him. And why did he kiss me? Another distraction? A way to stop me from complaining?

Well, it sure worked, didn't it? I hadn't just stopped complaining, I'd stopped thinking and breathing as well, and my heart continued to hammer even twenty minutes later. I replayed the moment over and over in my mind. The heat of his skin, the way he pressed into me, the taste of...

Stop it! How dare he? I'd made it quite clear I wanted no part of him, yet he still presumed he could take what I hadn't offered.

Except in a way I did offer, didn't I? My damn tongue had developed a life of its own when it touched his lips. I must have still been feeling the effects of the alcohol from last night; that was the only explanation. What had been in those cocktails?

After three attempts, I got my key into the lock and shoved open the apartment door. Despite having slept all day, I felt drained and in desperate need of something smooth, rich, and chocolatey. A vision of Oliver covered in chocolate sauce popped into my head. Freaking hell, had I gone crazy?

"How was court?" Imogen asked.

"I didn't need to go in the end. I ended up waiting around at the law firm all day."

"Oh, bummer. At least you missed the argument at Java. Some guy bought the last strawberry shortcake, and the girl behind him in the line went mental. Said it was the only thing that kept her sane in the mornings, and he'd ruined her life."

"Over a cookie?"

"That's what she said."

"Did he give it to her?"

"No. The asshole ran out the door with his latte in a to-go cup."

"Harsh."

"Yup. And Lance panicked and left me to deal with her while he made the coffees. I had to feed the poor girl two apple fritters and a chocolate muffin before she stopped crying. Apparently, it was the wrong time of the month, and she found her boyfriend in bed with another man yesterday."

"Ouch."

I guess that kind of put my Oliver issues into perspective. He may have been an arrogant asshole, but at least I didn't care about him. I didn't. *I. Didn't.* And I hadn't yet resorted to gaining my sugar fix by emotional blackmail.

"I made dinner," Imogen announced. "Sort of. I mean, I bought TV dinners and I've heated them up."

At least I didn't need to cook. "Sounds wonderful."

She laughed. “I’ll settle for edible. Come on, let’s put a movie on while we eat.”

By the time I woke up the next morning, I’d locked thoughts of Oliver firmly into the back of my mind. Okay, so they kept escaping, but each time one popped up unbidden, I shoved it away again. I needed to forget him and get on with life, starting with the 6:00 a.m. shift at Java. I felt slightly more human after yesterday, ready to face another day as I tugged on a pair of black skinny jeans and a white shirt. Waitress chic. And when I finished at twelve, I had three days off to look forward to.

Although at some point I’d either need to get more shifts at Java or search for a second job. Imogen was easy on the rent and right about the tips, but I’d never have any money left over at the end of the month. And that night out on Tuesday meant I’d be living on ramen noodles for a month.

But this weekend, I had free time, and I intended to make the most of it. Maybe I’d go for a walk, or read a book, or even look into expanding my social life. Goodness knows it needed help.

“Ready to go?” Imogen hopped out of her room, doing up the strap on one of her Mary Janes.

“As I’ll ever be.”

The first customer was already hovering outside as we opened the door, and trade didn’t let up for the first hour. I barely had time to blink in between noting orders, taking money, and putting cakes into bags. At that time in the morning, few people ate in, so at least I was spared from having to wait tables and wipe up spills.

And being busy was a blessing, because at least it kept my mind off Oliver. Until it didn't. He walked in at a quarter past seven, eyes on his ridiculous watch as he pushed through the door. For a brief second, I considered escaping to the break room, but then it was too late—he'd seen me.

Not that his face changed. Only his eyes latching onto mine gave the game away as he strode towards the back of the line. That contact was lost for a moment as the man ahead of him turned in greeting. A friend? A colleague? They certainly looked as if they knew each other.

"Uh, miss?"

The man at the front of the line brought me back to earth. "Sorry, what was that?"

"I'll have a mocha latte with whip and one of those banana muffins."

"Of course."

I got the man his order, but my gaze kept straying to Oliver, now engrossed in conversation. A couple of times, I thought I saw him glance in my direction as well, or was I imagining it?

"You want me to take a turn with the coffee?" I asked Imogen. Anything to avoid speaking to Oliver.

"No, I'm good here."

Rats. I'd found she preferred to make the drinks rather than speak to the customers. She said she'd had enough of faking niceness during her years with Octavia to do it every morning as well. And now there were only two people in front of Oliver.

"I'll have a cookie and fresh orange juice to go."

Make that one person.

All too soon, my nemesis reached the counter, and my stay of execution came to an end.

"So this is your new job?"

"No, I came in for a drink and they asked me to work the register."

"Good to see your hangover hasn't affected your fluency in sarcasm."

"Do you want to order something? Or did you just come in for the atmosphere?"

He looked me up and down, slowly, taking his time, as if I didn't have customers lining up out the door and Imogen frantically making drinks behind me.

"No, I came for the view."

Lucky for him I didn't have a drink in my hand, because he'd have ended up wearing it.

"Well, if you could stand to the side, I'd appreciate it, because the man behind you actually wants a coffee."

He laughed, then reached into his pocket for his wallet. "I'll have a grande Colombian, black."

"Sugar?"

"I don't usually like sweet things."

Was that a dig at me? Why did the man have to be so damned confusing?

I took the ten dollars he offered me, careful not to let our fingers touch, and didn't bother to thank him as he stuffed the change into the tip jar. I'd seen his office. He could afford it. And I avoided asking any more questions because I didn't want to hear his answers anyway.

Imogen made his drink, and rather than hand it to me like she usually did, she gave it straight to Oliver with a stupid grin on her face.

He looked at me as he said, “Thank you, Imogen.”

So he knew her name? Tell me he wasn’t a regular?

“That man is so dreamy,” she whispered to me as she turned back to the coffee machine. “He’s a lawyer on the Carter case, did you know that? Have you met him? I saw him on TV.”

Dreamy? No, he was more the stuff of nightmares.

“It’s a big legal team. I think I’ve seen him around.” I didn’t want to put my weird non-relationship with Oliver into words. “Does he come in often?”

“Once or twice a week since I started here. And he always tips well. Generous and hot—what more could a girl want?”

“He looks like the type to break a girl’s heart.”

“But I bet you’d enjoy yourself before he did it.”

“I’d rather have a man who cared about me.”

She put one hand on my arm. “Stef, most men are assholes, and I’m sure we understand that better than most. Sometimes you’ve got to keep that thought in the back of your mind and use them like they use you.” She giggled. “Either that or stay celibate the rest of your life.”

I watched Oliver’s departing ass, and I had to admit it was a nice sight. “You don’t think he’s a bit old?”

“That man’s like a fine wine. He’s going to age well. And you know what they say?”

“What?”

“With age comes experience. I can’t say I’d turn him down.”

Oh, how right she was. Oliver sure had experience, that much was clear. I clenched my thighs together just thinking about it. If I could turn the clock back, knowing what I knew now, what would I have done? If

I'd known he'd give me one amazing, unforgettable night then discard me like a piece of trash afterwards, would I still have slept with him?

I didn't want to answer that question, and I hated myself for even asking it.

CHAPTER 13

I BLOCKED OLIVER from my mind for the rest of Thursday. I bet he didn't give me a second thought after he saw me in Java, and he didn't deserve any of my headspace either.

Instead, Imogen and I spent the evening pampering ourselves, and it turned out she had enough beauty products to open her own spa hidden away in the bathroom cupboard.

"How do you even pick what colour to do your nails?" I asked, surveying the array of polish.

"I work on a rotation system." She picked up a bottle of hot pink. "Today, it's Wild Strawberry with black accents. Want me to do yours?"

At least then the decision would be out of my hands. "Would you mind?"

"Heck, no. I'll do them first—that way I won't smudge mine."

She pulled out several bottles—pink, peach, yellow, and blue—and set to work. At first, I thought she'd made a mess, but as she layered the colours, sunsets emerged. Then she added white accents for the waves and started to paint tiny people and palm trees in black.

"Wow. You're really good at this."

"I've always loved art, and when I was working at

Rubies, I trained as a nail technician in my spare time. One day I'd love to own a salon."

"Why do you work at Java? Why not get a job in a nail bar?"

She shrugged. "Money. I've got a few private clients, but nail girls don't earn that much, and between Java and the restaurant, I can put a bit aside each month in my start-up fund. I tried looking for investors, but it's tough out there at the moment. And nobody wants to rent a store to a girl with no business experience and no security deposit."

"It's a great goal. And let me know if you need help with a business plan. I was a business major before I dropped out."

"You'd help? I'd love that." She made a face. "I did art history. I enjoyed the studying, but it's not much use in the real world."

"Sure. We could start tomorrow?"

"I have a couple of manicures to do in the morning, and then I'm working at the restaurant in the evening. How about Saturday?"

"It's a date." I sat back and sighed, resting my finished hands on the arms of the chair, fingers spread. "I need to find another source of income as well."

"What do you want to do?"

"I'm not sure. I always wanted to manage a business. Maybe a spa, or a restaurant, or a bar. Somewhere that I'd enjoy going to work because all the customers would be having a good time. But I doubt that'll ever happen."

"Why not?"

"There are too many people out there who did manage to graduate from college."

Imogen settled herself back on the sofa and began to paint her own nails, nestling the bottle of polish between her knees. "It might be difficult to get what you want, but never give up. Would you be interested in shadowing the manager where I work? You know, to get some experience? I could ask if you like. He's nice."

"You think he'd agree?"

"On a quiet day, maybe. Like a Sunday or Monday. Not Friday or Saturday nights—the place is packed then."

"I'd like that."

"Then I'll talk to him." She reached over and patted my arm, careful not to touch her nails. "You'll make it; don't worry."

How I wished I had her confidence.

With Imogen out on Friday, I had a little time to reflect. Apart from Oliver popping up at awkward times, my move back to Richmond had gone better than expected with my new job and a comfortable home. And best of all, I'd made a new friend.

I didn't click with many people, not in the way where I knew they'd be a friend for life, no matter what shit got thrown at us. I first got that feeling from Mason, then Chrissie, and now from Imogen. It was as if we'd met years ago rather than days.

And heaven knew I needed a friend like that.

I tried to make myself useful by giving the apartment a clean, which only made me think back to the way Chrissie and I would do anything possible to avoid household chores. We used to kid around and pretend one day we'd get a housekeeper, but we never made that much money.

And now it looked as if I never would.

Once I'd finished clearing the last bits from my room, which involved six trips to the communal dumpster and a slightly twisted ankle, I flopped back onto the sofa. It was officially movie time.

Only Imogen had other plans. No sooner had the opening credits rolled, when my phone rang.

"Stef! Thank goodness you picked up. Are you at home?"

"I'm watching TV."

"I might have a better offer for you."

"Really?" For a moment, I thought she meant another nightclub, then I remembered she was at work. Good—I couldn't take another hangover like Wednesday's.

"You said you wanted extra money, right?" She didn't wait for me to answer. "Well, Veronique called in sick, and Louis can't get hold of anyone to cover. So I thought of you. How about it?"

"You mean waitressing?"

"It's not much more difficult than Java, and I'm sure Louis would take it easy on you. Plus if you want him to agree to the work shadowing, working this evening would give you a good chance to meet him."

Part of me groaned. The last thing I wanted to do on this chilly Friday night was carry plates of overpriced food around, but Imogen was right—the opportunity was too good to pass up.

"Okay, I'll do it. But what should I wear? And where's the restaurant?"

"Oh, thank goodness. Louis's gonna love you. I'll

meet you by the bus stop on Juniper and show you where to go. Just call when you're about to arrive, and I'll come out. And we all wear a white shirt with a black skirt. There's spares in my closet if you don't have anything suitable."

"I'm sure I do, but thanks. I'll be there as soon as I can."

Apprehension mixed with excitement as I pulled on a pair of pantyhose, careful not to snag them with my fancy nails. At the beginning of the week, I didn't have a job, and now I sort of had two. Good thing I'd taken a shower and blow-dried my hair this afternoon, because it meant all I needed to do was dress in appropriate clothes and leave. Things like that were important when you got paid by the hour.

And Imogen said the restaurant sometimes had celebrities visit. Armand Taylor a couple of months ago, if that was to be believed, although I couldn't fathom why Hollywood's biggest heart-throb would have wanted to visit Richmond. Still, I couldn't help wondering if I'd see anyone interesting.

The bus ride took twenty minutes, and the heater was broken. By the time I got to the stop, my teeth chattered due to an unseasonably chilly evening. I glanced up at the sky and saw the stars twinkling down at me. On nights like this, I liked to think Chrissie and my daddy were up above, lighting up each other's lives.

As promised, Imogen was right there when I stepped onto the pavement, arms wrapped around herself as her breath misted.

"Hurry up. It's so cold out here."

I didn't need to be told twice, and a minute later, she cut down an alley and motioned me through a side door that she opened with an electronic pass, straight into a bustling kitchen. At a counter, a small blond man in chef's whites waved his hands while he chewed an assistant out in a very French accent for burning something or other. What had I gotten myself into?

Imogen must have understood my worry, because she gave my arm a squeeze. "Just ignore Gaston. He's always like that, but he doesn't mean anything by it. He just cares about his restaurant and wants it to run well."

"Gaston's the owner?"

"Yes."

"I guess it's good he cares."

Even so, I made a mental note to stay out of Gaston's way. Getting yelled at in front of everyone wasn't my idea of fun.

"And this is Jean-Luc."

A smiling man with dimples glanced up from a row of tiny cakes decorated with gold leaf, then leaned in to kiss me on both cheeks.

"No hands while I'm preparing food. Lovely to meet you, chérie." Then to Imogen, "I'll save one of these for you later."

Imogen giggled then led me past rows of counters and ovens to a tiny office, where a dark-haired man in a suit sat at a cluttered desk. "This is Louis, the manager."

Louis skirted past piles of brochures and paperwork to shake my hand. "Thanks for helping out at such short notice. It's a full house tonight."

"It's always good to be busy."

He grimaced. "Usually I'd agree with you, but Scott Lowes just turned up with his wife, and the paparazzi keep trying to sneak in."

"Scott Lowes? No way."

"Lovely guy, but the circus that follows him around always makes life difficult. Don't worry, though—we'll keep you away from all that as it's your first night."

Chaos or not, I couldn't help being disappointed that I wouldn't get to see a man I'd drooled over so many times on the big screen. "What would you like me to do?"

"I thought you could look after the private dining room. It's only eight guests, and they're having some sort of business meeting. They should be easy enough to look after, and they've already ordered. Just take in their meals, keep their drinks topped up, and clear away the dishes." He handed me a small black box. "Clip that to your waistband and stand outside the dining room door. If they want something, it'll vibrate. Otherwise, don't go in without knocking."

A waitress poked her head around the doorjamb. "Louis, a photographer just shoved his way inside. Can you help?"

"Excuse me, I need to go. Good luck."

This place was a heck of a lot different from Marnie's Diner, and a summer working there plus my short stint at Java was the sole extent of my waitressing experience. The Daily Grind didn't count since I'd rarely left the counter. Still, Chrissie always used to tell me to "fake it till you make it," and once again, I took her words to heart.

"Shall I show you where the dining room is?"

Imogen asked.

I took a deep breath. I could do this—I had to believe that.

"Sure."

Chapter 14

I COULD HEAR the bedlam coming from the front of the restaurant as Imogen led me to a door at the back. When I was a little girl, I'd dreamed of being a movie star, but if this was their reality, I was glad I'd grown up a nobody.

"Just wait here until they call you," Imogen said, pointing at a spot next to an ornamental tree. "It'll be easy. You'll see."

She'd already set me up with a pad and pen, plus a copy of the menu to read through, although she said most of the food required Google Translate to interpret. Now I was on my own.

While I waited, I took in the corner of the dining room I could see from my sentry post. Artfully placed screens gave the illusion of privacy and meant my attempts to catch a glimpse of Scott Lowes were foiled. Plush furnishings absorbed most of the conversation, and the black-and-white décor was set off by silver accents that reflected glimmers from the chandeliers above. The understated elegance scared me. What if I dropped a plate? Or spilled a drink? What if...?

I jumped as the box on my hip buzzed, but I quickly swallowed down the lump in my throat. *Here goes nothing.*

The door wasn't as heavy as it looked, and it swung

both ways, making it easy to carry food through. I shouldn't have been surprised. Whoever designed this place had obviously paid attention to detail.

As the door closed behind me, I got my first look at my customers for the evening. Eight men in suits, ranging from their mid-twenties to sixty at a guess. Seven corporate clones. And Oliver freaking Rhodes.

I'm sure every drop of blood drained out of my face at the sight of him, and I certainly swayed on my feet. He, on the other hand, didn't blink, just looked down at the black box in his hand.

"If I'd known this would summon *you*, I'd have pressed it sooner."

The rest of the men tittered, and I wanted to sink through the floor. Right after I'd impaled Oliver's testicles on an ice pick.

But I wasn't rich enough to allow myself that luxury.

Instead, I forced a smile onto my unwilling face and met his eyes. "How can I help?"

He glanced at the wine list in front of him. "Could you bring us a couple of bottles of the Chateau Musar?"

"Certainly. Sir," I added as an afterthought.

He raised an eyebrow, then started a conversation with the man next to him. I was dismissed—a feeling all too familiar.

The buzzer went off a dozen more times that evening. More drinks, clear the plates, more drinks, take the dessert order, more drinks, clear another pile of plates, more drinks, more drinks, more drinks.

At least there was plenty to watch as I maintained my vigil beside the door. First, a man proposed to his girlfriend with the ring in a glass of champagne. A little cheesy, but cute, at least until she choked on it. A doctor dining two tables over gave her the Heimlich manoeuvre, so at least she got to enjoy dessert. And she still had a better evening than the couple at the table in the corner. The man's other girlfriend called while he visited the bathroom, and the ensuing argument was something to behold. Louis had to ask them to move it to the street because the other diners were looking a tad uncomfortable.

Finally, my customers began to leave, filing out one after the other. I counted up to seven, and then the damn buzzer went off.

Oh, how I longed to ignore it, but if I hoped to get another shift here, I couldn't afford to. Butterflies with razor-sharp wings flew around my stomach as I pushed the door open.

"Can I help?"

Oliver leaned back in his chair at the far end of the table. "That depends."

"On what?"

"On whether you still wish me bodily harm. I saw the look on your face earlier."

"With the things you do to me, are you really surprised? And why are you here? Are you stalking me?"

"I could ask you the same thing. First, you turn up at the coffee place I've used for years, and now you're in my restaurant."

"*Your* restaurant? Isn't that overstating things a bit?"

"I'd have thought the name would have given the game away."

I thought back to the menu I'd studied earlier in the

evening. The silver logos on the plates and cups. The embroidery on the apron I'd been given to wear. *Rhodium.*

I collapsed on an empty seat with a bump. "I thought Gaston owned it."

"He owns a percentage. I'm the majority shareholder."

A tear dripped down my cheek unbidden. "I'd never have come here if I'd realised."

Oliver moved from his seat and crouched in front of me, caging me in with a hand on each of the chair arms. "Why?"

"Because I don't want to be near you."

"Why?"

He reached a thumb out and wiped the errant tear away.

My voice dropped to a whisper. "Because you're bad for me."

"Sometimes bad can be good." He smiled and my insides flipped. "And I noticed you used the present tense earlier."

"What are you talking about?"

"You said 'the things you do to me.' Not 'the things you did to me.' In your mind, it's still ongoing."

I shook my head. "You're wrong."

He moved his hands from the chair to my legs. "No, I'm not."

His thumbs ran up my thighs, stopping just short of the crease where my legs met my body. Heat burst through me like a bomb going off, and it probably left as much damage in its wake.

"You can't do this."

He leaned forwards until his lips were half an inch

from mine. "You want me to stop?"

I hesitated too long. I knew that, but my mouth wouldn't say yes. Even though my brain instructed it to. Even though it was the only sensible option. Even though I strongly suspected how this would end.

"No," I whispered. "I don't want you to stop."

I thought Oliver would kiss me, and I closed my eyes, waiting for that spark to ignite, but instead, he took my elbows and helped me to my feet.

What was he doing?

"Sit up on the table."

"Why?"

"Because I'm asking you nicely."

He didn't wait for me to comply, just lifted me until I was positioned the way he wanted—facing him, my legs spread as he pulled the chair closer and sat on it.

One leg at a time, he lifted my feet and positioned them on the arms of the chair so this time I caged him in. Although that didn't feel like the case, because we both knew it was me who was trapped.

And when he reached forwards and pulled me along the polished surface, I realised what was going to happen.

"No," I whispered. "You can't."

"I can, and I will. Now lie back."

Everything about this screamed bad idea. What if someone walked in? I could hear people moving around on the other side of the door—the voices of other customers and my colleagues. Imogen was out there, for crying out loud. And Oliver was an asshole. But as he caressed my thighs with magic fingers, the devil inside me threw caution to the wind and I did as he said.

The cool wood was a contrast to the warmth of Oliver's fingers as he inched my skirt higher, and I tingled just from the anticipation. How could a man do this to me with barely a touch?

Ripping filled the air as he tore apart my pantyhose, and I nearly fell off the table when his fingers brushed my nub through my panties.

"You'll notice I didn't order dessert tonight, princess. I decided to save myself for you."

I gasped at his words. "You knew this would happen?"

"From the moment you walked in that door."

"You bastard." I tried to get up, but a row of his kisses on my inner thigh stopped me. "I hate you," I mumbled.

"So you keep saying."

My back arched as he moved my panties to the side and blew warm air over me.

"It's true."

He just chuckled. "Pity. I'm enjoying myself. I knew it was a good decision to offer a private dining room. And this buzzer system? Genius."

He unclipped the box from my waist and pressed it between my legs. Then he pushed his button, and I bit my tongue to stop myself from screaming.

"I enjoy seeing you like this, Steffie."

"What? Out of my mind?"

"No, turned on. Aroused. Your cheeks go pink and your breasts get fuller." He pushed my panties aside again, only this time he swiped his tongue across my sweet spot. "And you taste delicious."

He quickly followed up his tongue with a finger, pushed deep inside me. "And judging by the state of you, I'm not the only one who was looking forward to the end of dinner."

"I was not."

His finger made a squelching sound as he removed it, and he trailed its wetness across my skin. "Liar."

The buzzer came back, and it turned out it kept vibrating the whole time he kept his button pressed. By the time he let up, juices ran down me, and I'd stuffed my own fingers into my mouth to keep from crying out. And when he sucked my most sensitive spot, long and hard, I could take no more.

I fell apart on the table, next to a half-empty glass of wine and a vase of black-and-white flowers, crystal sparkling overhead. Freaking hell, I couldn't even remember my own name.

As I floated back to earth, Oliver leaned forwards and kissed me hard on the mouth.

"Taste yourself," he told me.

Like I had a choice.

Once again, it wasn't as disgusting as I thought, and if I was honest, my arousal combined with the faint taste of Scotch from Oliver took me halfway to heaven again. I was still shaking when he pulled me upright.

"Princess, I just found my favourite dessert, but that one's not going on the menu."

I didn't have words. None of my senses worked. "Mmmm."

"Is that all you've got to say for yourself?"

A fraction of my faculties returned. "I think so. Yes."

He knelt down and peeled off the remains of my ruined pantyhose, removing one shoe at a time then kissing my insteps before he replaced them.

"Can you stand up?"

"I don't know."

"Try."

I slithered off the table and balanced on wobbly legs as he tugged my skirt into place. Didn't he want anything in return? Most men I'd met liked to bask in their own pleasure, and any the women got was merely incidental. But apart from a significant bulge in his pants, Oliver showed no signs of being affected.

"I'll call you a car," he said.

I'd been expecting something like that, but I couldn't deny how much it stung. I simply didn't understand the man. How could he be so into me then switch all that off?

"Don't."

"Steffie, I don't want you travelling home alone."

"I won't be. My roommate works here too, and I'm going home with her."

He looked me in the eye. "Really?"

"I'm not a liar."

How dare he doubt me that way? I may have been stupid and weak-willed around him, but never dishonest.

He ran a hand through his hair. "Sorry. I shouldn't have asked that. Shall I arrange transport for both of you?"

"No, because then she'll ask questions."

He grinned, and it made him look years younger. "So now I'm your dirty little secret?"

"Whatever. This isn't happening again."

He didn't say a word, just held the door open as I marched from the room, praying I didn't smell too much like sex. With that in mind, I scurried to the ladies' room and fished around in my bag for the tiny bottle of perfume I always kept in there. I'd just given myself a couple of squirts when Imogen walked in.

"How did it go? I didn't see much of you."

"Okay. One of them was a little demanding, but the rest were fine."

"Sounds typical. Say, weren't you wearing pantyhose earlier?"

"I got a huge run and thought I'd better take them off. Good thing I shaved my legs this afternoon."

Imogen laughed. "Always good to be prepared. You never know, you might even get lucky. There's some decent men in a place like this."

"You read too many romance novels."

"Tell me you haven't thought about it."

"Not really. Hey, did you get to see Scott Lowes?"

"OMG! Louis assigned me his table, and when Scott passed me his credit card, he touched my hand. I'm never washing it again."

I swung my bag over my shoulder. "That's not very hygienic."

"I don't care. I mean, *Scott Lowes*."

By the time we got out to the restaurant floor again, only a few patrons remained at scattered tables and Oliver was long gone. But what came in his place was a sense of disgust. How could I have let him use me like that? I couldn't even claim ignorance this time, because I knew damn well how it would end.

Never again, I promised myself. Never again.

CHAPTER 15

IMOGEN WAS STILL talking about Scott Lowes over breakfast the next morning. His eyes, his hands, his smooth voice.

"Didn't he have his wife with him?" I reminded her.

"Yes, and the way he looked at her broke the heart of every other woman in the restaurant." She looked downcast for a second, then perked up. "But I forgot to tell you, we have dates tonight."

I spluttered on my orange juice, nearly losing it over the kitchen table. "Did you just say 'we'?"

Imogen grinned and bobbed her head. "You can thank me later."

Two slices of toast popped out of the toaster, and she abandoned her mug of coffee in favour of slathering them with butter. It took me a few seconds to process everything.

"But I don't want to go on a date." Curiosity got the better of me. "With who?"

"Aha, I knew you couldn't resist." She waved a slice of toast around after she'd taken a bite from it, and I groaned at the crumbs now dotting the kitchen I'd spent ages cleaning yesterday.

"I *can* resist. I'm just interested in finding out how much of a disaster you've tried to set me up for."

"Don't be like that. You liked him."

"Who?"

For a moment, a picture of Oliver popped into my head, but I soon blocked it. Imogen didn't know anything about my involvement with him—I'd been very careful to avoid any mention of the man I absolutely shouldn't be thinking about, especially after what he did to me last night.

And in a freaking restaurant! The door wasn't locked, and anyone could have walked in. What would have happened if one of his dining companions had forgotten their umbrella or something? And the buzzer... Someone would be wearing that clipped to their waistband tonight, completely unaware of where it had been. That thought alone should have made me feel ill, but I felt a tingle between my legs reminiscent of that caused by the buzzer itself. What the hell was wrong with me?

Imogen finished chewing her mouthful of toast, blissfully unaware of the disaster my sex life had become. "Two of the guys we met in the club on Tuesday night. Well, Wednesday morning. Landon was really into you, and the way you danced with him, I could see the feeling was mutual. So I accepted on your behalf."

Try as I might, I couldn't recall anything of the early hours after nearly singeing my eyebrows off with a flaming sambuca. "I don't remember anyone called Landon."

She giggled, and more crumbs dropped onto the floor. "Boy, you really got wasted, didn't you?"

"That part I know."

"Good thing I can hold my drink, isn't it? Landon's a cutie, and his friend and him want to take us out for dinner."

How did I feel about that? At that stage, it would have been easy enough to back out claiming alcohol-related amnesia. But I hadn't been on a proper date for ages, and no, Oliver most certainly did not count. Perhaps I needed this? An evening with a normal guy, doing normal things like dinner, dancing, and maybe more without money changing hands, and definitely without me coming over the dining table.

"And you're sure I liked him?"

"Honey, you grabbed his ass in the club and told everyone it belonged to you."

Hear that *thunk*? That was my jaw hitting the table. "I didn't."

"Oh yes, you did. Don't worry, he saw the funny side."

"And he still wants to take me on a date?"

"You do yourself down. You're smart, pretty, and funny, and most guys would kill to have a girl like that. So yes, he wants to take you out on a date. Seven o'clock. Don't be late."

I mused over Imogen's comments as I curled my hair into soft waves that evening. She'd been way off base with her "most guys" comment. I seemed to attract the weirdos like a damn magnet—one of those huge electromagnets, sucking in every pervert and fetishist for miles around.

Other than the men who'd paid for me through Rubies, I could count the number of guys I'd dated since I started college on one hand, and none of them lasted more than a month. Then there were the men who wanted something else. Randy, who'd been obvious in his demands, and Oliver, who I still didn't understand. The only guy who'd showed any interest in the real me had ended up dead. I didn't have a great track record, did I?

So perhaps this would be my chance? Dinner with an average guy, and as Imogen had arranged it as a double date, I'd have moral support if it turned out terrible.

"Almost ready to go?" she asked, appearing in my doorway.

"Five minutes."

"That dress suits you. I never had the chest to carry it off, but on you, it's perfect."

I wasn't quite so convinced. The clingy dark-green velvet looked the part, but it felt like my girls were about to fall out of the plunging neckline despite the toupee tape Imogen had used to stick them in.

"I'll need to be careful if we dance."

She shook her own smaller pair, safely encased in a high halterneck that she'd teamed with capri pants despite the cold weather. "Just stick close to Landon, and that way if there's a wardrobe malfunction, nobody'll see."

I wasn't sure I wanted to live by those words of wisdom, but Imogen wasn't a girl to argue with over things like that. And now she stepped into my room and started rooting through my make-up bag.

After a few seconds, she held up a tube of mascara in triumph. "You need more of this. Or false lashes. Do you have any of those?"

"I hate wearing them. I always worry in case they

fall off."

"I went out to dinner with a client once, and another girl at the table had an enormous pair decorated with tiny crystals. One of them landed in her soup."

"You're not helping."

"Sorry. Okay, no false lashes, but you need to add more mascara. And darker lipstick."

Fifteen minutes later, once Imogen had "let my inner vixen out," I shoved my arms into my coat and walked out the door. The black trench wasn't particularly warm, but since my stint as Sable, I'd abandoned faux fur for good. I didn't need another reminder of my past life.

We splurged on a cab to take us to the restaurant, and I spent the trip racking my brain for some memory of Landon, however vague. But there was nothing. I only hoped Imogen's assessment proved correct.

The driver drew up outside Iberico, a mid-priced Spanish restaurant I'd never been to. It was too cheap for my ex-clients to consider eating there and out of my price range on a normal day. But with the extra money I'd earned at Rhodium, I figured I deserved a treat. And I had to smother a giggle at the irony—spending the money I'd made waiting on a man who was totally wrong for me on a date with a man who just might be right.

Imogen led me into the dimly lit bar, and I scanned the place for possibilities. Had Landon even arrived yet? The answer appeared to be yes, because when she led us towards a pair of men leaning on the bar, their eyes lit up in recognition.

The guy on the left wore blue jeans, a white T-shirt,

and a leather jacket—the biker look—but I figured him as too clean-cut to ride. His friend's style tended towards preppy, with skinny jeans and a Pringle sweater. Now, I hadn't dated enough to have a type, but if I had, I'm not sure either of them would have been it. The question was, which of the two was Landon?

I soon found out when Imogen marched up to Biker Guy and planted a smacker right on his lips. That left me with Mr. Abercrombie & Fitch. Now what? No way was I about to kiss him like Imogen did, but a handshake seemed weird.

Thankfully, he saved the day by leaning forwards and kissing me softly on the cheek.

"It's good to see you again, Stef."

"Likewise."

Imogen spun me around. "You remember Jamie?" she asked, knowing full well I didn't.

"How could I forget?"

I got a kiss on the other cheek from him, and then he motioned to his glass. "What can we get you ladies to drink?"

"Two glasses of white wine," Imogen told him, then added, "Not each."

He chuckled and ordered from the bartender. I'd already warned Imogen I'd be staying off the hard liquor tonight, even if I didn't have another appointment with Oliver tomorrow.

"We've booked a table," Landon said. "It'll be ready in a few minutes."

Thankfully Imogen steered the conversation, because I had no clue what I was and wasn't supposed to know from Tuesday. And Jamie had more to say than Landon, so between them, they did most of the talking.

Before the waitress showed us to our table, the topics cycled from a discussion about another friend who I also didn't remember from the night we'd met to news of a new bar opening nearby to a recap of last night's football.

Landon slipped into the same side of the booth as me, but he maintained a respectful distance and for that I was grateful.

"So, you work at Java with Imogen?" he asked.

"That's right. I started this week." And so much had happened in that short space of time, I almost couldn't believe it.

"Maybe I'll need to change where I buy my coffee."

"I'd be only too happy to serve you. With coffee," I hastened to add, in case I sounded like some kind of love slave.

He laughed. "Coffee sounds good to me. What did you do before you worked at Java?"

"I was a student here, and then I went home for a while."

"What did you major in?"

"Business at VCU, but I haven't graduated yet."

I wanted to get that out there, because letting him think I had a degree when I didn't would be worse than coming clean in the first place. Luckily, he didn't seem that bothered.

"I attended VCU on the business program too, but I graduated two years ago. Did you have classes with Professor Alanson?"

I smothered a laugh. "Yes, and his toupee still doesn't match the rest of his hair."

"It's fluffier than a chinchilla. I swear he used to get

a blowout every morning. You heard about the time the seniors stole it, right?"

And so the ice got broken. Despite my initial impressions, I liked Landon, and my worries about feeling uncomfortable over dinner proved unfounded. Imogen seemed to feel the same way about Jamie, given that she had her tongue stuck down his throat before the waitress brought dessert, and when the plates of churros did arrive, he fed her most of his.

I allowed myself one more glass of wine before we called it a night, and when Landon slid closer and draped his arm over my shoulders, I leaned into him rather than wishing I could get away. This felt good. Safe. Normal.

"I've enjoyed tonight," he said, clinking his glass against mine. "Can we do it again?"

I found myself nodding.

"But maybe without those two." He jerked his head at our two friends. "They really need to get a room."

I coughed, and Imogen looked up.

"Are you coming home?"

She took a few seconds to focus, her eyes a little dazed.

"What? Er..." She whispered into Jamie's ear, and he nodded. "I'm going home with Jamie. Do you want to catch a cab back with us? We can drop you off."

Landon answered for me. "It's okay. I'll make sure Stef gets home safely."

And he did. The boys insisted on picking up the tab, and then Jamie and Imogen dived for the first taxi, leaving us to wait for another. I didn't mind. It only surprised me they'd lasted that long. I'd half expected Jamie to toss her over his shoulder, caveman-style.

When the cab pulled up outside my apartment, Landon didn't try to invite himself in, and I was relieved about that. I had no idea what I'd have said if he did. For so long, I'd been a sure thing, and now I needed to reclaim some dignity. He gave me the space to do that, but he did lean over and kiss me softly on the lips before I got out.

And it was...nice. No sparks, no fireworks, but I didn't want that, right? This was the regular guy I'd been craving for so long. In time, the flutters of excitement would come. After all, Rome wasn't built in a day, the saying went, and yet it had lasted for thousands of years.

"Can I see you tomorrow?" Landon whispered, squeezing my hand.

"I'd like that."

CHAPTER 16

"ARE YOU GOING out with Jamie tonight?" I asked Imogen on Sunday.

She made a face. "I have to work. But he's picking me up afterwards."

"I take it I don't need to wait up?"

"Nuh-uh." She gave me a not-so-subtle wink. "It also means you'll have the place to yourself for your date with Landon."

"No way. That's not happening. Anyway, he's taking me out."

As of yesterday, new, sensible Stefanie had been born. My moves did not include letting men tie me to the bed or kiss me unexpectedly in elevators. Although I was sure if Landon tried the latter, he'd be a gentleman about it rather than walking off afterwards.

"Ooh, where?"

"I'm not sure. But he promised we wouldn't stay late, because I've got work tomorrow morning. Do you want me to call you to make sure you get up?"

"Nah, it's fine." Another wink. "Jamie's an early riser."

I tried to block thoughts of Imogen and Jamie and their

shenanigans from my mind as I waited for Landon to arrive. Without Imogen there to influence my dress sense, I'd opted for tight jeans and a scoop-neck top with enough sparkle to say "date" but enough coverage that I wouldn't be fidgeting with the neckline all evening.

I just had time to spritz perfume on and give my hair a last-minute brush before the door buzzer sounded, right on time. Another point in Landon's favour.

I picked up the entry phone. "Coming right away."

As the words left my lips, Oliver appeared in my head uninvited, and I grimaced at myself in the hall mirror. No. Oliver would *not* be joining me on this date tonight. Tonight was about a new man. A gentleman.

Landon offered me his arm as he led me to his car, a nearly new Ford Focus. I'd learned to drive back in Hartscross, even if the chances of me ever affording a car were lower than a heatwave in the Arctic. But at least I didn't need to take the bus tonight.

"Where are we going?" I asked.

"A friend of mine's having a party. I thought it would be fun for both of us to go. You might meet some new people."

I'd hinted at my loneliness last night over dinner, but not so much that I'd scare him off. How lovely that he'd taken notice. Even though I'd lived in Richmond for years, I'd never made real friends besides Chrissie. At school, I'd kept my head down and studied, and at Rubies? Enough said. Hanging out with people my own age whose sole reason for being there wasn't to get in my pants would make a pleasant change.

I did my seat belt up and Landon started the

engine, reaching over to give my hand a quick squeeze once he'd put the car in gear. I was pleased to see he concentrated on the road rather than chattering away. It meant we'd get to the party in one piece and gave me time to organise my thoughts.

Which were way off base. I'd been expecting a frat-boys type affair with beer pong, loud music, and dubious snack choices, but Landon pulled into a visitor space outside a fancy apartment complex.

"My buddy lives on the fourth floor," he said after he'd walked to the passenger side to open my door.

"This place looks really nice. Am I underdressed?"

I unbelted my coat so he could take a look.

He slipped an arm around my waist, under the coat. "You look perfect. There'll be a mix of people there, anyway."

A minute later, he knocked on the door of a condo, and a guy swung it wide open, holding out a hand to high-five Landon. "Good to see ya, buddy."

A glass of champagne soon found its way into my hand, and I gazed around the large apartment. The furniture was modern, all chrome and red leather, and the white counters in the open-plan kitchen overflowed with food and drink. Not the cheap kind, either. Bottles of wine jostled for space with the beer, and I even spotted smoked-salmon canapés.

Then I caught sight of the balcony and walked towards it, pulled along by an invisible string. When I stepped outside, the view over the gardens below was stunning, with trees and flowers lit up by artfully placed spotlights. A crystal-blue swimming pool twinkled off to one side, although I couldn't imagine anyone would be brave enough to use it at this time of year, even if it was heated.

"Great view, isn't it?"

Landon stepped up behind, one hand either side as he leaned forwards over the railing with me.

"It's beautiful."

"Not just the gardens."

I felt myself blush, heat rising in my cheeks. "Stop it."

He whispered in my ear, lips brushing softly against it. "It's true."

Why did I never quite believe men when they paid me compliments? Was it because the Rubies' men used to say things like that all the time, acting out their part as I did mine?

"I could stay out here for the whole night, watching."

He dropped a kiss on my hair. "You mind if I head inside? Catch up with a few people?"

"No, you go ahead."

The clouds cleared a little, enough for me to see the moon and a handful of stars, and I meant it: I could have stayed there all night. But Landon had gone to the effort of bringing me here, so I needed to be social. I found him in the lounge, drinking beer from a bottle as he chatted about baseball with a couple of other guys. Without breaking the conversation, he held his arm out and I slid beneath it, relishing the warmth when he tucked me against his side.

This was what a date should be like. Fun, good conversation, and enjoyable company. Sex didn't matter. Sure, it might make you feel good in the short term, but it wouldn't keep you company in your old age. If I tried that table trick with Oliver at sixty, I'd probably put my back out. Mind you, a few sessions with the chiropractor would be worth it for that sort of pleasure.

"Why are you smiling?" Landon asked.

Dammit, he'd caught me. "Just thinking how lucky I am to be here with you tonight."

"I'm the lucky one."

His buddies had headed over to the drinks table, and Landon moved so he pressed against me, arms wrapped around my waist. When he touched his lips to mine, a tingle spread through me, enough to surpass the mild buzz from the champagne. That was good, right? I mean, better than the last time? This was the kind of man who grew on you, that you learned to like, as opposed to one who stormed into your life and took whatever he wanted.

And Landon had a grin plastered on his face when he pulled back, so he obviously felt it too. Things were definitely heading in the right direction.

As I stepped down from my high, Landon took the empty glass from my hand. "Let's get you a top-up." He motioned at his own drink. "Don't worry. I'm stopping at one tonight so I'll be fine to drive."

And he was responsible too. I owed Imogen a huge thank you for organising my love life for me. Well, not love life, but definitely like life. You know what I mean.

Once I had a fresh drink in my hand, Landon led me deeper into the lounge. "Let me introduce you to some of these people. I think you'll get along with Mara and Alice."

He was right. After chatting with them for ten minutes, I learned stick-thin Mara modelled when she could get the work and waitressed when she couldn't.

Alice was a personal assistant to an accountant at one of the big firms in town.

"Dead boring, but it pays the bills," she said.

"I bet modelling's exciting. Do you ever travel abroad?" I asked Mara.

She grinned at me. "Sometimes. I did a shoot on the beach in Cancun last month, and they let me keep some of the outfits."

Alice cut in. "We can't all be lucky enough to have your figure, though."

"Oh, I know it won't last. I'm saving up to go to college when I can't resist the lure of donuts any longer. So, what do you do, Stef?"

"I work in a coffee place. Java."

"Ooh, that's my favourite," Alice squealed. "I go there on my break every afternoon for a cappuccino."

"I work the morning shift."

"Aww. Maybe I'll stop in early one day to say hi."

"I'd like that."

Landon had drifted off again, and when I saw him on the other side of the room, chatting with a group of girls, I couldn't help the way my body stiffened.

Mara reached out and squeezed my shoulder. "Don't worry about Landon. He's a hopeless flirt, but he only ever goes with one girl at a time."

Really? He laughed at something a brunette said, then took her glass to get her another drink. She was prettier than me. Thinner.

"I sure hope so. I've only known him a few days."

"You've got nothing to fear. I've never heard of him cheating, and we've moved in the same circles for years."

"What do you think of him?"

"Nice guy. If you've got a problem, he'll always try to help out. He's come up with the goods loads of times, and he's well-connected."

I smiled inside. "Thanks. I think I needed to hear that."

He refreshed the brunette's drink, then sauntered in my direction. Alice quickly turned the conversation to shopping in case he realised we'd been discussing him behind his back.

"Everything okay, beautiful?" he asked, offering his arm once again.

"Couldn't be better."

Tonight when he kissed me outside the apartment, I made more of an effort to respond, and things got a little heated as his tongue swept into my mouth to explore. The cold of the evening receded as he wrapped me up in his arms, and for a second, I rethought my decision not to invite him in.

But no, I had to stand firm on this. If we were to have any sort of future, there would be plenty of time for that later.

"Can I see you again this week?" he asked. "Maybe dinner or a movie?"

"I'm around every evening." Oh heck, did that sound too desperate? Should I have at least pretended to have a life?

Landon didn't seem to care. "I'll give you a call tomorrow. Sleep tight."

He leaned down and kissed me once more, giving me a lovely end to a very strange week.

Chapter 17

TRUE TO HIS word, Landon texted me on Monday morning just as the before-work rush came to an end. Did I want to go for dinner with him on Wednesday? I was about to reply in the affirmative when Imogen snatched the phone out of my hand.

"What are you doing?" she asked.

"Replying?"

"With a yes?"

My blush gave her the answer she needed, and she tutted at me. "Stef, you have *so* much left to learn. Landon didn't message you the second he got in last night, did he?"

"Well, no."

"So you don't reply to him right away either. Make him sweat a bit. Let him worry you might not be interested."

"But I *am* interested."

"I know that, you know that, but Landon doesn't have to. Give it a couple of hours."

"But..."

She pointed back to the counter. "You have a customer. I'll hang on to this until you understand the rules of proper texting etiquette."

It wasn't worth the argument, especially with the man waiting for coffee. I recognised him as a good tipper, so I hurried to serve him, and as usual, he didn't disappoint. A small flurry of tourists came in after that, most likely looking for somewhere to shelter from the rain. Their French accents sounded strange to my ears, and quite why they'd picked Richmond for their vacation as opposed to New York or even Virginia Beach, I had no idea.

I completely forgot my phone until after eleven when Imogen held it up. "Who's Oliver?"

"Huh?"

"Oliver. He just sent a message asking if you're free on Wednesday afternoon. Is there something you're not telling me? What about Landon?"

Oh. Just what I didn't need. More questions about the court case with his Royal Assholiness asking them. "It's nothing."

Imogen raised an eyebrow.

"Okay, it's to do with the Carter case."

"Ohmigosh. Not Oliver Rhodes?"

I crossed my fingers behind my back and cringed inside because I hated lying. "No, uh, another Oliver. He works at the same law firm."

She simmered down a notch but raised the other eyebrow. "Why did he thank you for an enjoyable dinner last week?"

That bastard. How dare he be so blatant? "He was eating at Rhodium while I was waitressing. I guess he thought I was efficient."

Imogen's grin broke through. "Ah, that explains it. I was worried you might be doing the dirty on Landon, and he doesn't deserve that."

"I never would. I promise." My encounter with Oliver didn't count. I hadn't even remembered meeting

Landon at that point. "How are things with you and Jamie?"

"Good. Really good. He treats me like a lady, apart from when he doesn't let me sleep."

I held up a hand. "I don't need all those details. Can I text Landon back now?"

She looked at her watch. "Yeah, you've held out long enough. Are you still going if this lawyer wants you on Wednesday?"

"The lawyer can wait."

I fired off two quick messages, one to Landon letting him know I'd love to go on Wednesday, and another to Oliver that wasn't so friendly.

Stef: I'm busy Wednesday. And there won't be a repeat of dinner.

A message came back almost instantly. Clearly, Oliver didn't follow Imogen's rules.

Oliver: I need to go over the case, so pick another day. Soon. And I've upgraded the buzzer system.

How arrogant could the man get? For that, he could wait longer.

Stef: Now I'm busy all week. And you can go buzz yourself.

Oliver: Next Monday, then. 3 p.m. Don't be late. And in the interests of full disclosure, I find your dirty mouth quite entertaining.

Stef: Stop texting me.

Oliver: Why? Is your phone set to vibrate?

That was it. Entertaining or not, the next time I saw Oliver, he was getting a tongue-lashing. And not in a good way.

"Everything okay?" Imogen asked.

"Fine, just lost network coverage for a bit, but it's

working now."

"Did you get your court thing rescheduled?"

"Yes, it's all good."

Of course, "good" was a relative term where Oliver was concerned. In reality, everything he touched was either amazing or awful. I hadn't yet seen any evidence he could do in between. But Oliver could wait until next week.

Because it was Wednesday, and I had a date. I'd begun counting down the hours until I saw Landon from the moment I woke up, and with twelve to go, I got a shock when he walked into Java.

My face lit up with a smile, and I was pleased to see it reciprocated. Imogen noticed who it was and sidled up. "Take a break. I'll manage for five minutes."

"Are you sure?"

After all, the place was busy.

"Positive."

Landon reached me as I stepped out from behind the counter.

"What are you doing here?" I asked.

"I couldn't wait until tonight to see you, and I needed coffee. This seemed like the perfect solution."

"What can I get you?"

He looked me up and down, and I laughed.

"From the menu, I mean."

"I know, but let a guy wish. I'll take an Americano."

"You want to wait in the break room?"

"Does that mean I get extras on the side?"

I stuck my tongue out. "Maybe. Okay, yes."

I definitely needed to work on this hard-to-get thing.

Five minutes went really fast when four and a half of them were spent locking lips with a cute guy. Good thing I'd put Landon's coffee in a to-go cup, because he didn't get around to drinking any of it, and all too soon, it was time for me to get back to work. Landon said he needed to do the same. He was interning at an advertising firm, which apparently didn't pay that well, but he hoped to move up the ladder soon.

He wrapped one arm around my waist and picked his drink up in the other hand, then we walked back out. Luckily, I'd only worn gloss rather than lipstick, although Landon's lips were kind of shiny now. He was no Oliver when it came to kissing, but... *Stefanie! Stop it.*

"Seven o'clock?" he asked. "I'll pick you up?"

"Wouldn't miss it for the world."

He gave me one last, sweet kiss on the cheek, and I looked up to find Mr. Rhodes glowering at me from his place at the front of the line.

"Later," Landon said as he hurried out the door.

"Can you get that next customer?" Imogen asked.

"No problem."

I paused to take a deep breath, then turned to face Oliver. No problem, my ass. The man was a walking definition of the word.

"What can I get for you, sir?" I asked, hoping I conveyed enough sarcasm there.

"Grande Colombian, black. I take it that's the reason you couldn't make this afternoon's meeting?"

"So what if he is?"

"I worry about you, Stefanie. You need to be

careful."

"What are you now, my dad?" I dropped my voice to a whisper and hissed, "I'll make sure I use a condom, okay?"

"That wasn't what I meant."

"I don't care. Butt out of my life."

His mouth set in a thin line as he handed over ten bucks, and I dropped the change into his hand from a couple of inches above, careful to avoid any chance of touching him. Horny Oliver scared me. Angry Oliver terrified me. Imogen passed me his drink, and I pushed it across the counter towards him. "Have a nice day."

He didn't answer, and I pretended I didn't care.

"So, have you done the deed yet?" Imogen asked first thing on Thursday morning.

And I meant first thing. I was still rubbing sleep from my eyes as I stumbled to the bathroom.

"I've known the guy, like, a week."

"Exactly my point."

"No, we haven't." A smile snuck onto my face. In a neat twist on dinner, Landon had packed a picnic and taken me to an old-fashioned drive-in theatre last night, although I couldn't have told you which movie we saw. "But I'm not completely averse to the idea."

I put my fingers in my ears as Imogen squealed and hugged me.

"Oh, I'm so happy you've finally found a guy you like! Are you going out again soon?"

"He's invited me to a party on Friday night."

"Jamie asked me to the same one, but I have to

work. Are you going?"

I nodded. After all, the last one had been fun.

"You want me to stay at Jamie's that night?"

"Would you mind?"

"You say that like it's a hardship. Believe me, it's not. And there's condoms in my nightstand and lube in the bathroom cabinet."

"Imogen!"

"Just saying."

We'd nearly come to the end of the Friday shift when Imogen's phone rang. Neither of us normally worked Fridays, but the regular Friday team had asked for a favour, and covering meant they owed us one. Imogen popped into the break room while I served a solitary customer, a stranger who needed me to explain the difference between every kind of coffee we sold.

She popped her head out a few minutes later. "Is it safe?"

"He's gone now."

"Did he buy anything?"

"A bottle of apple juice. I'm serious."

She shook her head in disbelief. "Some people." She held up the phone. "That was Louis. He wants to know if you'd like another shift at Rhodium. Apparently, he got good feedback on your performance last time."

From Oliver, no doubt. My gut clenched. That...that asshole! He probably had a stupid smirk on his face while he was talking to Louis.

"Tonight? Louis wants me to work tonight?"

"Yeah. I remember you said you were going out

with Landon, but I thought I'd double-check. Fridays are second best for tips, and you never know, Scott Lowes might come back in."

"I really want to go with Landon." But Imogen was right about the tips. I'd got my share last week, and it doubled my wages for the night. "It'll sound awful if I tell Louis I'd rather go to a party, won't it?"

She shrugged. "So don't. I'll tell him you're not feeling well. What do you want? Flu? Cramps?"

"Ugh, not cramps. That's too much information. How about food poisoning?"

"Sure. There's no way he'd want you near the restaurant then. Shall I tell him you're still interested for the future?"

Was I? Oliver would hardly eat there every night, would he? And with tips, the money was quadruple what I earned at Java. "Sure, but do you think I could do the main floor?"

She let out a throaty laugh. "Too many pervy businessmen?"

"Something like that."

"I had a group once that ran bets over who could pinch my ass the most times. Gaston spat in their dessert."

Nice one, Gaston, but I could hardly ask him to put something nasty in Oliver's. And I already knew he didn't order dessert from the kitchen.

"I think maybe it's best to avoid that room."

"If Louis offers again, I'll tell him."

"Are we going to the same place as last time?" I asked

Landon when he met me at my door.

He'd worn a button-down shirt this time, and I was glad I'd made the effort with a dress. I'd had it for a while, a gift from an ex-client, and it was a few inches shorter than I remembered. The back plunged so low I'd foregone wearing a bra and instead opted for some weird sticky cup things Octavia had given me. I might have to curtail my balcony time, if there was one, because my nipples kept threatening to poke over the top.

"No, this one's bigger. We're heading out to Rybridge."

"Really? Rybridge?"

I'd only been there half a dozen times, and I said a silent prayer we weren't going to one of my ex-client's homes. Now, *that* would be an embarrassment. Rybridge was Richmond's richest suburb, where houses regularly sold for seven figures and you needed an invite to get past the gates.

"A college buddy of mine has a house there. Well, his parents do, but they're away for the weekend." He turned to grin at me. "Eight bedrooms."

My belly did a little backflip. Was that a hint? "Have you been there before?"

"Plenty of times. And if you liked the balcony at the last place, you'll love the back deck." He held out his wallet. "Have you got room for that in your purse? It's making my pocket lumpy."

I gestured at my tiny clutch. "Sorry. I couldn't fit more than a handkerchief in here." And a condom. Okay, three. Imogen insisted.

Landon helped me into his car, and when he turned into a sweeping driveway half an hour later, I became confident I'd love more than the back deck. The house was spectacular, an architectural masterpiece of glass and steel. And it had a sound system befitting it—I heard the bass pumping before we left the car. Even better, I'd never seen the building before in my life, although I had visited a similar, but smaller, home a few streets over for the purpose of spanking a retired banker with a wooden spoon while he offered me stock tips. The man had bored me to tears, and I wasn't surprised his wife had left him for her gym instructor.

I had high hopes of tonight being more exciting. And as Landon caressed the bare skin of my back, the first frisson of what was to come ran through me. Would tonight be the night? Imogen had made a point of shoving the condoms into my handbag before she went to work, although I wasn't sure what Landon would say if I produced the strawberry-flavoured one.

He took my coat as soon as we got through the door, giving me a moment in the hallway to admire the wire sculpture that dominated the room—a man and woman intertwined, but the man seemed to have three hands. No, four. A stylistic representation of Mr. Rhodes.

Landon blew cool air across my shoulder blades, making me jump. "Ready to go through?"

"Of course."

He leaned across and whispered, "I love the dress. Especially the back."

"Me too."

He settled one hand on my quivering spine and steered me through to a huge, open-plan lounge. Someone had set up a bar on a closed grand piano, and the champagne was in full flow.

Mara spotted us and raced over with a couple of drinks. “Great to see you!”

I took a sip from the offered glass. “And you. Thanks.”

“Alice is over here. Landon, you don’t mind if I borrow Stef for a moment, do you?”

He laughed and dipped his head to kiss me. “Be my guest.”

We chatted for half an hour before he claimed me back, and I liked that he wanted me to meet other people. I imagined if Oliver were in the same situation, he’d threaten anyone who came near. Not because he cared for me as a person—he’d made his lack of interest abundantly clear—but because he was selfish and didn’t want anyone else to have me. I still remembered his glare at Landon on Wednesday. If looks could kill, Landon would have been on the floor of Java with daggers sticking out of his back.

I clenched my teeth and growled silently at myself. *Stop. Stop thinking about Oliver.* It was Landon who had his arm around me, and him who I planned to take home with me this evening. I needed to exorcise Oliver’s ghost, and Landon was the perfect man for the job.

“You want some food?” he asked. “There’s plenty in the kitchen.”

“I wouldn’t mind a bite to eat.”

If only to soak up the alcohol. Mara had picked up a bottle of bubbly and kept topping my glass up as we spoke, and I felt a bit wobbly on my heels. Good thing I had Landon for support.

We’d got halfway across the great room when the yelling started. Angry shouts, not just revellers having fun.

"What the...?" Landon started.

Men in black swarmed the room, and my guts seized. Were we being robbed? I'd seen a true-crime special about home invasions last month, and three people ended up dead. *Don't puke, Stef.* That wouldn't help us to escape.

The overhead lights went off, and flashlight beams cut through the darkness as screams echoed from every corner. Hands tore Landon away from me. I tried to keep hold of his arm, but I fell over something solid—a body? a table?—and the air squashed out of my lungs as I landed.

The next thing I knew, one of the unwelcome visitors clapped a pair of handcuffs on me and hauled me to my feet.

"What are you doing?" I screamed. "Let me go!"

He didn't answer, just dragged me through the chaos towards the front door.

Was this it? Was my life over? Or was the nightmare just beginning?

Chapter 18

THE HORROR OF the situation became clear when I got marched out of the house and shoved into the back of a police cruiser.

"What's going on?"

"You have the right to remain silent. Anything you say can and will be used against you in a court of law."

"Why are you saying that? Am I being arrested?" My voice rose to a shriek, clear even above the shouts and chaos coming from all around me.

"You have the right to an attorney. If you cannot afford an attorney, one will be provided for you. Do you understand the rights I've just read to you?"

A sob escaped, quickly followed by tears. "Why are you doing this?"

"Do you understand the rights I've just read to you?"

"Yes, I damn well understand them. Why am I in handcuffs?"

"I'm arresting you on suspicion of drug dealing."

"Drug dealing? Are you crazy? I've never even taken drugs."

Apart from a couple of puffs on a joint back in Hartscross when I was sixteen. I'd choked so hard I ended up with a huge black bruise on my back where one of my old school friends thumped me, and that was my first and last foray into the world of illegal substances.

"You'd be surprised how many people say that, ma'am."

"But it's true!"

"Best to save it for the interview."

He leaned in and locked my cuffs to a grille behind the front seats.

"Wait! You can't just leave me here."

All I got was a snarky grin. "I'll be back. Don't worry."

Tears streamed down my cheeks, and I couldn't even wipe them away. Not that I had any tissues—my purse had disappeared somewhere in the melee, complete with my phone and wallet. Through the window, I watched as Landon got the same treatment as me, the whole ugly scene lit up by security lights blazing from the side of the house. There must have been thirty cops there. It rivalled the scene after Chrissie's murder for sheer theatrics.

Jamie got led out next, wearing a pair of boxers and a blanket around his shoulders. A girl followed in similar attire, screaming bloody murder. Had they been together when this happened? I'd have put my head in my hands if I could. Imogen was going to be devastated, and I couldn't even let her know what was going on.

The door behind me opened, and I jumped, then twisted around in time to see Mara half falling into the seat beside me. She looked pissed rather than upset.

"I can't believe this," she hissed. "Daddy hates when I get arrested. The last time he bailed me out, he cut off my allowance for three months."

"Your allowance?" I asked hollowly. "You're worried about an allowance?"

"Why do you look so surprised about this?"

"Because the police just burst into a peaceful party and arrested everyone. Did the neighbours complain or something?"

She stared at me for a few seconds, then burst out laughing. "You really didn't know, did you? Fuck, you're so naïve."

"What are you talking about?"

"Your boyfriend deals the best coke in Richmond; that's what I'm talking about."

It was as if the world stopped for a minute as I took in her words and tried to make sense of them. Landon, a drug dealer? No way. I'd never seen him look remotely... How did someone behave on coke? I had absolutely no idea. But he'd always seemed so normal. So sweet.

"You're lying," I whispered, and she laughed harder.

"Think about it, little country girl. He takes you to parties and leaves you while he makes his sales. Then he takes you home and fucks you, right?"

"He doesn't..."

"If you don't believe me, that's up to you."

I didn't want to believe her, just like I didn't want to admit that Oliver had been right when he warned me to be careful. Once again, I'd managed to demonstrate an appalling lack of judgement.

Eventually, the cop came back and slid behind the wheel, and we lapsed into silence as he started the engine and drove us to the police precinct. Mara seemed unconcerned by the whole process, but I'll admit I was terrified. Even more so when we got hauled out at the other end and fingerprinted. Having my mugshot taken, mascara streaks and all, surpassed even Oliver's worst efforts as the most humiliating experience of my life.

"N-n-now what?" I asked the policeman accompanying me.

"We'll take you to the cells, and then you'll have an interview in the morning. Do you want to make your phone call?"

Who the hell should I call? As he always did at the most inopportune moments, Oliver popped into my head, but I couldn't bring myself to phone him. Not like this. No way would I beg him for help. That left Imogen or my parents. My parents were out too. Mom would freak, and Chester would blame me for her nervous breakdown. And Imogen? How could I call her from jail so late at night with this sort of news?

"Can I make it later?"

He shrugged. "Suit yourself."

I soon found myself shoved into a holding cell with a dozen other women. Half were clearly off their heads on drink or drugs, and the others looked mean enough that I gave them a wide berth. I spotted Mara at the far end and went to sit next to her, even though I didn't like her much either anymore.

"You told me Landon was a good guy. Why did you say that?" I asked her.

"I figured you were looking to score. He's always been generous with freebies."

I leaned my head against the wall, feeling sick. My beautiful dress had a tear across the middle, and either dirt or bloodstains streaked the grey silk. And I'd broken one heel of my shoe, so when I walked to the cells, it was with a bizarre skip-hop that made me look drunk. How had I gotten myself into such a mess?

I'd lost track of time when a policeman called my name through the bars. "Stefanie Amor. You're up."

"Up for what?"

Beside me, Mara stretched out under a thin blanket. "Interview, stupid."

Thanks. How had I ever liked that girl? I dreaded talking to the police because I had no idea what to say, but at least in an interview room, I'd be away from Mara. I walked to the door, and the policeman let me through then cuffed my hands behind my back.

"Is it morning now?" I asked.

Because I certainly hadn't slept, and it didn't seem as if enough time had passed for it to be Saturday. I stifled a yawn as he led me along a corridor.

"Four a.m."

"You do interviews at that time?"

"Depends on who it is."

He stopped outside a door and reached for the handle.

"Wait. What happens? Do I need a lawyer? The cop told me in the car that you'd give me a lawyer."

I didn't know what awaited me in that room, but I knew I didn't want to face it by myself.

"Your lawyer's already in there."

Of course he was. The cop swung the door open to reveal Oliver sitting on the far side of a metal table, and he looked pissed. Like, really pissed. His lips were so thin I could hardly see them, and he barely looked at me with stone-cold eyes as the cop led me over to the chair beside him and sat me down.

"You can lose the cuffs," Oliver told him.

"I'm not sure..."

"She's a twenty-two-year-old barista, not a hardened criminal."

Every one of his words pierced the air like a knife.

The cop reached down and unlocked me, and my left hand went straight to my hair the way it did every time I got stressed. I'd barely managed to twist one lock around my fingers when two more policemen came in and sat opposite us. Right now, I wasn't sure whether to be relieved that a half-competent lawyer had shown up or cry because it was the one man I really didn't want to see.

The police asked questions. About Landon and Jamie and the parties I'd been to. And worse, they wanted to know what happened on our dates, and after them. I tried to answer as best I could, but Oliver interrupted constantly, warning me not to speak, telling the cops their questions were irrelevant, pointing out all the ways in which they were wrong.

After a while, I gave up on talking and just let him get on with tearing the two grown men opposite me into tiny pieces, and, if I wasn't mistaken, taking pleasure in it. And sitting there beside him, I understood two things. Firstly, that he'd been easy on me in his office so far, and secondly, why he charged the big bucks for his work.

And all the time, his silver pen flipped around in those long fingers, twirling, flashing, occasionally being used to write neat notes on a yellow pad. I should have listened, but my head was fuzzy and the only thing I wanted to do was crawl under a duvet and sleep. No, not sleep. Hide. I wanted to hide.

The clock on the wall told me just over an hour had passed when the men stood up. I'd long since lost track of the conversation. A combination of confusion and aching tiredness had caused my brain to shut down, and when Oliver took my elbow and lifted, I could barely stand.

"Am I going back to jail now?"

"No, you're going home."

I trailed behind him as he led the way through a maze of corridors, and then we were in the parking lot.

"Uh, I don't suppose I could borrow a cab fare?"

And perhaps a door key because I didn't know where Imogen was. She'd said Jamie gave her a key to go to his place straight after work, but without him there, would she have stayed? Then a horrible thought struck me. If he was mixed up in all this, would the police have raided his place as well?

"Imogen..." I mumbled.

"Is at home." He opened the passenger door of a black Porsche. "Get in."

"Is this your car?"

He'd driven a Mercedes the last time I saw him at Riverley.

"No, it's the fucking tooth fairy's. Get in."

He scared me, but what choice did I have? Either I went with Oliver or I stayed stranded in a parking lot with the wind whistling through the hole in my dress. Goose bumps popped up on my arms, reminding me how cold I was, and worse, my nipples were standing to attention.

I lowered myself into the passenger seat, and he slammed the door. Hard. He gave the driver's door the same treatment once he'd gotten behind the wheel.

"Are you taking me home?" I asked, hating the tremble in my voice.

"Yes, Stefanie, I'm taking you home."

I was surprised he didn't get arrested himself, the way he spun the wheels leaving the parking lot, but no flashing lights followed. Probably they wouldn't have kept up anyway. Buildings whipped past, and he blew through at least two red lights. It wasn't until he stomped on the brakes outside a fancy apartment block that I realised I had no idea where I was. A shutter in the side of the building rolled up, and he pulled forwards into an underground parking garage. Expensive cars stretched in all directions—BMWs, Audis, and even a Corvette.

"This isn't where I live."

"No, Stefanie, this is where I live."

Oh. Shit.

Chapter 19

"CAN YOU TAKE me back to my apartment? Please?" I clung to the seat belt like a lifeline.

He waved a hand at me. "I'm not taking you back to Imogen in that state."

I looked down at my body. With all the moving around, the tear in the dress had got longer, a white slash against my stomach, and I realised my pantyhose had a huge run in them as well.

"Does she know what happened?"

"I sent someone to pick her up from Jamie's place before the police broke through his door. I had enough on my hands tonight without having to bail her out as well."

"Bail? I'm on bail?"

"Did you not listen to anything back there?"

"I didn't understand."

"Yes, you're on bail. You need permission to leave the state."

I leaned forwards over the dashboard, fighting down the bile that rose in my throat. "Who paid it?" I didn't have that kind of money, and I doubted Imogen did either. "You?"

"I couldn't. Conflict of interest."

"So who?"

"Dan di Grassi."

If I'd had a gun at that moment, I'd have stuck it in my mouth and pulled the trigger. So much shit kept happening to me, and I couldn't stop it. And now more people knew the sordid details of my shambles of a life.

"But I barely know Dan."

"*I* know her. And she likes you, the little she saw of you before you disappeared back to Georgia."

I slumped over and stared out the window, unseeing. "You must have realised why I did that."

"Yes."

That was it. Just "yes." He understood he'd upset me enough that night to send me running through three states, but he didn't care enough to talk about it. The silence stretched between us, filling the car until he finally spoke.

"We should go inside."

"Stop changing the subject. Or better yet, take me to my own freaking home."

He walked around the car, then stooped down and lifted me out, setting me on my feet as he closed the door and bleeped the alarm on. How dare he do this?

I tried to walk away, but with my broken shoe, I didn't get very far. I kicked both of the pumps off and went barefoot instead, but I'd only gotten a couple of yards when Oliver threw me over his shoulder like a rag doll and strode towards an elevator in the far corner. Asshole. I beat on his back with my fists, but it made no difference. He adjusted his grip slightly and kept walking.

The elevator took off with a *whoosh*, and I watched the floor numbers tick by. Thirteen, fourteen, fifteen... Did he live in the penthouse? Oh, who was I kidding—of course he did. We emerged into a white hallway on the twentieth floor, the starkness broken by a single abstract painting hanging on the wall opposite the elevator, and he took a key out of his pocket and unlocked the only door in sight.

"Where are all the other apartments?"

"I'm the only one on this floor."

Great. Nobody would hear me scream.

Without further ceremony, he pushed the door open and flicked on the lights. From my bumpy upside-down position, I barely saw the apartment as he strode through a huge, open-plan living room—white, white, and more white—and along a corridor. Then I found myself dumped on a bed.

I stared up at him. He still hadn't smiled once, not that he was the epitome of cheerfulness on a good day, but he didn't usually look at me like a piece of lint he wanted to flick off.

"Now what?"

I half expected him to try some kinky game, especially since I was sprawled out on a mattress, and I wanted to take pleasure in telling him where he could stuff it.

"Get some sleep. I'll talk to you in the morning."

He backed out of the room and closed the door behind him.

That was it?

After his show of testosterone carrying me in here, he just walked off and left me? I truly didn't understand the man.

Sleep, he'd said. How did he expect me to do that? Sure, I might have been tired earlier, but after the ride in the elevator, I was wide awake. The man lived in his own damn crazy world.

I stretched luxuriantly, revelling in the sound of silence. Imogen usually put the TV on first thing in the morning, so I figured she must have overslept as well. I gave my head a little shake, trying to get rid of the nightmare that had plagued me last night, the one where I'd ended up in jail and Oliver had charged in to rescue me like some dark knight.

I reached a foot out, half expecting to find Landon beside me, but I only got empty sheets. Weird. I didn't remember my bed being that big. And why didn't he spend the night? I was almost certain I'd planned to invite him in.

Maybe he'd left early? I cracked an eyelid open, then sat up in a hurry when instead of my pale-pink walls, I saw a white sheepskin rug on a white-tiled floor, a navy-blue leather sofa, and the hint of a roof terrace through sheer floor-to-ceiling drapes.

Then it all came flooding back.

My nightmare had become a reality, and now I was in Oliver's damn apartment.

I lifted the comforter and peered underneath, finding myself in the remains of the silk dress I'd once loved. With anyone but Oliver, I'd take still being clothed as a good sign, but that didn't seem to bother him the last time. I slipped a hand between my legs, breathing a sigh of relief when I felt the lace of my most expensive pair of panties—the ones I'd planned for Landon to remove last night.

Landon. How could I have been so stupid? A drug dealer. A freaking drug dealer!

I'd had it with men. As soon as the court case ended, I'd become a nun. Life in a convent looked positively idyllic compared to what Richmond had to offer.

But meanwhile, I still had to get out of Oliver's apartment.

I was filthy, not just on the outside but on the inside too, and I knew that kind of dirt wouldn't be easy to wash off. For now, I'd have to settle for making myself appear presentable, just as a temporary measure. I looked around the room again, and this time I spotted the paper carrier bags stacked near the door, three of them. What did they hold?

Still wobbly, I swung my legs over the side of the bed, relishing the feel of the fluffy rug between my toes more than I should have, and padded over to the bags. The first held dainty silk underwear, all in my size, the second contained a pair of Converse, and the third yielded a pair of jeans and a pale-green cashmere sweater.

Were they for me? I wanted to assume yes—firstly, because I hated to imagine how many other women Oliver brought home with him, and secondly, because I didn't want to leave the safety of the bedroom with a dress that gaped in the middle.

But first I needed to use the bathroom, and while I was in there, I caught a glimpse of myself in the mirror. Wow. If Oliver hadn't been disgusted with me enough last night, the sight of me with mascara smeared all over my cheeks and dried snot under my nose would have been enough to put him off for life.

And that was a good thing. Of course it was.

Not wanting to face him again like that, I slipped

my arms out of the loose sleeves, and grey silk pooled at my feet. The shower was one of those complicated affairs with so many knobs and buttons it could only have been designed by a man. With a bit of experimentation, I managed to get a stream of steaming water, and I couldn't help sighing as I stepped underneath. A wire shelf held luxurious lotions and potions—a mixture of Molton Brown and Bvlgari, all the bottles new and unused—and I shampooed and conditioned my hair. I felt almost human by the time I wrapped myself up in a towel.

Then I felt like an errant child again when I stepped into the bedroom, because Oliver was sitting in the chair by the window, watching me.

I clutched the towel tighter. "Do you make a habit of walking into people's bedrooms?"

"No."

"What if I'd been naked?"

He didn't say anything, just smiled for a second, the grin of a predator closing in on his prey. Then his mask slipped back into place, evening out his features.

"Can I get dressed?"

He waved a hand in my direction but didn't move. "Be my guest."

Ugh, that man. I snatched up the bags and slammed the bathroom door behind me. I wasn't sure the clothes would fit, especially the jeans, seeing as I had enough trouble buying them for myself, but it was as if everything had been made to measure. How did Oliver know what sizes to buy?

I shoved my ruined dress into the tiny trash can in the corner, where it stuck out the top like a bunch of withered flowers. Time to face the music.

"Uh, thanks for the clothes."

"You need to thank Bradley, not me."

That explained it. Bradley was the personal assistant to Emerson Black, a friend of Oliver's, and one more person I'd met during the search for Chrissie's killer. Like every other woman, I'd adored Bradley, and I wished for a moment I hadn't left so suddenly afterwards.

"Maybe I could send a card? And something for Dan?" I had a hazy memory of Oliver saying she'd paid my bail.

"Or you could go and visit them?"

"I can't. Not after..."

I groaned just thinking about it. Even though I'd skirted the law during my time as a Ruby, not once did I ever get arrested. It was bad enough Oliver knowing what happened last night, without the world finding out. Although I'd embarrassed myself around him so many times already that once more didn't make much difference. Dammit, I wished he hadn't told Dan about my mistake, even if it meant staying in jail.

Come to think of it... "How did you find out I'd been arrested?"

How *did* Oliver magically turn up at the police station when I hadn't even made my damn phone call? Last night, I'd been too busy panicking to wonder, but now that I could think clearly, I realised he'd never give up his corner office to work as a public defender.

"I had someone keeping an eye on what was happening last night."

"What? Why?"

He looked away from me, towards the window, and sighed. "Because I wanted to make sure Landon Bishop didn't slip through the cops' fingers again."

"You knew? You knew he was dealing drugs and you didn't tell me?"

"I recognised him on Wednesday." Oliver met my gaze, his eyes steady. "You weren't supposed to be there. Imogen said you were ill."

Well, I certainly felt that way at the moment. "That's why I got offered the shift at Rhodium?"

"Yes, Stefanie. Only you lied."

"It was just a little fib."

"Do you know how Bishop got away last time?"

"How?"

"He got his girlfriend to carry the drugs for him. She's serving eleven years for her own stupidity."

I thought back to the conversation we'd had when Landon picked me up.

"He asked me to carry his wallet," I whispered.

Oliver just nodded.

That could have been me. Eleven years locked away in an eight-by-ten concrete box.

"Why didn't you say something?" I screeched. "Why didn't you tell me?"

"Would you have listened? I saw the way you looked at him."

Oliver's eyes flashed, a rare show of emotion from him and a hint as to what he was thinking.

"You were jealous? So you thought you'd send us both to prison?"

"As I said, you weren't supposed to be there."

Right. I was on a roll now, and the words kept flowing. All the pent-up frustration from the way Oliver treated me at Riverley Hall and Rhodium came tumbling out.

"You didn't want me, but you didn't want anyone else to have me either? You fucked me, then you left me, and now you think you've got some say in my life?" I pointed down at the bruises on my wrists—a reminder of the chaos last night. "You'd rather this happen than let me go?"

"That's not true."

I stormed past him, out of the bedroom. Which way led to freedom? I guessed left, beyond relieved when I found myself in the entrance hall. The front door, or rather doors, were huge wooden affairs more suited to a French chateau. I fumbled with the lock, cursing as Oliver's footsteps sounded on the tiled floor behind me.

"Stefanie, can we talk about this?"

"No.

"Please?"

I turned to face him, tears dripping as I fought to maintain a shred of dignity. "For once in your life, do the right thing and let me leave."

He came closer, reached past me, and opened the door.

"My elevator code is zero two zero seven."

I ran past him, feeling his eyes on my back as I waited for the elevator doors to open. The second they slid back, I dashed inside and hit the buttons to take me to the first floor.

It was only as I stepped out into the lobby and forced my breathing to slow that I truly processed his parting words.

The elevator code, the numbers I'd punched in to make my desperate escape...

Zero two zero seven.

The seventh of February.

My birthday.

CHAPTER 20

I REALISED TOO late that I'd run out of Oliver's building with no phone and no money. Either the police had them, or they were in the shambolic remains of a glass-and-steel edifice in Rybridge. I could add cancelling my credit card to the list of things to do today, although if someone found it, they were welcome to my bills.

Without the means to contact anyone, I stopped a lady walking a chihuahua and asked where I was. She gave me an odd look but helped with directions back to my apartment. Sick to my stomach from the events of the last twenty-four hours, I set off on the two-mile walk home.

Imogen answered the entry phone almost immediately, sounding breathless.

"Stef?"

"Can you let me in? I don't have my bag."

The buzzer sounded, and with the elevator out of order, I climbed up to the fourth floor wearily. All I wanted to do was go back to bed, even though I'd just got up. As I exited the stairwell, Imogen rushed out the door and threw her arms around me, pressing her face into the crook of my neck as she stood on tiptoes.

"He said you were okay, but I wasn't sure I believed him until you got here."

I hugged her back, grateful at least one person in the world was happy to see me.

"He?"

"A guy came to Jamie's and told me he knew you and I needed to leave, that the police were on their way to search the apartment. I wasn't sure about going, but he was really hot."

I didn't know whether to be happy she got out or gnash my teeth at her.

"Imogen, you understand that just because a guy's hot, it doesn't always mean he's safe, right?"

Oliver wrote the rule book on that one.

She pulled back and rolled her eyes. "Duh, I totally get that. But he had an ID badge for some security firm. And a Camaro."

Oh, Imogen. "What security firm?"

"Uh, I'm not sure. Black-something?"

Blackwood. It had to be. "Promise me you'll be more careful next time."

"Okay, okay, I will. So do you know him? Can I get his number? I was so busy worrying last night I forgot to ask."

"I don't know who he was. He must have been a friend of a friend."

"Malachi, that was his name. So, can you ask your friend?"

"We had a bit of an argument this morning." She opened her mouth, and I could feel questions coming, so I cut her off. "Anyway, what about Jamie? You seem to have got over him really quickly."

"Malachi said he was dealing drugs, so I figure it's not a good idea to hang out with him anymore. I don't want to get caught up in any trouble. What exactly happened to you last night, anyway?"

"Can we discuss it later? I need to lie down first."

I stayed in bed until Sunday. Cocooned under the comforter where no monsters, ghouls, or lawyers could get me. Although I kept yawning, every time I closed my eyes and tried to sleep, I ended up back at Friday night's party, and once I'd relived my arrest for the sixth time, I gave up and planned what to say to Imogen instead.

I still hadn't entirely decided when she knocked on my door.

"I brought coffee."

Those words would usually be the equivalent of "open sesame," but this morning, I barely contained my groan. "Thanks."

She pushed the door open and peered around the edge. "How are you feeling?"

"Like I got run over by a truck."

And it didn't help when Imogen sat down on the end of the bed with a bump. The ripples made me queasy.

"So what happened? You can't keep me in the dark any longer."

I recounted the whole sorry chain of events at the party, from the moment Landon picked me up until I got thrown in jail. When I got to the bit about Jamie stumbling out with a half-naked girl in tow, Imogen's eyes narrowed.

"That's it! I'm gonna cut his balls off with a pair of nail clippers."

"Is that even possible?"

"I don't know, but I intend to find out. Or a potato peeler? What do you think of a potato peeler?"

"I think it's a good thing Jamie got put in jail."

"I hope they lock him up for good, the asshole. Still, I can't believe it took them almost a whole day to let you go."

"Well..." If that was what she thought, who was I to correct her? At least that would avoid awkward questions about where I'd stayed for the remains of Friday night. "The cops were really busy. I guess they had a lot of people to interview."

"Malachi said your lawyer had things under control."

"Yeah, he did. He did most of the talking, and then they let me go."

She took the coffee out of my hand and gave me a hug. "I'm so glad you're back. Next time, I promise I'll vet our dates better. No cheaters, no dealers. Perhaps I should go scouting at the library or something."

Fun though it might be to see Imogen skulking through the stacks of books, I needed to let her know where I stood.

"I've decided I'm going celibate. In fact, if you even see me near a man, shoot me."

"No way."

"I'll join a convent. It's the only option. Men are rats."

Except for Oliver. Oliver was more of a lion but with the ethics of a mosquito.

"But celibacy? That's a bit drastic."

"I still have fingers."

"Fingers don't wine you and dine you first."

"I'm not drinking again either. It only gets me into trouble."

"Well, aren't you gonna be the funnest person on earth."

"Maybe I'll take up a new hobby?"

"Like what? Needlepoint?"

Imogen left for her shift at Rhodium at four, which gave me the evening with ice cream and a movie. They didn't have the same effect they used to. Instead, I thought back to all the times I'd snuggled up with Chrissie as we drowned our sorrows in a pint of double chocolate chip. If only I could turn the clock back a year, knowing what I knew now... How different things would be.

I fell asleep before Imogen came home, but she still got up before me on Monday morning. I tried to match her smile as we walked to Java.

Not easy, as she was positively beaming.

"Guess what? One of the other waitresses at Rhodium is having her appendix out this week. Louis sent her home yesterday in agony, right before the Ghost came in. She was really pissed."

"I'm sure he'll be back."

The Ghost—also known as Ethan White—was another celebrity, a DJ and music producer who'd adopted a spooky stage name, and Oliver probably gave him a discount seeing as they were friends. He'd also gotten tangled up in the Carter mess through no fault of his own.

"I hope so. He's hot. Anyway, she's off for at least a

week, so I've got all her extra shifts. Isn't that great? Louis wants to know if you'd be interested in the ones I'm already working?"

"Uh, I'm not sure..."

"Consider it. I don't have to get back to him until this afternoon."

"Okay."

My answer would be no, but I knew Imogen would try to convince me otherwise, and it was too early for me to think of a response. I needed at least two cups of coffee in me to come up with something plausible.

But I'd only had one before Monday morning got a whole lot worse. I was taking a rare turn at the coffee machine when Imogen nudged me and hissed in my ear. "Hot stuff alert. Your go."

And then I felt him. Before I even began to turn.

After everything I'd said to him on Saturday, Oliver still showed up for a plain black Colombian as if nothing had happened. Not that I remembered his order or anything. Anyway, the man must have the hide of a rhino. And if the contents of his guest bathroom were anything to go by, he probably treated it with three-hundred-dollar moisturiser morning, noon, and night.

I forced myself to unclench my jaw and walked up to the counter. "What can I get you?"

"Grande Colombian. Black."

"I'm on it," Imogen called out.

There was an awkward silence for a few seconds before Oliver lowered his voice. "How are you?"

"Fine."

A pause. "I'll call the police this morning and see what's going on with the Bishop case."

"Thanks."

"And you're still coming this afternoon?"

I'd been trying to block the visit to his office from my mind.

"I wasn't aware there was a choice?"

"There isn't."

Imogen handed me his coffee, I slammed it onto the counter, and he dropped a hundred-dollar bill next to it. Prick. Was I supposed to be impressed by that? It would eat half our change. I fished out his ninety-six dollars and fifteen cents, only when I went to give it to him, I saw the back of his hand-tailored suit disappearing out the door.

Oh no. No way. He didn't get to dump all that change on me like some bribe for my services later.

"Back in a sec," I muttered to a startled Imogen, then took off after him.

He'd abandoned his Porsche in a tow-away zone across the street—no surprises there—and he bleeped the locks as I burst out of Java.

"Wait!"

He looked across at me, then shook his head and opened the door. Red mist clouded my vision as I pushed into a run, hand outstretched. If he wouldn't accept the money, I'd throw it into his damn car.

The first indication I got that something was wrong was a slight widening of Oliver's eyes as he glanced to my right. The second was a streak of blue, and the third was the searing pain in my left ankle as the truck hit me. The driver didn't even stop, just squealed his tyres as I rolled into the gutter. Asshole. And kind of ironic. Someone had attempted to run me over on purpose a few months back, and I'd escaped, but now I'd gotten hurt through my own stupidity.

"Fuck!" Oliver was beside me in an instant.

Great. As if being hit by a truck wasn't bad enough.

"Where does it hurt?"

"My ankle." I tried rolling to one side to get up, only to rethink that as a white-hot dagger of pain stabbed my left wrist. "And my wrist. Could you help me up? I need to go and sit down."

"The only place you're going is the hospital."

Visions of past medical bills swam through my mind—the main reason I'd ended up in this mess in the first place. "I'll be fine. I just need a couple of painkillers and a rest."

"No chance. Your ankle's swelling already."

I made another attempt to get to my feet, and the world went blurry as another wave of agony shot through my leg. "I'm not going to the hospital."

"Yes, you are." He already had his phone in his hand.

"No, I'm not. I can't afford it, okay? I don't have insurance."

"I'll take care of it."

"No, you won't. I'm not being indebted to you."

"So you'd rather not be able to walk?"

A scream sounded from the other side of the road, and Imogen ran across. Thankfully there was no more traffic, because she didn't look both ways either.

"What happened?"

"I had an accident."

"A car hit her," Oliver said helpfully.

"Holy Stromboli. Have you called an ambulance?"

"I'm trying, but Stefanie here doesn't want to see a doctor."

Imogen grabbed the phone out of his hand. "Don't be ridiculous. Of course she does."

Oliver smiled triumphantly while Imogen made the call, although he soon stopped looking so smug when I leaned to the side and threw up on his leather wingtips. Freaking hell, I hurt. The pain was so bad I didn't even get a chance to feel mortified, although as this was the second time I'd puked in front of him, he should have been used to it by now.

The ambulance must have been close, because the siren sounded a minute later. I closed my eyes and prayed for drugs as a pair of medics jostled me onto a stretcher.

"Would you like something for the pain?" the female medic asked.

I managed to nod, teeth clenched together.

She inserted an IV line into my hand and patted me on the shoulder. "That'll start to work in a minute, lovely." She looked out at the crowd. "Who's coming to the hospital with this girl?"

Imogen stepped forwards. "I will, but I'll need to get rid of the customers and lock the shop. Can I catch up?"

Then Oliver's voice sounded from the side. "Take your time. I'll go with her."

"Are you sure?"

"Positive."

I tried to speak, but it came out as a croak. "I'll be fine on my own."

Imogen shook her head. "Oh, Stef. The drugs have sent you silly already." She glanced over my shoulder, then looked back. "And he's hot," she mouthed.

Hot? Oliver was the second circle of hell.

CHAPTER 21

A BIZARRE SENSE of déjà vu overcame me as I lay in a hospital cubicle waiting for the results of my X-rays. Had I broken something this time? I had a horrible feeling the answer would be yes.

At least today I didn't have to wait so long to get seen. When I damaged my wrist before, I'd sat on one of those hard plastic chairs for hours before someone came to help.

Today, Oliver had made a phone call and a doctor materialised almost immediately. At least the asshole was good for something other than sex and, well, lawyering.

Not that he hung around. When Dr. Beech wheeled me back to a cubicle after my X-rays, Oliver was nowhere in sight, but Imogen had arrived and somehow convinced the staff to let her through.

She leapt up the instant she saw me. "Are you okay? Did you break any bones?"

"I'm not sure yet."

The white-coated cutie hovering near Imogen squeezed her arm. "I'm sure your sister will be just fine. I need to go check on some patients, but call if you need anything." He gave her a grin that spoke of years at the orthodontist. "Like, anything."

She gave him a little wave, watching until he

rounded the corner out of sight.

"Fast work, Imogen."

"Practice makes perfect. Anyhow, you can't talk—your hottie's still hanging around outside on the phone. Getting hit by a car? Genius. I've never thought of that one before."

"I didn't plan it."

"So why did you go running after Oliver Rhodes?"

"He forgot his change."

Imogen rolled her eyes. "You should have put it in the tip jar. I bet your subconscious told you he was some kind of white knight. And did you see his car? That thing's top of the line."

"I might have broken bones here. Trust me, my subconscious didn't ask him to save me."

She settled into the chair beside the bed. "So, how long until you get the test results?"

"Who knows? Ages, probably."

At least the nurse had given me more painkillers now. Before, just breathing made my limbs hurt.

"I'm not so sure about that."

I turned my head and followed her gaze. Dr. Beech approached, chatting to Oliver as though they were old buddies. The pair of them stopped next to the bed, and Dr. Beech consulted my chart. I tried to read his expression, but his frown mixed with a lopsided smile didn't give much away.

"Well, Miss Amor, you've been quite lucky. A hairline fracture of your ankle and a grade-two sprain of your wrist. Six weeks, and you'll be well on the way to recovery."

"Six weeks?" I groaned and sank back into the pillow.

Another six weeks of not earning any money would put me on the breadline, but there was no way I could serve customers fast enough with one hand. I'd probably spill coffee everywhere. And this time, I didn't even have any savings.

"Give or take. The nurse will organise a cast for your ankle and strap your wrist up. You'll need to put plenty of ice on it for the next couple of days to take the swelling down."

My last stint in a cast had been hell, and I'd needed Chrissie's help with everything from washing my hair to cooking dinner. I hadn't known Imogen anywhere near as long, and she'd barely be around next week anyway.

"I'll have to go home," I mumbled.

Except I couldn't go back to Georgia, could I? Not when I was on bail and banned from leaving the state. Shit.

"Oh no, not back to Georgia?" Imogen perched on the side of the bed and held my good hand.

"I can't do everything by myself for six weeks, not with a cast and bandages."

My eyes prickled, and I blinked back the tears. After the experience with Randy, not one little bit of me wanted to return to Hartscross, even if I was allowed to go.

"But you don't have to leave. I'll cover next month's rent, and I'll see if I can get time off work to help you. Louis'll just have to find someone else to cover Katie's shifts. I'll tell him it's an emergency."

"That's not fair. You'll lose money."

"Don't worry; I've got some savings, and you're more important."

"But if you take time off work, that'll cost you even more money. Maybe if I explain the situation to the police, they'll understand and let me take the bus home."

"Stef, you can't go on the bus with a broken leg and a bad arm. How long does it take? Eight hours? Nine?"

"About ten, but I'll have painkillers."

Dr. Beech cut in. "You'll also need to have a check-up on those injuries in two weeks, Miss Amor. It's already been paid for here."

"What? By who?"

He didn't answer, but cut his eyes to my dark-haired nemesis.

Imogen smiled triumphantly. "See? You have to stay in Richmond now."

"Stefanie can stay in my apartment."

Three heads swivelled to look at Oliver, who looked as surprised as anyone by the words that had just left his mouth.

Oh no. No way. Not in a million years.

"Really?" Imogen asked.

Oliver shifted from foot to foot. "I spend most of my time at the office. My housekeeper can look after Stefanie during the day, and the building's concierge is available all evening."

Hello, stop talking as if I wasn't there.

"Imogen, no. Remember what we spoke about this morning?"

"About you wanting to become a nun? You weren't serious, were you?"

"About the 'men are rats' part," I hissed, trying to keep my voice down.

"But he's not a rat." She snuck a glance at Oliver.

"He's a lawyer. And he's hot."

From the slight smirk on his face, he definitely heard that last part.

"And I bet he's got a great apartment. Yes, you should definitely go."

"No!"

She turned to Oliver. "Don't worry about my friend. Her judgement's been a little off lately."

Imogen didn't know the half of it. And she completely ignored me as she carried on.

"If you write down your address, I'll drop some of her clothes off later. Can you give her a ride there from the hospital?"

Oliver plucked a card from his wallet and handed it to her. "If you call this number, my assistant will arrange to pick up Stefanie's things."

"Do I get any say in this?" I asked.

They both turned to me. "No."

In the hospital parking lot, I tried another feeble protest while Oliver slid the passenger seat back as far as it would go and lowered me into it.

"You don't have to do this. I'll manage at home."

"Why should you have to 'manage' when you can have help?"

I didn't have an answer, and secretly, a tiny part of me liked the idea of being attended to by a housekeeper for a week, if only so I could eat proper food. Even affording groceries would be difficult right now—I'd really struggled with that last time. Besides, I soon found out Oliver was serious about spending most of his time in the office.

That first night, he led me into the elevator and we soon whizzed up to the penthouse. He held out an arm when the doors opened, but I shook my head.

"I need to get used to walking with a crutch."

Two crutches would have been ideal, but my injured wrist put an end to that idea. Instead, I set off at an awkward hop-shuffle that took more out of me than I cared to admit. In the lounge, I collapsed back on the white leather sofa, grateful to rest and half-asleep from the medication. I was still dressed in the black skirt I'd worn to Java, which now sported a two-inch tear on one thigh, and the nurse had found me a top to wear that would fit over my bandages—one of those baggy green ones doctors wear. I was a mismatched mess in Oliver's immaculate home.

The man himself trailed me in and took a seat in the chair opposite. "Can I get you anything? Something to drink? Dinner?"

I wanted to say no, that I'd be fine, but I couldn't ignore the gnawing hunger caused by not eating for a day. "I wouldn't say no to some food."

"Italian okay?"

"I'll eat anything."

Oliver raised an eyebrow, and I realised I'd said something really stupid.

"I mean, I like Italian."

He walked over to a table by the door and picked up the phone, then spoke for a minute in what I could only assume was Italian. Once he hung up, he took his seat again.

"There's an Italian restaurant in the lobby if you get hungry. Just dial star twelve. And Rhodium will deliver here. Plus Claude's, if you want French cuisine."

Of course they would. Oliver lived in a different world, one where the two best restaurants in Richmond, neither of which even offered a delivery service, were at his beck and call. "Thanks. I'm sure I can find something here, though." Something that didn't require me to take out another credit card.

"Bridget keeps the cupboards fully stocked."

"Bridget's your housekeeper?"

He nodded. "You'll meet her tomorrow—she usually starts around eight. Do you want something to drink?"

As well as my stomach being empty, my throat was parched. "Yes, please. But I shouldn't have alcohol with my pain pills."

"Water? Juice?"

"Juice is good."

The doorbell rang as he came back with two glasses of OJ, and rather than move to the dining table, we ate from our laps in the lounge. Oliver's version of delivered food didn't come in cardboard containers—it arrived on china plates complete with cutlery and condiments. Even so, from the awkward way he sat, I got the impression he didn't usually eat informally like that.

I ate so quickly I barely had time to talk, and in any case, I didn't know what to say. Oliver chewed more slowly, and a couple of times, I caught him watching me as I carved off pieces of lasagne using the side of my fork.

"Are you left-handed?" he asked.

"Why do you want to know?"

"You look uncomfortable eating with your right."

I forked up the last mouthful and slid the plate onto

the glass coffee table. “Yes, I’m left-handed. I can’t even write until these bandages come off. I’m basically screwed.”

He abandoned the last few mouthfuls of his cannelloni and loaded the plates back onto the tray they arrived on, then bent and pressed his lips to mine. No tongues, just a hard, closed-mouth kiss, so quick I didn’t have time to act indignant.

“Not tonight, princess. I have to go to the office.”

I glanced at the clock on the wall behind him, a three-foot-tall homage to minimalist art in shades of green, and a rare splash of colour in the apartment. “The office? But it’s a quarter to nine.”

“Yes, I’m aware of that. And I still have a day’s work to catch up on.”

“I’m sorry. That’s all my fault. Is there anything I can do to help? I mean, I know I’m incapacitated, but…”

“Shh.” He stooped, and before I realised what was happening, he’d picked me up, one arm under the crook of my knees and the other under my back. “You need to get some sleep.”

He carried me into the bedroom I’d used before and balanced me on my good foot while he flipped the comforter back. That was…strange. So far, I’d seen asshole Oliver, hard-nosed lawyer Oliver, and sexy Oliver. Kind Oliver was new, and I wasn’t quite sure how I felt about him.

“I’m sorry…” I tried again.

Oliver placed a finger over my lips. “*I’m* sorry you got injured.”

Stealthy fingers slipped behind my bottom and slid down the zipper on my skirt. It fell to the floor, and he helped me to step out of it. Next went my top, peeled over my head and discarded beside the skirt. I felt decidedly unsexy standing there in my plain white underwear, two limbs decorated with bandages.

Oliver must have thought so too, because rather than touch me the way he had in the past, he lowered me to the mattress and gently tucked the covers around me. All I got was a kiss on the forehead before he backed towards the door. Hardly surprising—I looked like an ancient Egyptian mummy who'd started to come unravelled.

"I'll see you later," he whispered.

And then he was gone.

CHAPTER 22

OLIVER'S VERSION OF "later" turned out to be different to most other people's, because when I put on the robe hanging on the back of the bathroom door and shuffle-hopped out to find some breakfast the next morning, the only person in the kitchen was an older lady, in her late fifties at a guess.

As I walked through the door, she left the stove and pulled out a stool for me to perch on. "You must be Stefanie?"

I nodded. "But call me Stef. And you're Bridget?"

"Yes, I am." She looked me over with undisguised curiosity. "Can I get you something to eat?"

"Maybe something light?"

"Toast? Cereal? Eggs?"

"Toast would be good."

Such a simple task, but I couldn't even spread butter right now.

Bridget bustled around, setting out a place mat and cutlery then fetching me a glass of juice. It looked like orange, but it didn't taste like it.

"What's in this?"

"Mango and carrot. Full of vitamins."

If someone had suggested I drink carrot juice, I'd have wrinkled my nose, but it was surprisingly tasty. I finished the glass, and Bridget poured me another. She moved around the kitchen as if she cooked in it every day, which she probably did. How much involvement did she have in Oliver's life?

"Have you worked for Oliver long?"

"Eight years now."

"That's a long time."

"It's passed quickly. Too quickly. My children were teenagers when I started here, and they're both married with families of their own now."

"How many children do you have?"

"Two—a boy and a girl. Lawrence moved to Europe and Veronica's in New York now. She works for one of the big publishing houses, although she swears it's not as glamorous as it sounds."

"It's probably more glamorous than waitressing."

"Is that what you do?"

Bridget slid my toast over as I nodded. Wholemeal bread, but at least she'd been generous with the butter.

"At one of Oliver's restaurants?"

Restaurants plural? "He's got more than one?"

A slightly peeved look flitted across her face. Why? It was just a simple question.

"Yes, dear," she said. "He has more than one."

"He only mentioned Rhodium."

"He also part-owns the Italian place on the first floor."

I realised how little I knew about Oliver, only his occupation and the fact that he could send me into ecstasy with a touch of his fingers. Oh, and that he had assholic tendencies. What else could Bridget tell me?

"So what other investments does he have, besides the restaurants and the law firm?"

"This and that. You'll need to speak to him if you

want the details."

I guess the answer was that Bridget could tell me a lot, but she wouldn't, and suddenly she didn't sound so friendly anymore.

"I bet everything must keep him really busy."

"It does. And just because you've wormed your way into his home, it doesn't mean you'll get into his affections or his wallet as well."

Oh, hell. She thought I was a gold-digger. "I-I-I didn't mean it that way. I don't want anything from him."

"That's what the last girl to stay here said."

What last girl? Oliver had always given me the impression he didn't do serious relationships, but he'd lived with a woman? Mind you, I was staying in his home, and I didn't even want to be here.

"I don't know anything about her, but the only reason I'm here is because I got hurt and my roommate's working all week. She and Oliver insisted I stay. I'd gladly go home if I could."

"So you're only here for this week?"

"Yes. Imogen, my roommate, she's got extra shifts at Rhodium this week because they're short-staffed, but next week she'll be home more."

Bridget gave me a little smile. "In that case, I'm sorry for biting your head off. So many women have tried to get their claws into Oliver over the years, and he's like a second son to me. One who doesn't always know what's best for him."

"It doesn't matter. Everyone needs somebody to look out for them."

I'd love to have my own Bridget. Mom and Chester cared, but they'd never gone out of their way to fight in my corner. The closest I'd had was Chrissie and now Imogen.

"So you met Oliver through your roommate?"

"No." I might as well tell Bridget. If she was close to Oliver, she'd most likely find out anyway. "We met through the Carter case. I'm a witness."

She regarded me again, eyes narrowed. "Oh, so you're that Stefanie."

I nodded, blinking back tears. I'd never escape the judgemental looks and condescending words when people realised what I used to do for a living.

"Yes, I'm that Stefanie. But don't worry, as soon as the case is over, I'll have nothing to do with your precious Oliver again."

I slid off the chair and grabbed my crutch from where I'd leaned it against the breakfast bar, then shuffle-hopped back to my room. No, not *my* room. The room where I'd be sleeping for the next six nights until I could escape back to normality.

I stayed in bed for the rest of the day, staring at the ceiling until I found the remote in the drawer of the nightstand. Then I switched on the TV and watched old black-and-white movies until it got dark. Back in those days, life was so much simpler. Men were gentlemen, not mercurial assholes with psyches more tangled than Rapunzel's tresses in the middle of a hurricane.

And my own hair wasn't much better. It had gone lank and greasy, and although I'd managed to wipe my face with a washcloth, there was little I could do about the other parts of me without help.

When I'd broken my arm before, Chrissie had taped a plastic bag over it then hopped into the shower with me to sort out my hair. Doing the job we once did meant we had few inhibitions when it came to such things. I still recalled her hoots of laughter as she kidded about setting up a webcam and making our fortunes that way. The thought of asking Bridget to do the same resulted in a weird snort, and I thanked my lucky stars no one was around to hear me.

I could probably ask Imogen to give me a hand, but not before next week, and until then, I had to put up with hair oily enough to tempt a US invasion.

And right now, I had another problem: hunger.

When my stomach growled for the eleventh time, not that I was counting or anything, I ventured back out into the dragon's layer, only to find the apartment silent. No Oliver, no Bridget. And no lights. I squinted into the gloomy hallway, searching for the switch, but it eluded me, and I had to shuffle slowly to the kitchen, trying not to bump into the walls or the furniture. I made it with only one bashed elbow and, thankfully, managed to turn on the spotlights above the kitchen island.

Now what? There was a limit to what I could make with partial use of my left hand, and I settled on reheating a pot of cooked spaghetti I found in the refrigerator, most likely leftovers from the restaurant downstairs. Oliver's restaurant.

Except this evening, there was no Oliver to share the food with me. Was he coming home tonight? Did he come home last night? I thought back to my day on the sofa in his office, wrapped up in a blanket drenched in his dark musk. How much time did he spend in the same place, doing the same thing?

The only sound in the apartment was the faint hum from the refrigerator as I wrapped the last strands of spaghetti around my fork, chewing slowly. Was sleeping at the office a regular thing for Oliver? Or was he avoiding me?

I began to suspect the latter when he didn't appear on Wednesday either. Bridget made me toast in the morning without a word, and then I retreated to the bedroom once more. I longed to pull back the drapes in the lounge and sit in there to enjoy the view over the roof terrace with the city beyond, but Bridget's presence lingered in the room like a malevolent ghost.

So I fell back into the same routine as yesterday—hiding out in my room until it was safe, then rummaging for food in the kitchen like a tramp searching through dumpsters at the end of an evening. As I poured muesli into a bowl, I cursed the ridiculous situation. Bridget would help, Oliver said. This would be so much better than staying at home.

Well, he was wrong. Damn wrong. Tomorrow, I'd call a cab and go back to Imogen's, where I should have insisted on staying in the first place.

Chapter 23

THE SOUND OF the front door closing made me jump, and I looked around guiltily even though I had every right to be there. That feeling of being unwelcome had become ingrained in me over the last few years. Selling yourself did that.

Shoes slapped on the tile in the hallway, and seconds later, Oliver strode into the kitchen and flicked on the rest of the lights. I'd tried to bundle my nasty hair into a ponytail, but I looked awful and no doubt smelled worse. In complete contrast, he still wore a tie, and despite the late hour, his suit didn't have a single wrinkle.

"Why are you sitting in the dark?" he asked. "And eating cereal?"

"I couldn't find the light switches, and I'm not so great at cooking at the moment."

"Why didn't you ask Bridget to help?"

What was I supposed to say to that? I couldn't think of a single answer that didn't make me sound like a whiny first grader tattling to the teacher. And to cap it all, my eyes went itchy, and I blinked to hold back the tears.

Oliver came closer, invading my personal space. "Stefanie, tell me."

"Uh, I don't think Bridget likes me," I squeaked.

"But it's okay. I'm gonna go home tomorrow."

"No, you're not. What did she say?"

"It doesn't matter."

He raised my chin, forcing me to look at him. "Yes, it does."

"She told me I couldn't worm my way into your wallet, and then she asked how we met and I told her it was because of the Carter case and she realised who I was and looked down her nose at me like I was trash." I barely paused for breath in that vomit of words, and now I gulped in air as the first tear trickled down my cheek.

Oliver stepped back and mouthed a curse, not looking at all happy. "I'll speak to her. She can be overprotective, but I thought we were past this."

"Honestly, it's fine. I'd rather be at home, anyway. I don't want to upset Bridget, and I don't want your money either."

"I know you don't."

He closed the gap again then leaned in to kiss me on the head, but I twisted away before his lips could touch the horrors of my hair.

"What's wrong?"

"My hair's yucky," I mumbled. "The rest of me too. I can't manage in the shower with these dressings."

"Steffie, don't ever describe yourself as yucky." Despite my protests, he kissed me.

"But—"

"Shh. No buts. And what's with the cereal? Why didn't you call Il Tramonto? Or Rhodium?"

"I didn't want to put anyone to any trouble."

He muttered something that sounded suspiciously like "for fuck's sake" and pulled out his phone. Two seconds later, he jabbered away in Italian, then hung up.

"Dinner's on its way."

"You didn't have to do that."

Rather than replying, he picked me up, and I caught a whiff of my own body odour as he carried me through to the dining area. Could this evening get any more embarrassing? The white table was polished to such a high sheen I could make out the dark circles under my eyes in my reflection as he set me onto a seat. Oliver shrugged off his jacket and hung it carefully over one of the chair backs, then sat down opposite.

"Aren't you going to change? I mean, I'm feeling really underdressed here."

A bathrobe versus a suit—that was hardly fair.

"Into what?"

"Jeans?"

"I don't have any of those."

"You don't have jeans?"

"I don't need them."

"Do you own anything but suits?"

"Gym gear."

"That's it? Nothing casual? Not even a pair of chinos? Or pyjamas?"

Oliver shook his head then gave me a wolfish smile. "I sleep naked."

Okay, maybe I shouldn't have gone there with the pyjamas. "What do you do to relax?"

He stared towards the darkened drapes for a few seconds. "I don't."

"What, nothing?"

"Sex, sometimes. I run if I need to let off steam."

"You don't even relax during sex. You do all the

work."

I clapped a hand over my mouth, hardly able to believe I said that.

He just laughed. "True. I guess I like to call the shots. But you enjoy that."

I went pink and tried to steer the conversation back onto a more appropriate track.

"There must be something else. Reading books? Watching movies?"

"It's been a long time since I did anything but work."

The doorbell chimed, and he stood up, preventing me from asking more questions. Oliver didn't have a single hobby? No wonder that stick never came out of his ass.

He returned a minute later carrying another tray. What had he ordered?

"Veal calabrese," he said as he set the food down in front of me. "If you don't like it, I'll ask them to bring something else."

I'd only eaten veal a couple of times before, both with clients, but I didn't mind giving it a go.

"Thank you. Aren't you eating?"

"I had a dinner meeting."

"Oh." Conversation was hard with Oliver. We lived in such different worlds, and I had no idea what to say. "The restaurant cooked it very quickly."

"Yes, and they'll do the same for you if you call them."

"Bridget said you part-owned the restaurant?"

"I do."

"So you like food? That's kind of a hobby."

"I like money, and it makes a profit."

I tried a forkful of the veal, and it melted in my mouth. Oliver had made a good choice. Screw the pain pills—I needed alcohol. The red wine that came with the food slid down smoothly as well, a palate of rich fruitiness that certainly didn't come from the bargain bin.

And with alcohol came courage.

"So we're getting somewhere. You like sex, and you like money. What else?"

He leaned back in his chair, thinking. "I like to win."

"You mean in court?"

"I always used to say that winning a big trial was better than sex. I don't know whether I'll still feel that rush, but I damn well want to find out."

"Are you nervous about Carter?"

"I wouldn't admit it if I was."

"I'm terrified."

"Don't be. I'm not intending to lose."

"I meant I'm terrified of getting on the stand. About spilling my secrets to a bunch of strangers and the media too."

Oliver fixed his gaze on me. "It'll be okay. Trust me."

"I don't know you," I whispered.

"But *I* know *you*."

"Most of the time I barely know myself, either."

He scraped his chair back across the floor and stood up. Was he leaving? What did I say? I went to get up too, but he waved me back down again.

"Sit. Enjoy your food."

"Where are you going?"

"Always so curious, Steffie. Eat."

I ate every last morsel on the plate, and Oliver still hadn't reappeared. Worse, when he'd carried me over to the table, I'd left my crutch in the kitchen, so unless I wanted to hop all the way back to my room, I was stuck.

Some might say I was lucky, being stuck in a luxurious apartment like that, but Oliver confused me beyond measure, and I didn't want to face Bridget the next morning, even if Oliver did say he'd speak to her. I craved my little bed at Imogen's with the flowery linens I'd bought from the sale bin and the shelf full of battered books next to it. Luxury sucked.

Then Oliver reappeared and picked me up again. Okay, so maybe some parts of my stay weren't so bad. Being cradled against his chest beat hobbling. Except we bypassed my bedroom and carried on to the next door along.

"Why are we going in here?"

He didn't answer, just pushed the door open. It was another bedroom, but the only light flickered from the en suite bathroom in the corner. Candles?

"What is this?"

"Close your eyes."

"Why?"

"Because you need to learn to trust me."

"But—"

He whispered in my ear, his lips brushing the edge. "Do it, princess."

Oliver's voice sent shivers through me the same way it had on our first night together. I closed my eyes.

I knew he'd taken me into the bathroom because the background light changed, and when he set me on my good foot, the tile was cool underneath. A gentle tug at my waist and the robe I wore fell undone.

Humid air caressed my body, and I felt Oliver's eyes on me as well, more invasive than any touch. My skin prickled under his gaze. He slid the robe off my shoulders, leaving me in my underwear, then with one light touch from his fingers to the clasp, I spilled out of my bra. He removed that as well, leaving me before him in only white cotton panties, accessorised by a cast and a bandage. I shouldn't have felt sexy in the slightest, but as he moved around me, a fire sparked to life in my belly. It started as a slow smoulder, but with every light caress, the flames grew hotter.

I gasped as he drew one nipple into his mouth, biting gently on the peak as it hardened. After giving the other the same treatment, he trailed the tip of his tongue along my collarbone. Did I ask for this? No. But perhaps Oliver had been right earlier when he said he knew me. Because even if I struggled to admit it, I wanted his hands anywhere he cared to put them.

And right now, they swept down my stomach, lower, lower, avoiding the sweet spot completely as he parted my thighs. I felt a twinge of disappointment as I'd been hoping for something else entirely.

"Patience, princess," his soft voice came again, low and throaty.

Dammit. He really could read my thoughts.

A trail of soft kisses across each of my cheeks made my toes curl. Then, far too slowly, he hooked his thumbs in the sides of my panties and slid them down my legs. One hand cupped my mound.

"I love that you're bare down here."

Oh, thank goodness I waxed.

I pressed into him, desperate for friction to relieve the building ache, but all I got was one stroke and a chuckle. Then he stepped back entirely, and I heard the rustle of clothing behind me. Oh, please tell me Oliver was getting naked this time? In both of our previous encounters, he'd stayed fully clothed, and like he said, I had a curiosity problem.

I nearly sang hallelujah when he pressed back against me, flesh on flesh. And by the feel of him, there was muscle underneath, no fat. He wasn't stacked like a bodybuilder, but he said he ran and his physique backed that up.

"Open your eyes now, Steffie."

I did so, and the first thing I saw was my reflection in a giant mirror over the bathroom vanity, my cheeks flushed as need coursed through me. Oliver stood behind and swept my hair to one side, then kissed my neck before moving up to my jaw, my cheek, and finally my lips. Gasping, I broke eye contact with myself and turned my head. Then I saw the bath.

The bedroom I slept in had a corner tub in the en suite, complete with whirlpool jets and expensive toiletries. But this bathroom came with a giant oval tub in the centre of the room, the kind of thing I'd thought only existed in movies. And it was two-thirds full of water and bubbles.

"Ready?" Oliver asked, sliding his arms around my waist.

"You're giving me a bath?"

"You'll need to hook your cast over one side and your arm over the other."

Before I could think further, he lifted me up and stepped into the tub, then lowered us both so I nestled between his legs. Well, this was a new experience, possibly the most intensely erotic one of my life and a far cry from the superficial liaisons I'd gotten used to as a Ruby.

The hot water bordered on painful, and the sensation wasn't helped by Oliver heating things up further. But with little choice other than to stay in the bath, I relaxed back against his solid chest as he used a cup to wet my hair then lathered shampoo into it. Whimpers I couldn't control escaped as his fingers dug into my scalp, removing days' worth of tension with a few minutes of magic. He repeated the process with conditioner and combed it through to the ends.

"Were you secretly a hairdresser?" I asked.

"Never been anything but a lawyer."

"If you ever need an alternate career…"

"Naked shampooing?"

"Women would pay a fortune."

He leaned forward, closer to my ear. "I'm not for sale."

And neither was I anymore. Never again, no matter how poor I might end up. Oliver knew who I'd been, what I'd been, and yet he still gave me this. I realised at that moment I'd take everything he offered, no matter how lonely the nights got. Oliver's touch was my drug.

Once he'd rinsed the conditioner out, he took a washcloth and started on my body. I swear he didn't miss an inch, and he saved the most intimate part for last. When his hand reached between my legs, he discarded the cloth and let his fingers do the work. Bolts of pleasure shot down my legs as he circled my nub, and I begged him in my mind to go for the centre. But of course he didn't. With agonising slowness, he touched me everywhere but, driving me crazy until he slid a finger deep inside. I arched back, giving up on any sort of dignity as I surrendered to the sensations he unleashed. Then his thumb joined in and I fell apart.

Luckily, he kept hold of me so I didn't drown, and I melted back into him as the ripples subsided.

"You never look more beautiful than when you come," he whispered.

"How about you?" I wiggled my butt, and his hard cock rubbed against me.

"Tonight's about you, princess, not me."

"Why can't it be about both of us?"

I leaned forwards a smidgen then reached behind me to grasp his length, and I couldn't help feeling a certain satisfaction when he groaned. He always fought so hard to stay in control, and I wanted to see him lose it, just a little.

"I don't want to hurt you."

"My arm and ankle are fine."

"I didn't mean in that way."

I got what he was saying, but I'd come a long way since he first walked out on me. I'd never pretend to understand Oliver Rhodes completely, but I knew not to expect commitment. That offer wasn't on the table. My head got that, and my heart would have to work with it. My body? My body wanted him in every way possible.

"I'm not looking for hearts and flowers, Oliver."

Now when I twisted to look at him, I got a lopsided smile.

"I can do the flowers if you want."

"I'll settle for another orgasm. And maybe some freesias."

He chuckled and pressed forwards. "Are you on the pill, princess?"

"Yes, and I'm clean. I got tested after Rubies, and I haven't been with anyone but you since."

"My results were clear two weeks ago, and I haven't wanted any other woman since that night at Riverley."

I'd barely had time to process that confession when he tilted me forwards and slid inside. Bath sex was a new experience, but I liked it already.

Oliver moved slowly at first, smooth strokes as our bodies adjusted to each other. Each time he pushed in, that little bundle of nerves hidden deep inside sent me a thank-you note. I gripped the side of the bath as Oliver thrust harder, faster, both of us ignoring the water sloshing over the sides. He reached a hand between my legs again, ensuring I exploded at the same time as him. The stars bursting behind my eyelids eclipsed the candles as I came down from my high, and Oliver brushed soft kisses over the back of my neck.

"Maybe you don't need a new hobby," I told him once I could speak again. "This one's just fine."

"It beats knitting."

I lay back in his arms, enjoying the feel of him around me until the water went cold. I tried to ignore the goose bumps popping up on my arms, but Oliver didn't.

"Time to get you to bed."

He rose, dripping, and lifted me with him. My right leg had gone to sleep where it met the edge of the tub, and I wiggled my toes to try and work some feeling back.

Oliver wrapped a towel around my hair then patted me dry with a second. I used the time to sneak glances at him, seeing as he hadn't bothered to cover himself up. I'd wondered after the evening at Rhodium whether he was shy about his body, but I knew now that he had no reason to be. Yes, Imogen was one hundred percent right. Oliver was hot as hell. I longed to reach out and trace his abs with a finger, but I wasn't sure how he'd react, and after what he'd just done for me, I didn't want to risk upsetting him.

That time was past.

Once I was dry, he picked me up again and carried me back to my room. He'd already laid a towel on my pillow and turned back the comforter, and now he tucked me underneath it.

"Sweet dreams, princess." He leaned down and kissed me softly on the lips.

"Will you stay with me?"

His eyes clouded. "I can't."

"Why do you always leave?"

"It's the only way I know how to do this."

"But—"

Oliver shook his head. "Don't, Steffie. If you want me to stop, I will, but I can't offer more."

I longed to pull him into the bed with me, but I'd gone into this with my eyes open and I wasn't about to beg. Instead, I took his hand and brought his knuckles to my lips.

"Will you be here tomorrow?"

"Do you want me to be?"

There were two answers to that—the sensible one and the only one I could give.

"Yes."

He nodded once, then backed away.

"I hope you have sweet dreams too," I whispered.

CHAPTER 24

WHEN I GOT to the kitchen the next morning, feeling both human and out of this world, there was no sign of Oliver, but Bridget was stirring something in a mixing bowl.

"Toast?" she asked, giving me an obviously forced smile. Her lips may have curved up, but her eyes were hard.

"Yes, please."

She rinsed her hands and walked to the refrigerator. "Oliver said I'm to make sure you eat lunch."

Oh, so he *had* spoken to her. It didn't seem to have made much of a difference to her attitude.

"I won't need much. More toast is fine."

I didn't want to be a burden, an annoyance, or anything else that would make both our lives more awkward.

"I'll bring it to your room."

Guess I knew where I'd be staying today. She obviously didn't want me hanging around her, and I had to confess to the feeling being mutual.

The front door slammed, and we both jerked our heads around. Had Oliver come back? I found myself wishing he had, because I needed help to thaw the frosty atmosphere, and I got half my wish.

"Morning!" Dan called out from the doorway.

She held at least six bags in each hand, and she dumped them all on the floor just inside the kitchen before rushing over to hug Bridget.

The older woman smiled properly this time, proving that those muscles did work. It was just me she hated.

Once Dan let go, she looked over at me and raised an eyebrow.

"Miss Amor is staying with Oliver this week," Bridget informed her.

"Awesome!"

Bridget's pursed lips said she didn't share Dan's sentiment, and Dan gave her a nudge with her shoulder.

"Oh, lighten up, Bridgie. Stef's one of the good guys."

"Someone has to protect that boy from making mistakes," Bridget muttered, loud enough for me to hear.

"I know, but you don't need to worry with Stef, I promise. She's not another Kelly."

Kelly? Who was Kelly?

Dan left Bridget and headed over to me, but before I could say anything, she engulfed me in a hug.

"Oliver said you'd had an accident, but I didn't realise he'd squirrelled you away here, the sly old git. That's great, though. I haven't seen you for ages, so we can have lunch." She looked at her watch. "Well, brunch. I have a meeting at twelve."

Her screwed-up face told me she didn't relish the thought of it.

I pointed at my leg. "I can't get very far."

"We can go to Il Tramonto. They don't officially open until lunchtime, but the chef will cook us something if I ask nicely."

"Are you sure you're not too busy?"

"I'm always busy, but taking a break for Mario's food is never a hardship, believe me." She shoved my plate of half-eaten toast away. "Go on, get dressed and then we can go."

Bridget came to her senses and half-heartedly chided Dan. "You can't leave all those bags in the doorway."

"I'll shove them into the lounge while Stef's changing." She turned back to me. "Oliver's coming home tonight, right?"

"Uh, I don't know for sure. I think so."

She pulled out her phone and started typing out a message. "He'd better be. He can't avoid his birthday completely."

"It's his birthday?"

"Yeah. He hates a fuss. Bradley arranged a surprise party seven years ago, but he made a rare mistake and an all-male troupe of hula dancers turned up. Oliver got mauled, and since then, he's refused to have any kind of celebration." She jerked her head at the bags. "So I've brought his gifts over."

"I didn't realise. I haven't got him anything."

"He won't care. It's not as if he told you what day it was, and he won't want a party." She winked. "But maybe you can come up with a nice surprise." She put a certain emphasis on the word "come."

"Uh, it's not like that..."

"Sure it isn't. What are you still doing here? Go change."

She went back to the bags, leaving me to shuffle-hop to the bedroom. My suitcase had appeared in there yesterday, presumably from Imogen, so at least I had something other than a bathrobe.

Oh, I forgot. Imogen packed. The case contained four cocktail dresses, a sexy nightie that wasn't mine, lacy underwear, and in a nod to practicality, a single ballet flat. Perhaps I'd be wearing the bathrobe after all.

I was still staring at the contents when Dan barged in without knocking.

"What's keeping you?"

I pointed at the garments I'd laid out on the bed. "My friend packed, only I think she misunderstood the situation."

Dan twirled a pair of barely there panties on her finger. "Really? I'd say she did quite well."

I snatched the panties back. "None of this exactly screams 'brunch,' does it?"

"Fair enough. Look, I'll call Bradley. He can send a skirt or something."

"I can't ask him to—"

"Trust me, Bradley lives for shit like this."

She plopped down on the bed and sent another message, then motioned for me to sit beside her. I did so gingerly, lifting my cast up onto the comforter.

Awkward.

She waved the phone at me. "Oliver's coming back at seven. I've made reservations for you at Claude's. He should do something nice for his birthday, even if he doesn't think he wants to."

"I'm not sure that's a good idea. I mean, I'm only here because Oliver felt sorry for me, not because he wants to go out for dinner."

"Nonsense. If Oliver felt sorry for you, he'd have rented you a hotel room and sent flowers. This is his home, and he's given you the run of it. Believe me, you're here because he wants you to be."

"I'm sure it's not unusual."

She threw her head back and laughed. "You know how many women Oliver lets in here? One: Bridget. And now you."

"And you."

"He doesn't have a choice over that. I'd just pick the lock and let myself in, so it's easier to give me a key."

"What about Kelly?"

Dan's eyes clouded over, marring her normally cheerful disposition.

"Forget I ever mentioned Kelly. She was a mistake, and one we'd all rather forget."

My curiosity was piqued, but Dan's expression warned me not to push any further. Who was Kelly, and why did Dan dislike her so much? I longed to ask, but instead, I turned to something a little safer.

"So, have you known Oliver long?"

"Yeah. A decade? No, longer..." She counted on her fingers. "Eleven years."

"How did you two meet?"

"In a bar. Where else?"

"I thought maybe work. He said he doesn't do anything but work and run."

I left out the sex part. I didn't know if he and Dan had or they hadn't, and I wasn't sure I *wanted* to know either.

"He forgot to mention the bar-hopping. Although he hasn't done that so much over the last few months. Not since the Carter thing blew up."

"I can't imagine Oliver out drinking."

Dan stared beyond me, gaze fixed on the wall. "He's like I used to be, although he never gets raging drunk."

"What do you mean, how you used to be?"

I'd only known her for a few months.

"I'd fuck to forget. For an hour or two, I'd lose myself in the comfort of a warm body, but the fix never lasted long. In the morning I'd hate myself, but fifteen hours later, I'd go out and do the exact same thing again." She met my eyes once more and smiled, but with sadness rather than joy. "I was broken; I understand that now. I was broken until Ethan fixed the cracks."

"And Oliver's broken?" Every new bit of information I found out changed my view of him, and right now, I struggled to reconcile broken Oliver with the man I sort of knew. Oliver was put-together, in control. I was the damaged one.

"He hides it well."

"With made-to-order suits and silk ties? He told me he doesn't own any casual clothes."

"True, but have you any idea how many women go for a man in a suit?"

Okay, she had a point there. I mean, he did wear them well, and he didn't skimp on the tailoring either.

Dan shrieked with laughter. "You just licked your lips."

"I didn't!"

"You definitely did."

"Maybe they were dry or something. I need lip balm."

A new voice sounded from the doorway. "I didn't bring lip balm, but I have two skirts, three tops, and mascara."

"Bradley!" Dan leapt up to hug him.

I tried to clamber to my feet—well, foot—but before I got halfway, Bradley sat on the bed and slung an arm around my shoulders. "So this is where you've been hiding, sweet cheeks."

"I haven't been hiding."

"Then why haven't we seen you for months?"

"I went home to Georgia for a while."

"Well, it's a good thing you've come to your senses." The bag he'd dropped on the bed lay on its side, and he pulled a skirt out of it. "What do you think? Fifties style, so it'll work with the cast, and I've brought a matching sweater."

Dan helped me dress while Bradley rearranged Oliver's lounge. I bet he'd be thrilled when he found the pink candles on the coffee table. Down in Il Tramonto, we picked out a table by the window, and one of the kitchen staff brought a menu over.

"I'm having ice cream," Bradley announced. "Three scoops. Surprise me."

Dan rolled her eyes, something I imagined she must do a lot with him around. "I'll stick with salad."

"Salad for me too, please."

When the employee disappeared, Dan leaned forwards on her elbows. "How are you holding up? This case is taking a toll on everyone, huh?"

"I've mostly been trying to avoid it."

"Wish I could."

"I heard they found another body?"

"Yeah. Carter's most recent victim, we think. He killed her a week or two after Christina and buried her in the remembrance garden at the retirement complex his company was building. Sick, huh? He even planted a rose bush over the top."

"My gosh. So do you think the rumours about him being a serial killer are true?"

"For sure. He even admitted it. But he won't tell us where any of the other women are buried, and finding them isn't easy. We're working on the assumption that he took the lazy option and buried them at the bottom of pre-dug holes in his developments, but if they're in the foundations, we might never find them. Who's gonna start tearing houses down on the off-chance there could be somebody buried underneath? We can do soil analysis, and there's this new technique testing the gas composition in air pockets, but even so... The whole thing's a multi-jurisdictional logistical nightmare."

"Sure sounds like it. How did you even find that one girl?"

"Emmy. We took a trip out to the Winter Pines development and walked around, and she bet me fifty bucks Carter would have buried a victim in that spot for the irony. Turned out she was right, the freaky bitch."

Suddenly, I wasn't particularly hungry anymore. "Can't she visit the other complexes?"

"We're working our way through them, but they're spread from coast to coast. Right now, the cops are going over the golf course at Carter's development in Fort Lauderdale with a cadaver dog and ground-penetrating radar. The twelfth through seventeenth holes. Carter kept a condo there, and that's the view from his bedroom balcony. I'm betting on the thirteenth hole."

"For luck?"

"Now you're getting it."

"Do you think you'll find anything?"

"Yeah. If not there, then somewhere else. We also need to check all the houses he rented. Carter told me he killed fifteen or sixteen other women besides Christina, and our analysis has identified forty-seven possibles from the missing persons' lists in areas where he's lived. Chances are, we'll find a couple at least."

"Why didn't he kill me?" I whispered.

I'd considered that question far too many times to count. From what I recalled, Carter had just been an average guy, normal by Rubies' standards.

"Honestly? We'll probably never know. Best not to dwell on it."

The food arrived, and Bradley waved a spoonful of ice cream in my direction. "What she said. Don't dwell on it. Dwell on clothes and jewellery and shoes instead." He glanced down at my cast and the ballet flat. "Well, shoe."

I forced a smile. "Okay."

But I still felt quite sick.

Bradley turned the conversation to the new Disney movie, then a dress his friend Ishmael had designed that looked like a birdcage. I shoved all the bad things out of my head, but the downside of that was that I forgot to thank Dan for posting my bail until after they'd both left. How could something so important have slipped my mind? Since that first night with Oliver, I'd turned into a scatterbrained fool. Before him, before Carter, I'd been the epitome of organisation, with lists, calendars, and timetables galore. Now I struggled to remember whether I'd eaten breakfast. Could a person go senile at twenty-two?

Back in Oliver's apartment, I tried to phone her before I forgot again, but her assistant answered. No, I didn't want to leave a message, not with a stranger. I sent a text instead, although that probably wasn't much better.

Stef: Thank you so much for posting my bail. I don't know what I'd have done otherwise.

A few minutes later, my phone pinged.

Dan: Don't worry about it. That's what friends are for.

Friends. I didn't have many, but those I did have, I was determined to hang on to. There and then, I vowed not to run away again, not to Georgia or anywhere else. Richmond may have dealt some cruel hands, but it was up to me how I played them. If I folded, I'd lose for sure.

CHAPTER 25

AS DAN SEEMED determined Oliver and I were going to Claude's, I did what I could with my hair and used some of the make-up Bradley had couriered over this afternoon. He'd wanted to help me get ready as well, but Emmy had an event to attend this evening that required his services, and I assured him I'd be absolutely fine by myself. Hmm... What to wear? I was tempted by one of Imogen's cocktail dresses, but with only one hand, I didn't stand much chance of getting into it. If Oliver wanted me to dress up, he'd have to help with the zipper when he got back.

At least my wrist hurt a little less today, and maybe I imagined it, but I could have sworn the swelling had gone down. Oh, how I longed to lose those damned bandages and live normally again. Funny how you didn't really appreciate the simple things in life like flossing your teeth until you couldn't do them anymore, wasn't it?

Bridget went home at four, so I ventured out into the lounge to wait for Oliver. The sofa was more comfortable than it looked, and I settled in for one movie, then a second, until I realised the giant clock had struck seven and he still wasn't back. Disappointment welled up inside me, and I cursed myself for feeling that way. How could I have allowed myself to get my hopes up over a man who'd told me he didn't commit to anything? Not even dinner, it appeared.

The front door didn't open until half past seven, and I pretended to ignore the *clip* of Oliver's brogues on the tile as I hugged a cushion to my chest. It didn't matter. None of it mattered.

His footsteps quietened as he hit the carpeted area, and he soon reached my side. I tried for a smile.

"Did you have a good day?" I asked.

Up close, his face looked worn, and tiny lines not usually present marred the skin around his eyes.

"I'm not sure I'd describe it as good, but it was productive. You look pretty, princess."

He leaned forwards and planted a soft kiss on my lips, then looked slightly surprised at himself.

"Dan said we were going out this evening," I said softly.

"Oh, that. I cancelled it. Sorry, I should have sent you a message."

"It doesn't matter."

"Yes, it does. Dan just doesn't think sometimes. I'm a prosecutor at the moment, and you're a witness in the case I'm working on. If someone saw the two of us together, I'd be up for a disciplinary and the case against Carter could collapse."

"Oh." I hadn't even thought of that. "So I really shouldn't be here, then?"

"No, you really shouldn't."

"The sensible thing for me to do would be to go home."

Oliver pressed into me again, and this time his kiss was deeper. "Yes, it would."

"Do you want me to go?"

"No, Steffie, I don't." Another kiss, this time with tongues. "What I want is to strip you naked and take you over the back of the sofa, but Claude's delivering dinner at eight, so that's not entirely appropriate."

I wound my good arm around his neck, holding him close. "Later, then?"

"Later."

I'd only eaten at Claude's once before, and that evening, I'd been so busy freaking out about my dining companion, a sweaty banker who insisted on pawing me across the table, that I barely tasted the food. Even worse, he'd paid me to spend the entire night with him, so I felt more than a little nauseated.

But I had no such problems tonight. Oliver shed his jacket and tie, and I struggled to decide what was more delicious—my pan-seared beef fillet with bordelaise sauce or him.

Or dessert.

"Bradley put them up to this, I know it."

Oliver clenched his jaw as he opened the two-foot-high cake box and peered gingerly inside.

"What is it?"

He pulled the lid back further, revealing a miniature jail in cake form, complete with bars, an exercise yard, and a tiny prisoner in an orange jumpsuit. I leaned closer. "Is that Carter?"

"I suspect it's meant to be. Bradley's always had the most appalling taste in cakes."

"At least he's got faith in you. To put Carter in jail, I

mean."

"And it's big enough to feed everyone in the building."

"It's still sweet. Bradley cares."

"Let's see if you feel the same way after you've eaten half of it." Oliver sighed, exasperated, then shrugged. "I suppose it's not as bad as the one he got Dan for her thirtieth. Giving a cake shaped like a set of dentures to someone with a concealed carry permit is never a good idea. Luckily, she only shot up the cake and not him."

Laughter bubbled inside me, and even Oliver couldn't help smiling.

"I wish I'd seen that," I giggled.

"Stick around long enough, and there's bound to be another crime against taste." He picked up a knife. "Guess we'd better make a start on this."

I spotted a package taped to the side of the box.

"Wait! Are those candles?"

"So what if they are?"

"It's your birthday. We have to light them."

"But I'll only blow them out again."

"That's not the point. Find me some matches."

For a second, I thought Oliver would argue, what with him being a control freak and everything, but he rolled his eyes and meandered off to the kitchen while I started sticking the candles into the roof of the prison, counting as I went. How old was he? His dark-grey hair gave him a distinguished air, but the rest of him didn't match the colour.

He came back just as I placed the last candle. "You're thirty-five?"

"Yes, Steffie, I'm thirty-five. Does that bother you?"

Twelve years older than me. Did it? The honest

answer was no. I'd been with older, and I'd been with younger, but none of them made my insides fizz the way Oliver did. Age was just a number. I shook my head and held out my hand for the matches.

"You're as old as the woman you feel."

That was the first time I'd seen him laugh properly, and he pressed against me as I lit the candles.

"Good answer, Miss Amor."

"Now you have to make a wish."

He leaned forwards and blew them out. "Done."

"What did you wish for?"

"I'll keep that to myself for now."

He twisted to kiss me, and behind him, the candles burst into life again.

"Uh..."

He followed the direction of my pointing finger and groaned. "Fuck it, I forgot about Bradley's obsession with relighting candles. Plus I thought he'd stopped all that since Emmy used a fire extinguisher on one of his creations last year."

"So what do we do?"

"Drown them. It's the only way."

Oliver carried the flaming cake to the kitchen, leaving a multitude of swear words floating in his wake as I shuffle-hopped behind, and we soon had a pile of smouldering candles in the sink. I caught Oliver yawning as he reached for the knife again.

"Tired?"

He dropped a kiss on my cheek. "Not that tired."

But he was flagging—I saw it in the way he slouched back on the sofa rather than maintaining his usual uptight posture—and while he nibbled on part of the wall from the exercise yard, I came up with my own idea for a birthday gift.

I swallowed my last bite and took a mouthful of the champagne Bradley had thoughtfully included. I was about to put one of the most valuable tricks Chrissie had taught me into practice.

"What are you doing?" Oliver asked as I wriggled forwards and dropped a cushion in front of him.

"You'll see. Sit back and forget your shot-calling for a few minutes."

I dropped to my knees in front of him, and at first, I thought he might object as I reached for his belt. But he leaned back and slid his ass forwards along the leather to give me better access.

He was already getting hard as I drew his zipper down, and I resisted the urge to make a "not bad for an old man" joke. Totally inappropriate. And considering half of my more mature clients had needed the talents of a vacuum cleaner combined with a handful of little blue pills to get them going, Oliver gave me an easy ride.

I supported myself on the couch with my left elbow, then gripped the base of his cock with my right hand as I drew his length into my mouth. Not the most elegant of positions, but tonight needs must.

Oliver fisted his hands in my hair as I sucked him deeper, and deeper, and deeper. I locked my gaze on his as I opened my throat and took him all the way to the base, loving his look of surprise when he realised what I was doing, and even more so the long groan he let out.

Sure, I knew he was only allowing me the illusion of control, but tonight, I planned to take advantage of it.

In all my time as a Ruby, I'd never once enjoyed

giving a blow job, but tonight with Oliver, things were different. I relished every half smile, every dirty word he muttered, every twitch of his cock, and by the time his control slipped further and he started flexing his hips, I longed to reach between my own legs to relieve the ache building there. But with one wrist bandaged and my balance precarious, I had to settle for clenching my thighs together as he fucked my mouth.

I knew he was about to come when his legs started trembling, and I gripped one of his ass cheeks with my good hand as he exploded into my throat. And "exploded" was the only word for it. You'd think he'd been fasting for months rather than a day.

The only sound in the room was Oliver's laboured breathing as he hauled me up onto the sofa.

"That sure beat the cake, princess."

"Tasted sweeter."

He groaned again and lifted me so I straddled him. "Are you comfortable?"

I managed a nod as his hand slipped beneath my skirt. One long kiss and a few strokes of his fingers later, he wasn't the only one having a happy birthday.

Chapter 26

I WORKED MY jaw from side to side as I walked into the kitchen the next morning. Oliver was bigger than most, and I was out of practice, so a touch of stiffness had set in overnight.

Oliver looked up from the paper he was reading at the breakfast bar. "Sore?"

"A little." A blush rose up my cheeks. "What are you doing here?"

"I live here."

"I mean, why aren't you at work?"

He patted the stool next to him, and I shuffle-hopped over and took a seat. Out the corner of my eye, I saw Bridget watching from her position by the stove as Oliver kissed me softly on the lips. I waited for the scowl, but all I got was a twitch of her mouth.

"We need to go over those questions this morning." He squeezed my hand. "I'm sorry. If I could avoid the interrogation, I would, but I can't. I thought we'd do as much as possible here then finalise things in the office at some point."

Annnnnd bump. Back to earth after the magic of yesterday evening. "Okay. But I can't pretend I'm looking forward to it."

"Understandable. Let's have some breakfast, and then we can start."

"I'm not really hungry." Funnily enough, my appetite had just flown out the window. By jet.

"Are you sure? There's plenty of cake left."

"I think I'd throw up if I ate another mouthful of that. Besides, I have a new favourite dessert."

"Steffie, if you say things like that, I'll never get any work done."

"You could take a day off."

He stared as if I'd just morphed into Medusa. "I don't take time off."

"Maybe you should start with an hour." I looked around to check Bridget was out of sight before I slid my hand into Oliver's lap. "Then work your way up."

"You're a bad influence, princess."

I grinned at him, although it was a little forced because dread was already building over the interview.

"That's what I'm aiming for."

Oliver's study in the penthouse, his man cave, was a replica of his office at work—an oversized desk, a leather sofa, and shelves and shelves full of boring books without a novel in sight. He took a seat in the high-backed chair behind his desk while I plopped onto the couch.

That feeling of déjà vu hit again when he got out a legal pad, twirled an expensive fountain pen around his fingers, then glanced at the watch that cost more than any car I could ever hope to buy.

"Are you ready to start?"

He popped the cap off the pen as I stuffed the ends of my hair into my mouth and started chewing. Stress made me do it, but for the last two days, I couldn't remember fiddling with my hair once. No, I wasn't ready to start, but I didn't have a lot of choice in the matter.

"I guess. Could you just not look at me?"

"What do you mean?"

"It's bad enough having to talk about this, but when you watch it feels as if you're judging."

Oliver shoved his chair back and walked over. "I promise I'm not."

"But that's what it feels like. And then you write down all the horrible stuff."

"Then let's try something different." He returned to his desk, opened the drawer, and took out a small object. "Digital recorder." He held it up as he sat down beside me. "Swing your legs onto the seat."

With a bit of shuffling, he arranged us so he faced forwards on the sofa, and I sat side-on with my back to him, looking out across the roof terrace as he wrapped an arm around my waist. Rather than seeing his eyes, I got a view of the Richmond skyline, and...

"Is that a hot tub?" It sure looked like one, nestled among pots of tropical foliage and minimalistic wicker-and-glass furniture. If only it were summer, I could have spent all day out there with a book or a magazine and escaped Bridget's evil glares.

"My questions first, and I'll record your answers rather than taking notes. That way we can just talk, okay? We'll build it up until speaking about what happened doesn't hurt anymore."

"Okay."

"So, let's start at the very beginning..."

For the next three hours, we went over everything I

remembered about Carter and my time at Rubies. Oliver's voice remained even and calm while mine wavered between a whisper and high-pitched horror. Putting my ex-career into words made me feel sick to the pit of my stomach, and if Oliver had never wanted to touch me again afterwards, I couldn't have blamed him. I was damaged goods, shattered on the inside while I worked hard to maintain a neutral facade.

But he kept his arm around me, occasionally stroking the skin on the back of my hand or kissing my hair when I described something particularly ugly. He lent me his strength, and boy did I need it. By the time he reached over to click the recorder off, I felt drained.

But then he whispered in my ear. "Yes, it's a hot tub. You want to upgrade from bath sex to hot-tub sex?"

"You still want me after all that?"

"It's your past, Steffie. Don't let it cloud your future."

In the last few days, I'd come to understand Oliver better. Dan said he fucked to forget, and I got that now. When I spoke about the men from Rubies, I felt their fingers on my skin again, their warm breath on my cheeks as they took their fill. And I needed to erase those memories, or at least overwrite them with something better.

Oliver wasn't the prince I'd dreamed of when I was a little girl, the one who rode in on a white horse and saved me from my sorry existence, but I could cast him as a magician. When he got his hands on me, he blocked out the bad.

"You didn't answer the question."

He didn't speak for a few seconds, and then he

sighed. My stomach sank.

"Yes, Steffie, I still want you."

A tiny bit of the heaviness in my chest fell away, banished to the abyss. "Then I like the sound of the hot tub."

He twisted my neck to claim my mouth, and this time he didn't hold back. I got tongue, teeth, and a little sweat.

"Just give me a minute to send Bridget on an errand."

Oliver carried me in from the chilly air, dried me off, and got me presentable in time for Bridget's return, then headed into the office. That left me to flop back on the bed and phone Imogen, because while Oliver had been demonstrating the features of his hot tub, she'd called four times.

"Is everything okay?" I asked.

"Yep, except I've got the morning off and I haven't spoken to you for three days. I've been a terrible friend, but I'm so..." She paused to yawn. "Tired."

"You haven't been terrible at all. You had a big week this week."

"It's almost over. Three more evenings at Rhodium and things'll be back to normal. How are you? Do you hurt?"

"I've been taking painkillers, so the bandages are more of an inconvenience than anything else."

"I bet. My sister broke her arm a few years back, and I had to wash her hair. Do you want me to help with yours? If it's really yucky, I could come tomorrow morning?"

I ran my fingers through it and found the ends still damp. "I'll be okay until Sunday."

"Has the hot lawyer been taking care of you?"

"Yes, he's been really kind."

"And has he been *taking care* of you?"

I almost choked. "Imogen! I can't answer that."

"I knew it!"

"You can't tell anyone! He could get into big trouble because I'm a witness on his case."

"My lips are sealed. I don't suppose you managed to get Malachi's phone number?"

"I forgot to ask."

"Pleeeeeease."

"I'll do my best."

Although exactly how I was supposed to phrase that with Oliver was a mystery. My horny friend wants Malachi's number because he's hot? I'd have to give it some thought.

"Thanks! So, girl time on Monday afternoon?"

"You bet."

"I'll make sure I buy chocolate."

Once Imogen had hung up, I sank back against the pillows and closed my eyes. Despite my rocky start here, the last two nights had blown me away. What would the weekend bring? And would I want to go home on Sunday?

And Friday night brought me...nothing. Nothing but a one-line text from Oliver.

Oliver Asshole Rhodes: Won't be back tonight—

client event. See you tomorrow.

The stilted message of a man not used to keeping a girl informed of his whereabouts. Even so, I figured I should probably change his middle name on my phone, seeing as he'd made the effort.

What was his actual middle name? Did he even have one? I knew so little about him, and most of what I did know confused the hell out of me. Oliver was bad, but oh-so-good at the same time. I'd always dreamed of a man who'd take care of me, who'd be there for more than a quick fumble in the dark, and Mr. Rhodes wasn't him. But when he touched me? He took me to a happier place.

No sooner had I updated his name to something more appropriate, the phone pinged again.

Oliver Rocky Rhodes: Sweet dreams. O.

Chapter 27

I'D HOPED BRIDGET wouldn't work on the weekends, but no such luck. When I cracked open my door on Saturday morning, she was dusting the picture frames in the hallway right outside.

"Breakfast?" she asked.

I almost said "no" and dived back under the comforter, but I didn't want to stoop to her level of rudeness.

"That would be lovely."

She'd already put bread in the toaster by the time I got into the kitchen, and I didn't dare tell her I'd rather have cereal. I hopped onto a stool at the counter as she slid a mug of filter coffee over to me.

"Thank you."

I took a sip, hoping she'd go away, but she kept hovering. Why? What was wrong? She made me nervous.

After a few seconds, she cleared her throat. "Look, I'm sorry we got off on the wrong foot."

Well, that was a surprise. "So am I."

Because I'd rather have spent the last few days back in jail than tiptoe-hopping around Bridget. At least the junkies and alcoholics hadn't constantly judged me.

"I just worry about Oliver. I don't like to see him get hurt."

"You mean like what happened with Kelly?"

"Exactly."

"Who was she?"

"We don't talk about that girl. Ever."

Whoa. I backed off in a hurry. "Sorry, I didn't mean to pry. And I assure you I don't want to hurt Oliver. I mean, I don't know exactly what's going on between us, but… I just enjoy spending time with him."

"That's what he said about you. So for his sake, we should try to get along."

He did? I forced a smile. "I'd like that."

The toast popped up, making me jump. Bridget hurried over to rescue it, which gave me a welcome reprieve from the awkward conversation.

"Very well. Do you want juice? Or a smoothie?"

"I'd love a smoothie, thank you."

With Bridget thawing a little, I risked spending the day in the lounge, where I could curl up on the sofa for another movie marathon. She even brought me popcorn and a sandwich for lunch, which meant when Oliver got back in the evening and asked me what I wanted for dinner, I wasn't particularly hungry.

"Something from Rhodium then? They do small plates," he suggested.

Despite working there, I'd still never tried the food. "Sounds perfect."

He ordered over the phone, then sank down onto the sofa next to me. "Good movie?"

"Yes, but we can watch something else if you want."

"You like the old stuff?"

"I do. Everything seemed so much less complicated in those days. Women got married young, had a couple of kids, and lived happily ever after. I guess I was born half a century too late."

"That's what you want? Marriage and children?"

"Yes. No. I don't know. When I left Georgia, I wanted to be a career girl, but now I'm so tired. After everything that's happened, I kind of wish someone would just take care of me."

Most men would run a mile at hearing that, but as Oliver had made it clear a relationship was off the cards, I felt safe revealing the truth. In some ways, he was easy to talk to.

"You've never thought of finishing college?"

"Every damn day. But that takes money, and I don't have it. I don't want to serve coffee for the rest of my life, though." I paused, not sure whether I should ask for a favour. But then I figured, what the hell? "Imogen thought Louis might let me work-shadow him at Rhodium to get some experience. Do you think he would?"

"You want to get into management?"

"It's what I was studying to do, but it's harder to get a foot in the door without a degree."

Oliver stayed silent for a moment, thinking. "Not Rhodium. But I can set something up with Giovanni at Il Tramonto. Would that be acceptable?"

So Oliver didn't think I was good enough for Rhodium? Even though I understood why, it still stung. But I couldn't afford to turn down his offer.

"I'd like that. Thank you."

"I'll speak to him tomorrow."

Dinner arrived, and I soon found out why Rhodium had the reputation it did. Every mouthful tasted delicious, and I forgot my lack of appetite as I dug into roast quail followed by chocolate mousse with caramelised bananas. I might never get to eat in the restaurant, but dining here with Oliver more than made up for that. Every so often, he'd glance over at me with a devilish glint in his eye, and I knew he was planning something. A delicious sense of anticipation built through each course, and by the time I licked my spoon, heat zipped through my veins.

This would be my last night here, and I wanted to remember it.

As soon as I'd swallowed, Oliver rose and helped me to my feet, supporting my weight as he led me out onto the roof terrace. From high up, the view was breathtaking, a patchwork of twinkling lights that spread as far as I could see.

A metal railing ran around the edge of the terrace, topping a row of glass panels. I gripped onto it with my good hand and leaned over. Luckily, I'd never been scared of heights. Tiny figures scurried like ants under the streetlights below, going about their business without knowing I was watching. I could just about make out a couple kissing, the man pressing his girl against the wall of the building opposite. I felt like a voyeur.

Oliver stepped up close behind me and caged me in, one arm on each side.

"It's beautiful," I breathed.

"It's more beautiful tonight."

I shivered, but not because of the cold. Why did he have to be so nice? It twisted me up inside.

"Do you come out here often?"

"It's a good spot to think."

I raised my eyes from the street and looked at some of the other buildings. We were the highest by a few floors, and I could see down into people's apartments. A man watching TV. A couple arguing. A dog lazed out on a couch. And... Oh!

I tried to look away, but Oliver turned my head again.

"We shouldn't be watching," I whispered.

A man in the next building lay back as a woman rode him cowboy-style, her head thrown back as she thrust her hips.

"Why do you say that?"

"It's... It's...wrong."

"Wrong how?"

"Because it's private."

He lifted my skirt and ran a finger between my legs. "And it turns you on."

I pressed my thighs together, but even as I did, a ripple of heat flooded through me. Down below, the woman adjusted her position, leaning forwards slightly as the man reached up and kneaded her breasts. I'd never watched two people together like that in real life, and I wasn't prepared for how it would make me feel. Oliver was right, even if I didn't want to admit it.

He slid one finger inside me, and I gasped. Everything about this was wrong, but I couldn't stop myself as I ground down onto him. The man made me wild.

"You like to watch, don't you, princess?"

"I don't know."

"I do." He swept my hair to the side and kissed his way up my neck. "I know you want to watch another woman come."

His finger disappeared and my insides pulsed with need. "Please."

"Please what, princess?"

His zipper sounded, and I realised what he was going to do.

"No! Not that! What if they look up and see us?"

He ripped my blouse open, baring me to the night air. "It's dark up here. Besides, they're busy."

Oliver didn't bother to remove my panties, just pushed them to the side and filled me. Of all the things he'd done, this one was the most illicit, the one I should have stopped but couldn't. I could only hang on to the railing as he found his rhythm, matching the man below. Every time the woman smiled, every time her eyes widened with pleasure, I felt it too. Then when she went over the edge, her mouth open in a silent scream, I fell with her.

The man pulled out and shot his load over her bare breasts as Oliver released deep inside me, biting down on my shoulder. Aftershocks ran through me as he held me up, and without his arms around my waist, I'd have ended up on the floor for sure.

Holy shit. What a ride.

Oliver carried me back to bed, and I still couldn't believe what we'd just done. Or how much I'd enjoyed it. Part of me wanted to scratch my eyes out. The other part longed to start at the beginning and do it all over again.

He tucked me under the comforter and knelt at my bedside.

"It's okay to enjoy it, Steffie."

"It's weird."

Maybe that view came from growing up in Hartscross, where anything other than the missionary position would surely cause a scandal. Or maybe my time at Rubies had conditioned me to be wary of anything out of the ordinary.

"Nobody ever rocked the world by taking the safe option."

"You rocked my world tonight," I whispered.

"You've rocked mine all week."

One more kiss and he disappeared, leaving me alone to think. And think I did. About him.

"Are you still planning to go home today?" Oliver asked on Sunday.

I wasn't aware I had a choice. But even if I did, it was for the best. All my pondering last night had led to the conclusion that Oliver was hot, but dangerous to a girl's heart. I didn't want to end up with mine broken.

"Yes. Imogen will be around more this week, my wrist hurts less, and I've gotten used to hopping around."

"Do you need a ride back?"

"I was planning to call a cab. Aren't you going into work?"

For a normal person, Sunday would mean a day off, but Oliver had already proven himself to be far from average.

"I brought the files I need home with me yesterday." He took a sip of his smoothie and made a face. "What the hell is in this?"

I reached for the bottle. "Blueberry, baobab, maca, and broccoli. According to the label, it's supposed to give you more energy."

"It's disgusting. I think Bridget's trying to kill me

with her health kicks."

I reached for the glass. "Can I try it?"

I certainly needed a bit of zing. I was still exhausted after yesterday, and I hadn't slept well.

He slid it over. "Be my guest."

I took a sip. "It's not that bad."

"Then you can drink the other six bottles in the fridge."

"I won't be here, so you're on your own."

"Take them with you. Please."

"Maybe one or two."

By four o'clock, I'd packed my suitcase, including the extra bits Bradley had sent. I took one final look around my big room, lingering for a second on the roof terrace. The rooms formed an L-shape around it, so all the bedrooms as well as the lounge shared the amazing view. I sure would miss it, especially the filthy memories of last night.

"Are you ready?" Oliver asked.

"As I'll ever be."

He wheeled my case as I shuffle-hopped to the elevator, and when he punched in the code, the silver doors silently closed on his world.

"Did you know your elevator code is the same as my birthday?"

"Yes."

Nothing else, just yes. I wanted to know why. Which came first? Meeting me or picking the code? But the words wouldn't come, and when we hit the basement, I still hadn't figured out how to ask. Nor was

I any the wiser by the time Oliver hefted my case into the back seat and closed the doors.

The man left me off-balance, and I especially wasn't prepared for the way he thumped the steering wheel.

"What's wrong?"

"Shit."

"Oliver, what is it?"

"I don't know how to do this."

"Do what?"

"This. Drive you back home and pretend the last few days didn't happen."

"Then don't pretend. Keep those moments as good memories." I laid a hand on his leg. "That's what I'll do. And they were good. Nobody's made me...enjoy things like that before."

He clasped my hand in his. "I'm all wrong for you. I don't do relationships, and you're a witness in my case, for fuck's sake. But I've never wanted to come home from the office before, and for the last couple of days, I couldn't wait to get out of there."

"So what are you saying?"

"I don't know. I haven't thought this through. Well, I have, but I didn't get very far." He shook his head. "Listen to me. Oliver Rhodes, the man who made his name by always knowing what to say, and I haven't got a clue."

"You want to see me again?"

"Yes. But I don't do commitment, so it isn't fair of me to ask."

"If you don't do commitment, what *do* you do?"

"Food. Fucking."

"So you want to have dinner and sex with me?"

He shrugged. "It's hardly the most romantic

proposal in the world, is it?"

No, it wasn't. But was I ready for romance? I mean, I'd thought so once, but my judgement was screwed right now, and look at what happened with Landon. At least Oliver was straight with me. And the dinner would come from a damn fine restaurant.

"Friends with benefits?"

"Something like that."

My insides still clenched every time I thought of last night. Or Thursday. Or Wednesday. Or the time over the table...

"Twice a week. I can do twice a week. No strings on either side. If one of us meets someone else, it ends."

"You're agreeing?" He sounded surprised.

To be honest, I shared his sentiment. If someone had told me last week I'd agree to be the plaything of a depraved lawyer who challenged the very boundaries of my sanity, I'd have laughed them right back to Georgia. But this week... This week, things were different.

"Twice a week," I repeated. "No more."

Twice a week should be enough to combat these wild urges I was getting in my nether regions but not enough for my heart to get any stupid ideas of its own.

Right?

Chapter 28

THIS NEW RELATIONSHIP with Oliver, if you could call it that, took a bit of getting used to. At eleven o'clock on Monday morning, I got the first text message.

Oliver Rocky Rhodes: I can free up evenings on Tuesday, Thursday, and Saturday this week. Which of those suit you? O.

When I'd suggested the twice-a-week thing, it hadn't really occurred to me that I'd be scheduling sex in like a hair appointment or a manicure. Or a Ruby. *No, Stef. Do not go there.* This thing with Oliver was totally different. Wasn't it? But mainly because he wasn't paying me.

I cast that thought to the back of my mind as I typed out a reply.

Stef: Thursday and Saturday. Imogen works Thursdays and she'll probably go out on Saturday. And you don't happen to have Malachi's number, do you?

Oliver Rocky Rhodes: I'll slot something in those days. Malachi's girlfriend wouldn't be too happy if I gave Imogen his number.

Slot something in? I bet he would. And I'd need to break the news about Malachi to Imogen gently.

Then there were the logistics to organise.

Oliver Rocky Rhodes: Shall I arrange a car to take you back in the evenings? Or do you want to stay over and I'll drive you home on my way to work?

After dinner, wine, and sex, the last thing I wanted to do was leave late in the evening. It was what I used to do most of the time in my former profession, and the way the cab drivers looked at me... They knew exactly what I'd been doing, and it made me feel so cheap.

Stef: Can I stay?

Oliver Rocky Rhodes: I'll ask Bridget to make up the spare room.

But for all the weirdness, during the evenings we spent together, Oliver did treat me like the princess he always called me. Imogen helped with my hair, and I made the effort to dress up, even if I didn't stay in my clothes for long—like the night he ate dessert off me, stretched out on the table. I'd never forget that experience.

Plus he kept his promise about speaking to Giovanni, and I spent two afternoons a week in the office at Il Tramonto while Giovanni showed me how the restaurant was run. And in week four, the doctor said I could take the bandages off my wrist, and I got the use of my hand back.

"Hallelujah!" I screeched as I shuffle-hopped around my apartment.

"Everything works again?" Imogen asked.

"It's stiff, but it only hurts a little, and the doctor said I should start using it to build up the strength again."

"Thank goodness. We've been stretched at Java. It's busier than ever."

"Want me to come in and help out? I can't stand for

long, but I could sit by the register and take the money."

"I don't think the boss'll pay three people for a shift."

"And I wouldn't expect him to. I feel bad about leaving you guys in the lurch, and I'm lonely here all day."

"In that case, we'd love to have you."

As well as getting me out of the apartment four mornings a week, being back at Java meant I could sneak in an extra few minutes with Oliver, because once he realised I was working there, he came in every day.

"If I tip you, will you chase me across the street again?"

"I would if I could run but not because of the money."

He handed over twenty bucks and lowered his voice. "I'd rather kiss you."

"That's Wednesday this week."

He leaned closer. "Princess, you're killing me. I jack off every night I'm not with you, and I'm getting RSI."

I almost choked, but thankfully nobody else heard what he said. He smiled that devilish smile of his and headed for the door before I managed to think up a reply. A girl drinking hot chocolate at the table nearest me watched his ass all the way, and I wanted to scratch her eyes out.

The man drove me crazy.

A couple of days after the bandages came off, Dan

insisted we go out for lunch. She acted bright, but the set of her jaw suggested a certain tension.

"Is everything all right?"

We'd gone to Il Tramonto, where the chef served us perfect crepes despite them being French rather than Italian, and Dan covered hers in chocolate sauce.

"Not much worse than usual. The court case is wearing a little thin. I just wish it was over."

"Me too."

"I don't know how Oliver does it. He's got all of Emmy's corporate stuff on top of two trials, and he's happier than I've ever seen him. Are you two still seeing each other?"

"Sort of. I don't know what we're doing." I cringed slightly as I gave her the bare bones of our arrangement. "I know it's weird, but I'd miss him if we stopped."

"You're probably what's keeping him sane right now. He's worked too hard for years; I've kept telling him that. You guys should take a vacation when the two trials are done."

Oliver had committed to one more big court case after Carter's, the prosecution of the man behind disaster number three, and Dan was involved in that one too.

"I don't think that's what he wants. That type of relationship, I mean."

"Convince him. The man needs a break."

"I don't..."

Giovanni interrupted us, beaming as usual. "Ah, my favourite girls. The staff are looking after you, *sì*?"

I nodded. "Yes, very well."

"You are still coming in tomorrow? I'll talk through

the new marketing campaign with you."

"Two o'clock?"

"*Perfetto*."

He grinned again, then headed for his office.

"You're working here?" Dan asked.

"Not really. Oliver arranged for me to get some work experience. One day, I'd love to get into hospitality management."

"I'm sure Oliver can help you find a job as well."

"I doubt that. He doesn't think I'm that great at it."

"Huh? He actually said that?"

"Not in those words, but I originally asked to shadow Louis at Rhodium, and he said no."

Dan burst out laughing.

"What?"

"He said no to Rhodium because he likes you, not because he thinks you're incompetent. Louis chases anything in a skirt, but Giovanni's gay."

"You really think that's the reason?"

"I know how Oliver's mind works. And if you don't want to ask him about a job, I can speak to Emmy. She's got fingers in every kind of pie you can imagine. Nick and Nate too."

"I don't want to put you to any trouble."

"It's no trouble. We like to look after our own."

I appreciated the sentiment, but I still wasn't sure I entirely fitted into their group. Every one of them was extraordinary in terms of looks and skills and intelligence, whereas I'd wound up knowing them by accident. I didn't want to push my luck.

Not with Dan, and not with Oliver.

I'd have loved to suggest three nights a week with him, or four, but apart from that comment in Java, he'd never shown any inclination of wanting more. And the way things were, I was happier than I had been in a long time. Imogen made me laugh, Bridget made me drink sometimes-awful smoothies, and Oliver made me come. The prospect of being alone again scared me more than the want growing inside me.

So I kept my feelings hidden.

The day the cast came off my leg, Oliver informed me by text message that he wanted to celebrate. It wasn't one of our regular days, but no way was I going to decline. I caught a cab from the hospital to his place, nodded at the concierge, who'd gotten used to me by now, and practically ran into the elevator. Zero two zero seven. Seconds later, Oliver met me at the door with a glass of champagne.

"Drink this. Then strip, because I want to pour the rest of the bottle over you then lick it off."

He didn't waste time, did he?

"Won't that get messy?"

"I'm counting on it. Then I'm going to fuck you in the shower, which I've been waiting to do for six damn weeks."

The last time I was here, he'd laid me on the bed and kissed me all over, the epitome of sweetness. Tonight, I got the Oliver who bent me over the table that night at Rhodium, and I wasn't sure which one I liked better.

Both. I wanted both. As often as I could get them.

I stripped.

Chapter 29

NOTHING GOOD EVER lasts, does it?

Oliver hauled me back to reality the day after our shower adventure with a reminder that I needed to go to his office for a formal interview. And it wouldn't just be him there. No, I'd have to spill the sordid details in front of his co-counsel and assistant.

And the court case was getting closer—it began in eight days. Oliver had avoided discussing it, but I saw the subtle changes in him—the deepening lines on his forehead, the way he'd zone out for a few seconds at a time while we ate dinner, the nights he'd head straight back to his study after sex, leaving me to lie awake and worry.

"What will happen?" I asked him one evening over dinner.

"I can't talk about it. I'm skirting ethical boundaries enough with you at the moment, and I need to keep that side of my life separate."

I understood that, but I hated to see him stressed.

"Is there anything I can do to help?"

"You already are, princess." He added more quietly, "More than you could ever know."

The day of the interview dawned grey and wet, a slow drizzle that soaked my shoes and made my hair frizz under my umbrella.

As I crossed the lobby at Rhodes, Holden and Maxwell, I thought back to the last time I'd visited. My embarrassment at Oliver's questions and the way I dashed out afterwards. I didn't doubt today would be just as uncomfortable, but how things had changed. Instead of wanting to cut out Oliver's tongue with a letter opener, I longed for him to wrap his arms around me and make this whole nightmare go away.

An immaculate receptionist who'd either arrived before the rain started or used a heck of a lot of hairspray showed me to a conference room. Three people were already seated on the other side of a long table—a stranger in the centre, Oliver to his left, and a younger girl on the right. From the way she kept clicking her pen, she seemed as nervous as me. An intern?

Oliver started off with the introductions. "This is Roy Heaton from the Commonwealth Attorney's office and his assistant."

I leaned over to shake hands, trying to keep the tremor out of my grip. When I got to Oliver, he gave me a little squeeze, as if to tell me things would be okay.

I tried to believe that, really I did. But as Roy asked question after question, laying my insides bare for the next two hours, little bits of my soul leached away, fluttering into the draught from the air conditioning. I caught myself chewing my hair too many times to count and forced my hands into my lap to keep from tearing it out.

By the time Roy flipped the cover of his legal pad

closed, I was tempted to exit the building via the window rather than the door. Each time I went through this, it got worse.

When it was finally over, Roy gave me a perfunctory smile and motioned towards the hallway. "Thank you for coming, Miss Amor. We'll call if we need anything else, although I've read through Oliver's notes and they're comprehensive."

What was I supposed to say? You're welcome? Because he wasn't. I opted for neutral instead.

"I'm glad to help if it means Carter goes to prison rather than a summer camp."

"We'll certainly do our best to make that happen."

I'd gotten halfway through the door when Oliver spoke up.

"Miss Amor? Would you mind staying for a minute or two? I have something I need you to sign in my office."

He hadn't mentioned that before, but since it was Oliver asking, I wasn't about to say no. Not if it meant I got to spend a little extra time with him outside our scheduled slots and coffee purchases.

"That's no problem."

Roy and the nameless assistant gathered up their belongings and filed out, with Oliver and me bringing up the rear.

"You mind if we take the stairs?" I asked. "The doctor says I need to get as much exercise as possible on my injured ankle."

"Of course, Miss Amor." Oliver motioned towards the door on the right of the elevators, now thankfully free of tape and contractors, and paused to speak with Roy. "I need to research a few things on that case we discussed, and then I'll speak to you this afternoon."

Roy already had his phone in his hand, checking his messages. "I'll wait for your call."

The assistant flashed Oliver a quick smile but wouldn't look me in the eye. Hardly surprising given what we'd just been talking about. I could barely face myself.

Oliver held the wooden door open for me to go through, and I found myself in a tiled stairwell. Metal railings guarded the central opening, and I couldn't resist peering over them, all the way down to the fancy mosaic floor in the basement. Somebody with money to burn had decorated this place.

"What do you want me to sign?" I asked, my voice bouncing off the walls.

He pressed up against me from behind.

"When I said 'sign,' I meant 'suck.'"

With one sentence, he set my heart racing.

"In your office?"

He spun me away from the railing and cupped my butt with his hands.

"I've spent the past two hours, thirteen minutes, and seventeen seconds watching your lips and thinking of them around my cock."

Then what were we waiting for? I grabbed his hand and pulled him up the first flight of stairs, but we only made it to the next landing before he backed me against the wall and touched his lips to mine, then nipped at my bottom lip and plunged his tongue into my mouth.

I twisted my head to the side as my heart threatened to pound through my ribcage.

"Stop! What if someone sees us?"

"Nobody ever uses the stairs. They're all too lazy."

He rubbed against me, hard already, and I reached for his zipper. Just a feel. Something to keep me going. Two and a half more flights of stairs suddenly seemed like a really long way.

"Princess, if you do that, we're not going to make it to my office."

But I didn't stop. I couldn't. My left hand slipped inside his boxer briefs and released eight inches of magic with a drop of pre-cum already oozing from the end. I swirled it around the tip with my thumb as Oliver groaned.

"Steffie, I mean it."

I brought my thumb to my lips and licked, and something seemed to snap within Oliver. Before I could swallow, he yanked my skirt up and pushed my panties aside.

"What are you doing?" I gasped.

"You asked for it."

"Freaking hell, are you crazy?"

He gritted his teeth, his mouth a thin line. "Around you, yes."

With one smooth motion, he slammed into me, and I closed my eyes. He'd lost his damn mind. We were in a stairwell, for crying out loud! Anyone could walk in. But a buzz of excitement ran through me at the thought of somebody doing just that, and I wrapped my arms around Oliver and pulled him closer, burying my face in his shoulder to quiet my whimpers.

"I won't last long, princess," he whispered, thrusting harder with every stroke.

"You don't need to."

My orgasm was building rapidly, and if Oliver

hadn't been holding me up, I'd have been on my knees.

Then a door opened above us.

"Stop! Stop!" I hissed, but he didn't.

Instead, his smile grew wider as he pumped into me one last time, and a starburst erupted in my belly as we both came.

Footsteps sounded, heading in our direction, joined by voices. Two people at least.

Oliver tucked himself away while I tugged my skirt down. What state was my hair in? I did a rapid finger-comb and prayed I looked presentable. Or, in fact, anything but just-fucked. Beside me, Oliver assumed a bland expression and took a step towards the next flight of stairs. How could he look so damn normal after what we'd just done?

"As I was saying, Miss Amor, the Virginia legal system allows the prosecution to call whatever witnesses they choose without having to give the defence prior notice. It gives us an advantage."

What was he talking about? He might as well have been speaking Swahili for all my brain understood of it. Still, I took a shaky step towards him so I didn't get left behind just as two men came into sight on the next landing.

"And that's why we plan to spring your appearance onto the defence as a surprise at the end of the trial. Our secret weapon, if you like. Mortimer Granville has no idea you're coming." Oliver paused to greet one of the men. "Morning, Todd. How's the wife?"

The nearest man grimaced. "Still spending all my money. I'm considering reporting my credit card stolen."

"Well, don't say I didn't warn you what would

happen the moment she got that ring on her finger."

All three men laughed, and the two interlopers carried on down the stairs as I sagged back against the handrail.

"You all right, princess?"

"No, I'm not. I can't believe you did that. Sometimes I really hate you."

He silenced me with another kiss. "I don't believe that."

I tried to look mad, but I was ninety-nine percent sure I failed. Although I couldn't stop shaking, it was mostly from exhilaration. What a rush! It may have been fast, but in my limited experience of orgasms, I'd never had one rip through me and destroy all my senses like that. Something I didn't dare admit to Oliver in case he wanted to try it again.

"Your cum is running down my leg."

He reached under my skirt, ran his thumb up my thigh, then offered it to me. "Suck."

I did so, tasting myself as well as him. How could I have enjoyed something so wrong?

"We can't do this again," I told him.

"We'll see."

"I'm serious."

He stilled, thinking for a few moments before he answered. "I think I might be too."

Was that a good thing or a bad thing?

"Are we still going to your office? I mean, do you have anything left?"

"I'm spent. But come anyway. We can have coffee before I deal with my emails."

"You're sure you've got time?"

"I'll make time." He took my hand and led me up

the stairs. “Once this trial starts, there’ll be precious little of that to spare.”

CHAPTER 30

ONCE AGAIN, OLIVER turned out to be right. When the trial started, it took over his life. Our two nights a week turned into a few snatched hours, and on one occasion, he fell asleep on the sofa before dinner even arrived. I didn't have the heart to wake him. Instead, I took off his shoes and tie then tucked a blanket around his exhausted body. He needed the rest.

I refused to watch the TV coverage of Carter, but it didn't matter. Imogen did it for me and recounted events in glorious detail.

"The whole thing's a circus," she said as we walked to Java one morning. "The Ghost's fans are outside court every day with banners and masks, but he hasn't turned up so far. And Oliver Rhodes has his own followers too. He was on the news signing autographs and posing for selfies."

"Really?"

"Yeah, and some girl interrupted his press conference yesterday and asked him to marry her."

Considering he still wouldn't share a bed with me overnight, I knew what his answer to that would have been, but I asked anyway. "What did he do?"

"Turned her down with an apology and said he was betrothed to his work right now. Betrothed. He actually said that." She gave a little sigh. "I'm so jealous. The guy I met last weekend could barely string a sentence together."

"Aw, no good then?"

"I'm not writing him off completely. He has other talents. But he sure ain't your rock-star lawyer. Does he look as good out of his suit as in it?"

I felt it appropriate to say, "No comment."

Imogen knew all about my arrangement with Oliver by now—it would have been impossible to keep it from her. But while she was happy to describe every detail of her dubious encounters, I preferred to keep mine private.

That didn't stop me from replaying them over and over in my head every night, though. Then I'd get hot and bothered, and the only way to get to sleep was to relieve the ache myself, imagining the whole time that it was Oliver's fingers touching me down there. The man had me obsessed.

But I didn't want it any other way.

"I hear you had a proposal?" I said to Oliver over dinner the next evening. He'd muttered something about a bad day, and I tried to lighten the mood.

He managed a smile. "Yes, I did. The cameras missed the one who got inside and flashed her breasts at me."

I couldn't help giggling. "Are you serious?"

"It's crazy. I got some attention when I used to do trials, but nothing like this. Ethan's brought all the kooks out of the woodwork. He's got this woman who keeps sending him socks with his face knitted into them."

"That's, er…sweet?"

"That's what Dan said, but he's still freaked."

"So have you had any weird gifts?"

He got up and returned with his briefcase, then rummaged through it.

"This arrived at the firm yesterday. My secretary had a fit."

I took the scrap of material he held out and burst into laughter.

"It's a thong? An elephant-shaped thong?"

"Who even came up with that idea?"

"I don't know, but you have to wear it."

"No, I don't." He pulled the offending item out of my hands and threw it across the room. "I'm going to burn it."

"Spoilsport."

"And proud of it."

"The Ghost's giving evidence today," Imogen told me, two weeks into the trial. "He turned up to court in a mask, and they had to call extra police in."

I felt sorry for Ethan and what he was going through. When I thought he'd killed Chrissie, I'd wished every kind of evil upon him, but I changed my mind when I got to know him. I wasn't the only person this trial was taking its toll on.

When Ethan finished, twelve-year-old Caleb testified by video link, and then Dan took her turn. Because of Oliver's long-standing friendship with her, which was apparently allowed as it predated the trial, his co-counsel took over the questioning, and I knew it hurt Oliver to watch her on the stand. As the main witness, Dan's testimony took over a week and left Oliver visibly drained.

But Dan was one of those people you couldn't keep down, and she and Ethan snuck into Oliver's apartment and joined us for dinner one evening.

"Thank fuck that's over." She flung her coat over an armchair and flopped onto one of the sofas. "I need wine."

Oliver came back moments later with a bottle of red and four glasses. "Speak for yourself. Two of us are still going."

"Sorry. But Mortimer Granville's an asshole. He's so fucking arrogant I want to punch his teeth out."

"He's a defence lawyer. He's only doing his job. People have accused me of the same thing."

"Yeah, but Granville's a jackal. He stalks you then goes in for the kill. And afterwards, he circles like a vulture and picks off what's left."

"Dan, stop talking."

"Actually, he's more like a rattlesnake. Sneaky."

"Dan..." Oliver glanced in my direction. "Shut the fuck up."

"And he kept staring at my tits. Stef, when it's your turn, wear something baggy. The man's a pervert."

Oliver sighed. "Yes. Wear something baggy. You'd look good in a burka."

"I'll wear something demure, okay? Can we change the subject now?"

Dan's words left me feeling queasy. I had two days until my day in court, if everything went according to plan, and I was dreading it. In all honesty, a burka didn't sound like a bad idea, because that way I'd avoid the hordes of photographers hanging around outside.

"Thank you for doing this," Ethan said quietly.

"It's for Chrissie as well, and all those other girls."

Dan clapped her hands. "Enough! Enough talking about shit we can't do anything about tonight. Let's eat Rhodium's finest and focus on the happier things in life. Like vacations. I fucking need one after this."

By the time we got to dessert, Dan and Ethan had decided to take Caleb on his first skiing trip, and I'd found out Oliver grew up in Colorado and hated snow. What else didn't I know about him?

Almost everything, but I was too tired to find out tonight. I needed my bed. Funny how I'd come to think of that room at Oliver's as mine, wasn't it? Especially when all I had in there was a few toiletries on the vanity in the bathroom and a handful of spare underwear stuffed in a lonely drawer.

"You don't have to get home to Caleb tonight?" I asked Dan as we stumbled from the dining room.

"He's having a sleepover with Vine and Trick. Bradley's allegedly supervising, but as long as the emergency services don't get called, I can live with it."

Dan was such a laid-back mom, but it was clear how much she loved that boy. I only hoped I could emulate her one day. But not with Oliver. I was sure of that much, and it hurt. Even more so when he walked off to the master suite, leaving me to go to the guest corridor with Dan. That left me feeling rejected, like I was good enough to eat dinner with but not good enough to keep.

She caught me staring after him, and in her typical way, she knew exactly what I was thinking.

"Don't be upset by it. He's doing this in the only way he knows how. He never spends the night with anyone."

"Even Kelly?"

"Kelly slept in the room at the other end of the corridor. He wanted her as far away as possible." She gave me a sad smile. "Your room belonged to Darcy."

And on that bombshell, she joined Ethan in their room, leaving me alone and more befuddled than ever.

CHAPTER 31

I TOOK DAN'S advice to heart, and for my day in court, I dressed appropriately—a loose, knee-length skirt, a boring cream blouse with a big bow at the neck, and a shapeless navy-blue blazer. My flat shoes were the unsexiest I could find and would have been more at home on an octogenarian.

"How do I look?" I asked Imogen, giving her a twirl.

"Like an advert for celibacy. I definitely wouldn't do you."

"Good. That's what I was hoping for."

"But you'll be on TV. Don't you want to look good?"

"Nope. I want to look dull, boring, and unmemorable."

"In that case, you're perfect."

Even Oliver did a double take when he saw me. We met at Rhodes, Holden and Maxwell beforehand, and he looked delicious in yet another made-to-measure suit.

"Nice shoes, grandma."

"Very funny. You were the one who told me to dress like this."

"Actually, it was Dan. I just agreed with her." He leaned closer. "But I'll be the one to peel you out of that ugly outfit later, princess."

Roy strode over, briefcase in hand, and stopped

things from getting any more heated.

"What's the plan?" he asked.

"Miss Amor would rather avoid the media, so I'll distract them while you take her inside."

Roy smirked at Oliver. "Planning to add to your collection of panties?"

"Huh?" I stared at him.

"The ladies have been throwing underwear at Oliver here. Not sure pink's his colour, though."

A vision of Oliver in something lacy popped into my mind, and pink certainly became my colour. I turned away to hide my blush while Oliver darted into his office for his briefcase. Then we could put it off no longer. It was time to go.

Oliver rode to the court building on North Ninth Street each day in a town car, and today, Roy and I caught a ride with him. I heard the shouts from outside before he opened the door, and the second he got out, the cameras started flashing.

Roy rolled his eyes. "Don't know how that guy does it. He's got this weird natural charisma that makes women flock to him, but he never shows the slightest interest."

The driver leaned over and gave us a knowing wink. "Reckon he might be gay."

I hastily turned my choke into a cough. "That's quite an assumption."

"Temptation throwing itself in his face like that, it's the only explanation."

Roy clutched my elbow. "Enough chat. Ready to

go?"

Not in a million years.

"Yes, I'm ready."

I kept my head down as we hurried into the courthouse, but even so, I felt the eyes and cameras of the world's media upon me. Everyone involved in the case was suffering from its reach, but this time tomorrow, my part would be finished. Done. I clung to that thought as Roy navigated us through corridors, up stairs, and along a hallway. He pushed an unmarked door open.

"Wait in here, please. There are some people I need to talk to."

"When do I have to go in?"

"Not long now. Someone will fetch you."

The room was sparsely furnished, just a couple of bare tables and uncomfortable plastic chairs. I perched on the edge of one and forced my fingers to release the end of my ponytail. Part of me wanted to put my appearance off forever, but at the same time, I longed to get it over with so I could carry on with my life. Anything but waiting in this limbo with the clock ticking down.

A few minutes before nine o'clock, the door clicked open. Was this it? Did I need to go in?

"Are you okay, princess?"

Oh, it was Oliver. "I thought you'd be in court by now."

"I should be, but I wanted to see you first."

He came closer, and I couldn't help tucking myself against his chest. I needed to feel his strength one last time before we faced the judge and jury.

"I'm so nervous."

He gave me a soft kiss on the lips and wrapped me up in his arms.

"I know, Steffie. I know. When you get on the stand, just keep looking at me, okay? Granville will try to intimidate you, but he's only got words. That's it. Just words. I'll do my best to keep his questions to a minimum. Answer honestly, don't elaborate on anything, and it'll be over before you know it."

"Can I stay with you tonight?"

We'd already had our two nights this week, but I needed him. I always swore I wouldn't become that girl, the one dependant on a man, but tonight I didn't want to be alone.

"Of course, princess." He paused a second, then reached for his briefcase on the nearby table and pulled out a key. "Take this. Let yourself in, and I'll get there as soon as I can."

A key to his apartment? Yes, it was only for today, but he'd never done that before. Did it mean anything? I didn't dare to hope.

"Thank you."

He hugged me to him once more and pressed his lips to mine. One last kiss before the nightmare began.

Only it started early.

The door opened behind me, and Oliver looked up sharply. I couldn't see who'd come in, but from the way Oliver's eyes widened infinitesimally, it wasn't good news.

"Rhodes. Hardly appropriate to be entertaining ladies before court, is it?"

The voice sounded vaguely familiar, but I couldn't place it.

"Morning, Granville," Oliver said.

Oh, shit! Of all the people to walk in, it had to be the damn defence lawyer. Now what? I tried to pull back, but Oliver held me where I was, squashed against his chest, and when I glanced up, I saw him smirk.

"I can't help it if the ladies downstairs find me irresistible."

A chuckle came from behind me. "I'd always assumed you were gay."

"I'm full of surprises."

"The usher's looking for the first witness. Don't suppose you've seen her anywhere?"

"I'd suggest trying the ladies' room."

"I'll tell her that. Hurry up, would you? This case has dragged on for long enough."

The door clicked closed, and I started shaking.

"Now what? Granville saw us together. What if the case falls apart and you get disciplined?"

Oliver gritted his teeth and closed his eyes. "Fuck. This isn't good." His eyes popped open again. "He only saw you from the back. Take your jacket off. You'll look different with only the blouse on."

I wrenched my arms from the sleeves and stuffed the ugly garment into Oliver's briefcase as he grabbed my ponytail and pulled the elastic out of it.

"And wear your hair loose. With any luck, he won't recognise you."

"What if he does? What if he realises?"

"Keep your fingers crossed and deny everything."

CHAPTER 32

OLIVER STRAIGHTENED HIS tie and picked up his briefcase.

"Wait!"

I wiped my lip gloss off his face. Watermelon pink wasn't a good look on him.

"Thanks."

Then he was gone, and I shot along the corridor to the nearest ladies' room to do the rest of my panicking there. According to Oliver, I was the last witness for the prosecution. What if I screwed everything up? What if Carter's insanity defence succeeded and it was all my fault?

I wiped my nose and blotted my eyes just in time for a lady to call my name.

"Stefanie Amor?"

"In here."

"You need to hurry up, darlin'. They're waitin' for ya."

"I'll be right out."

Now I understood how prisoners on death row felt, walking to their execution. Actually, maybe not. At least they got a decent meal first, whereas I hadn't eaten since lunch yesterday. My hideous shoes squeaked on the tile, the noise eclipsed only by the blood whooshing in my ears as my heart worked overtime.

Beside me, the usher pushed the door open, and I got my first look at the courtroom.

The public gallery was full to bursting, and all heads turned towards me as I shuffled to the front. The judge was already seated, and to his left, a twelve-person jury gawked in my direction. Oliver may have practised asking me a hundred questions, but nothing could have prepared me for this. Tension hung thick in the air as I looked towards the two tables before the judge.

Oliver turned from his seat, the one nearest the jury, with Roy at his side. I longed for a smile, but I didn't get it. Of course not. Oliver was far better at hiding his emotions than me, and his face was perfectly blank.

The usher led me towards the witness stand, which was next to the defence table, and then my day got worse.

First Carter turned to stare at me, and when I say stare, I mean stare. His clear blue eyes locked onto mine until I tore my gaze away. And do you know what scared me most? He didn't look like a monster, the kind you imagine under the bed as a child. He was a man. A plain, ordinary man. And a killer. If ever there was a reminder that the escort business was bad for your health, he was it.

Then the man next to him swivelled in my direction, and honestly, I thought I'd have a heart attack. Mortimer Granville, I presumed, but that's not what I knew him as.

No, on my weekly visits to the illustrious defence lawyer, the one who Dan called a jackal and a vulture, I'd only ever called him Timmy.

He called me Mom.

It had started out as a favour for Octavia, not something through Rubies. A friend of hers had a girl go sick, and knowing I'd do the weird stuff if it didn't involve a cock in the wrong place, she'd given me a call.

"It's a straightforward job. The guy's a fruitcake, but he won't hurt you. He likes to play dress-up and suck on your tits; then you give him a hand job and tuck him into bed."

"So what should I wear?"

"Something demure. Plain white underwear."

The clothes I'd worn to court, in fact. The skirt and blouse were both leftovers from my time with Timmy.

Shit, shit, shit.

Because what Octavia hadn't mentioned in that initial conversation was that Timmy liked to dress as a baby. I'd nearly had a freaking heart attack when he opened the door to me in a diaper, but the money was good and, like Octavia said, he was harmless.

And when he asked for me again the next Friday, and the one after that, I took his fifteen hundred dollars and spanked his pasty ass.

But now here I was, stuck in the most serious situation of my life, about to be questioned on the sexual preferences of a murderer by the man I was secretly sleeping with and the overgrown child whose diapers I used to change. You couldn't make it up.

And by the look of him, Mortimer Granville realised the horror of what was to come about the same time I did. He might have been wearing a fancy suit today, but his eyes were those of a toddler caught with his hand in the cookie jar.

The usher gently tugged on my arm.

"Come on, darlin'. It'll be done before you know it."

I prayed for divine intervention as I stepped into the witness box—an earthquake, a tornado, something like that—but nobody up there listened.

Instead, the clerk stepped forwards. "Do you solemnly swear to tell the truth, the whole truth, and nothing but the truth, so help you God?"

"Yes," I whispered, only the microphone in front of me amplified my voice and made me jump.

Oliver stood up and shuffled his papers, and I forced myself to let go of my hair. What should I do? Should I say something? Oliver told me witness/lawyer relations were banned, and let's face it, it would be hard to get less appropriate than powdering the defence lawyer's ass.

But the room was full of people, and I'd rather have shot myself right then than admit to them what I did. And what would Oliver think? I'd never mentioned Timmy to him, seeing as he was a private client and had nothing to do with Rubies or Carter. Or so I'd thought.

The judge's booming voice interrupted my thoughts. "Miss Amor? Are you with us?"

"Sorry?"

"Would you like me to repeat the question?" Oliver asked.

"Yes, please."

And so it began. I remembered Oliver's words and focused on him as he took me through my night with Carter once more, and by concentrating on his lips, I managed to block out the rest of the courtroom and imagine we were back in his study, just the two of us.

Oliver had warned me of Timmy's penchant for interrupting, and he tried once or twice at the beginning, full of bluster and unable to look me in the eye. But Oliver cut him down, and I stared straight at Timmy, daring him to try again, and after that, the man-child didn't say another word. On a couple of occasions, I caught Oliver glancing over to the defence table as if he expected a comment, but nothing came. Even Carter seemed confused.

"So, in your opinion, is Mr. Carter a rational human being?" Oliver asked.

"From what I saw, he's as sane as you or I." I glanced over at the defence table, wondering why Timmy hadn't stopped this. Oliver had told me to expect the question, but he also said Timmy wouldn't allow it. "Or Mr. Granville here."

Finally, a weak, "Objection. The witness is not a psychiatrist."

Oliver grinned. "Withdrawn."

He returned to his seat, and the judge turned his attention to Timmy, who looked a little unwell. His colour had dropped several shades since I first saw him, and beads of sweat ran down his brow. He wiped them away with a sleeve.

"Your witness, Mr. Granville."

"Er, yes. Of course."

He stood and began pacing in front of the judge, and I watched every step. Up and down. Up and down. Up and down.

I risked a glance over to Oliver. He was tracking Timmy with his brow furrowed, and I wished I could tell him what was going on.

Then Timmy stopped right in front of me. "Miss Amor, you say you only spent one night with the defendant?"

He locked his eyes on mine in an attempt at intimidation, but it was hard to be intimidated by a man when I knew firstly, that he had a four-inch dick, and secondly, he needed pharmaceutical help to get it up. I used to crush his little blue pills and mix them into his bottle of warm milk.

"That's true."

"I put it to you that it's not possible to tell much about a man in such a short period of time."

"On the contrary. I learned to judge men quickly, and Mr. Carter didn't give me any cause for alarm."

"But you have no professional training in psychology?"

"True, but my profession taught me a lot. I don't need a piece of paper to tell me a man who likes to wear diapers isn't entirely normal. For example."

Sniggers ran around the courtroom, and the judge called for order. Timmy turned an alarming shade of puce.

"Motion to dismiss that last answer," Timmy mumbled. "It's irrelevant."

"Upheld," the judge said. "Do you have any more questions, Mr. Granville?"

"I'm done."

That was it? Really? I fought to avoid grinning.

"Mr. Rhodes?"

Oliver gave a tiny one-shouldered shrug. "I don't have anything else."

"In that case, Miss Amor, you're free to leave."

I walked out of the courtroom, and as soon as the door

closed behind me, I broke into a run. I had to get out of there. The key to Oliver's apartment burned away in my pocket as I scurried out the front door, remembering too late about the media camped outside. Dammit. Dammit! Flashes burned my retinas as I scoured the road for a cab. Nothing.

That momentary hesitation was my undoing. Paparazzi came at me in a horde, and I didn't know whether to back up the steps or sprint down the road. They yelled my name, and I covered my face with my hands. All that time I'd spent avoiding publicity, and I'd ruined it in a moment of gross stupidity.

Good going, Sable.

Then a limo pulled up and the driver wound down his window. "Stefanie?"

I nodded.

"Dan sent me. She thought you might need a fast getaway."

I practically dived into the back while saying a silent thank you to Dan. She'd proven once more that she was a true friend.

"Where to?" the driver asked.

I gave Oliver's address and sank back in the leather seat. I needed to get to my sanctuary, and right now, that sanctuary was a penthouse in downtown Richmond where a mercurial lawyer liked to do bad things to me.

Oliver arrived just after six, slamming the front door behind him. Bridget, who'd thawed out markedly over the last few weeks, had left me with a plate of chocolate éclairs and another weird fruit concoction, and I licked cream off my fingers as Oliver strode into the kitchen.

"You want to tell me what happened in court this morning?"

He dumped his briefcase onto the breakfast bar and raised an eyebrow.

"I'm not sure you'd believe me if I did."

"Try me. I've never seen Granville at a loss like that, and I'm not convinced it was because he recognised you."

"Oh, he recognised me all right, but not from the clinch this morning. The last time I saw him, he was sleeping in an oversized crib and sucking on a pacifier."

"Come again?"

I recounted the whole story, from the nursery hidden behind the bookcase in Timmy's study to the way I had to burp him, the musical mobile over the pillow, and Timmy's favourite toy unicorn. Oliver actually wiped away tears at the end, he laughed so hard.

"Fuck me. I thought my sexual tastes were unusual, but at least when I suck your tits, it's not for nutritional purposes."

"It's not funny," I tried to say, but I couldn't stop giggling.

"Steffie, it's fucking hilarious. But I have no idea how I'm going to look Morty Granville in the eye in court tomorrow."

"I can't help you there."

"Maybe you can help with something else?" He took both my hands in his and twined our fingers together. "Like distraction."

I stood on tiptoes and pressed my lips to his. "I'd be

only too happy to assist."

CHAPTER 33

TWO WEEKS LATER, Oliver walked into his apartment and dropped his briefcase in the hallway. He'd told me to keep the key so I could get there early on the days I was due to see him, and I tended to take advantage of his comfy sofa and giant TV.

"It's over."

I scrambled up, rushed across the room, and flung my arms around him. "The jury's out?"

"As of four o'clock."

He'd already told me this was the part he hated most, that period between the summing up and the verdict where everything was out of his control and all we could do was wait.

"Did it go okay?"

"I think so. I hope so. Granville lost a bit of his fire after your testimony, and I'd already argued a lot of his points down. But juries are fickle. Put twelve people together in a situation like that, and they sometimes do unexpected things."

I gave Oliver a quick kiss, which turned into something longer as he pressed me up against the wall, and by the time he moved back, I'd lost my appetite for food.

"Do you want dinner now or later?" I asked. "Giovanni's on standby downstairs."

"Later. First, I need to lose myself in you, princess."

"You can do that all night."

He closed his eyes and leaned his forehead against mine. "Will you stay longer? Until the verdict comes through? I know I've got no right to ask, but..."

"I'll stay."

And I found myself wishing the jury would take a very long time indeed to make their decision.

Like with so many things in life, I didn't get my wish. The call came two days later. Two days of lazing around in Oliver's apartment, pretending I didn't have to leave. Pretending that somehow, despite everything, I could have a normal life with the man I'd fallen in love with.

Because that's what had happened. Nothing about my relationship with Oliver Rhodes followed convention, but I loved him anyway. From his bossy manner in bed and the way he pushed my boundaries, to his warmth next to me on the sofa as he watched a movie he didn't like because I wanted to, and the rise and fall of his chest as he fell asleep during it.

His public persona, the confident lawyer, bordering on arrogant, wasn't the man I'd grown to know. The one I wanted to keep, but understood I never could.

And now he tossed his phone back onto the table. "Jury's back. I need to get to court."

"Do you want me to come with you?"

"No, stay here. It'll be a circus."

I paced for an hour. I chewed my hair, spat it out, berated myself for it. And finally, I gave in and switched on the TV. Oliver was front and centre, microphones shoved up in his face as he spoke calmly and assuredly.

"Justice was done today, and while it won't bring back Miss Walker, I hope her family and friends can take some comfort from that."

I sagged back on the sofa. He'd done it. He got his conviction. The tension seeped out of me like an oil slick, spreading thinner and thinner until it dispersed on the waves.

Carter was going to prison. He'd killed Chrissie, and now he'd spend his life in the hellhole he tried to send Ethan to. I didn't feel sorry for him. Not one bit.

Ethan himself didn't attend the press conference, which meant Oliver bore the brunt of the questions. Not that I could blame Ethan. He didn't ask for any of this hoopla either. His new manager did put in an appearance and conveyed his client's relief at the outcome, yadda, yadda, yadda, and informed the world that Ethan just wanted to carry on making music. I stayed glued to the TV, watching the sound bites over and over on repeat until the front door opened.

Oliver still had a little leftover swagger from court, but he deserved it today.

"You won!"

"*We* won. It was a team effort." He broke into a grin. "And it feels fucking awesome."

I curled my fingers around his lapels and pulled him closer. "So, are we celebrating?"

He grimaced then sighed. "I've got bad news about that."

"Tell me."

"Bradley's throwing a party tonight. Dan tried to stop him, but apparently he's been planning it for days."

"But you hadn't even won yet."

"Oh, Bradley doesn't let little things like that stop him. Will you come?"

"With you?"

"No, Steffie, I thought I'd send you on your own while I got some sleep. Of course with me."

"I'll have to go home and pick up something to wear."

He touched his lips to mine. "I'd drive you, but there are reporters camped out downstairs. I'll call for a car and meet you at Riverley?"

"Weirdly, I look forward to it."

When I arrived in the grand hallway at Riverley two hours later, streamers hung from the suits of armour flanking the front door and a banner on the wall proclaimed "Happy Conviction."

Emmy, Oliver's biggest client, faced Bradley with her hands on her hips. "Do you really think this is appropriate?"

"We haven't had a party in ages."

She pointed at the banner. "What next? Are we gonna have fireworks next time I shoot someone?"

"Hmm, now there's an idea..."

"No. Just no." She turned to me. "Hey, Stef. Glad you could make it."

Emmy had never been anything but nice, but she still made me nervous.

"Thanks for inviting me. Is Oliver here yet?"

"Try the kitchen. He went to find a drink, and I

can't say I blame him."

By eight o'clock, the party was in full swing. Bradley had got a bit ahead of himself with his electric-chair-shaped cake, and the waiters were dressed in orange jumpsuits.

"Would you like a lethal injection, ma'am?" one of them asked me.

"What? No!"

"It's only a cocktail." He held out a tray of giant syringes filled with purple liquid.

"What's in it?"

"Gin, lychee puree, Blue Curaçao, lemon juice, and grenadine."

"Okay, I'll try one. What am I supposed to do, squirt it into my mouth?"

"Exactly, ma'am."

It actually wasn't that bad. Beside me, Oliver stuck with a glass of red wine and rolled his eyes.

"Every time Bradley throws a party, I think it can't possibly get any more tasteless, and every time, he surprises me."

"Let's just go with the flow. It'll be over soon."

At the front of the ballroom, Bradley stood on a chair and clapped his hands.

"Time for the party games. First up, jailbird Twister. Each couple wears a pair of handcuffs."

He snagged Emmy as she walked past and clapped a bracelet onto her wrist. I didn't see exactly what she did, but two seconds later, Bradley was attached to a lamp and Emmy carried on walking.

"You don't play fair!" he squealed.

"I also don't play Twister."

Dan took pity on the man and released him. "I'll

play. Come on, Ethan, it'll be fun."

Ethan didn't look as if he shared her opinion, but he held up a hand. "Fine, get it over with."

Oliver's arm tightened around my waist. "I'm weighing up the benefits of being handcuffed to you against the downside of playing games."

"I'm not wearing any panties."

Oliver grabbed my hand and pulled me towards the door, but Bradley spotted us.

"Hey! Come back."

We got into the hallway and ran for the stairs, Bradley's cries echoing behind us. On the next floor, Oliver shoved open the first door on the left and we tumbled through into the library.

Whoa. I'd never been in there before, and the vast shelves full of old books were like something out of a fairy tale. Floor lamps cast a dim glow as I walked over to the nearest and ran my fingers over the leather spines.

"This room's beautiful. How old are these books?"

"I'm not interested in the books tonight, princess."

He stalked me as I toured the room, taking in the wood carvings, the oil paintings on the walls, the worn leather seats. All such a far cry from my normal world, where my collection of paperbacks fitted on the tiny shelf next to my bed. I imagined myself curled up here with a fire roaring in the hearth while I got lost in the old tomes. One of three sets of French windows opened to my right, and I stepped onto the balcony, staring out across the moonlit estate. Before I met Oliver, I'd seen pictures of places like this, but now I'd lived the reality, if only for a few nights.

"I feel like Juliet."

"Does that make me Romeo?"

"Preferably without the tragic ending."

I leaned on the stone balustrade, so cool under my fingers but rough from years of weathering. By now, I knew Oliver well enough that the sound of his zipper wasn't a surprise.

A sigh escaped my lips as he ran both hands up my bare thighs, stopping at my waist.

"You weren't kidding about the panties."

I spread my legs slightly, waiting. "Never with you."

He ran a finger between my legs, and I shuddered. "You're soaked, princess. You've turned into a little minx, haven't you?"

"Mmmm."

"I like that in a woman."

So did I. At Rubies, sex had felt dirty, bad, wrong, but Oliver had helped me to embrace my filthy side in a way I'd never have dared to do in the past.

He slid into me, and I revelled in the full moon as he worked his fingers in and out, gently at first, getting faster as he undid the buttons on the front of my dress. Yes, I'd picked that one out for a reason.

Each tweak of my nipples sent spasms through me, and I clung onto the stonework harder.

"Touch me. Please."

Oliver's hand moved to the sweet spot just as the door clicked open behind us. I froze, but Oliver only laughed.

"Someone's there," I whispered.

"I don't care tonight."

A brassy voice bit through the air. "For fuck's sake, dude. We've got eighteen bedrooms in this place, and half of them have got balconies. Private balconies."

"Get lost, Emmy. We're busy."

The door slammed, and I couldn't help giggling. "Finally caught."

"Yes, I have been."

One last stroke of his fingers almost sent me falling over the edge of the balcony, but Oliver held me close as he came. I sagged back against him, spent, and with the newfound knowledge I'd do anything he asked me to. Being caught gave me the hardest orgasm of my life.

"Shall we go and find one of those bedrooms?" he asked.

"Yes."

He picked me up and carried me back through the library, along the corridor, and up the next flight of stairs, peppering me with kisses as he went.

"We just need to make a quick stop, princess. I want to grab some scarves."

CHAPTER 34

OLIVER RECREATED OUR first night together in every way except the tears, including disappearing by morning.

This time, though, I was ready for it. I knew he'd be back, so I took a shower and got dressed. My overnight bag had magically appeared in my room, which meant at least I had underwear.

I didn't know which room Oliver slept in, so I hoped to see him at breakfast—well, brunch, seeing as it was eleven o'clock now. But when I got into the kitchen, only Emmy sat at the counter, contemplating a mug of coffee.

Wonderful. Of all the people I'd hoped to avoid this morning, she was the one sitting in front of me. I tried to cover my blush with my hands as she looked up.

"Don't worry. I only saw Oliver's ass, and it wasn't the first time."

What? I couldn't hold back my gasp.

"Oh, don't look at me like that. I haven't fucked him. He goes skinny-dipping in the pool some mornings."

I wasn't quite sure what to say to that. I couldn't imagine Oliver being so uninhibited.

"Do you know where he is?"

"Yeah." She sighed. "There's a bit of bad news. Well,

sort of. Depends on how you choose to look at it. I'm happy, but Oliver's had to go to the precinct."

My heart skipped. "The police precinct?"

"Carter killed himself in the county jail last night. Fucking coward."

"Ohhhh."

I didn't know what I'd been expecting her to say, but it sure wasn't that. How did I feel? Honestly?

Relieved.

"Give it an hour or two, and the media'll be hopping on the story like fleas. Oliver needs to make a statement about how sorry everyone is, blah, blah, blah, but hopefully he'll be back for lunch."

"I can get a cab home."

"Don't bother. Oliver'll pick you up when he's done."

"I don't want to put him to any trouble."

She laughed. "The dude's crazy about you. Trust me, it won't be any trouble for him."

"I don't think he is. What we have, well, it's more of an arrangement."

Oh dear, why did I tell her that? Oliver never broadcasted what was going on between us, and now I'd blurted out his secret. Yes, Dan knew, but Dan was closer to Oliver. What on earth would Emmy think?

She ticked off points on her fingers. "He's cleared two evenings a week for you in the middle of his busiest time at work ever. He stepped out of a meeting with me to text you the other day. And he brought you here."

Okay, less judgey than I thought.

"He says he doesn't do relationships, and he never spends the night with me. That's hardly commitment."

Would he ever offer more?

"He's scarred."

"I don't understand why." My voice dropped to a whisper. "Did he bring Kelly here? Or Darcy?"

Those were the two names I'd heard mentioned, and I had no comparison between them and me, only the knowledge that they'd both had rooms in his apartment. What did they have that I didn't?

Emmy raised an eyebrow. "You know about them?"

"Only their names. Oliver never talks about his past."

She sighed, then took a sip of coffee and set her mug down. "Oliver's past drives him. And in answer to your question, yes, he brought Darcy here, but never Kelly. I'd have run Kelly off the property and everyone knew it, including her."

Someone else who didn't like Kelly. "Why was Darcy so different?"

"Because Darcy was Oliver's daughter. Kelly was just the woman who gave birth to her."

The bottom just dropped out of my world. "His d-d-daughter?"

"Yeah. Cute kid, despite having the world's biggest bitch for a mother."

"You keep saying 'was'?"

"Darcy died when she was two years old."

My hands flew to my mouth and I gasped again. "What? How?"

"I'll tell you, because if you're going to have any sort of future with Oliver, you need to understand why he is how he is. But be bloody careful with the knowledge, yeah? He still won't talk about it, six years later."

"I promise. The last thing I want to do is hurt him."

"I know that. But sometimes it happens even when

you don't mean it to."

"I love him."

Well, wasn't I just one big stream-of-consciousness today?

Emmy closed her eyes for a second. "I get that too. Anyway, I didn't know Oliver well back then, but he's always been close to Dan. They used to go out drinking together. Kelly was a one-night stand that went wrong in the worst possible way."

"She got pregnant?" I whispered.

"Bitch probably poked holes in the condom. But when she told him a couple of months later, he tried to do the right thing and moved her into his apartment. She spent half a year abusing his credit card and irritating the shit out of him before Darcy was born. Dan even caught her drinking. We both went over there and informed her of the error of her ways."

"She sounds awful."

"And she only got worse after Darcy came into the world. She'd go out partying every single fucking night. Oliver hired Bridget to look after his daughter in the daytime so he could carry on working, then cared for her himself in the evenings. They'd come over here to escape the car crash in his apartment some weekends."

"So what happened to her?" I almost didn't dare to ask, but at the same time, I needed to know.

"Oliver was defending a guy who'd killed his neighbour's kid. Everyone knew he did it, but Oliver got the asshole off on a technicality. He had this 'win at all costs' mentality, and back then, he hadn't learned how to pick the right battles. Plus Kelly was spending his money faster than he made it, so he couldn't easily afford to turn down work."

"I didn't realise he was like that. I mean, I know him being with me during the trial wasn't ethical, but..."

"Once upon a time, honey, you both screwed people for money. But you've changed and so has he. Darcy's death taught him a lot. Anyhow, there were threats. The neighbour told Oliver he'd feel the same pain, then disappeared. The police searched for the man, and we looked for him too, but every time we got a sniff of him, he vanished again. Oliver told Kelly to stay inside, but it was Bridget's morning off and Kelly just had to get a fucking manicure, didn't she?"

"She took Darcy out with her?"

Emmy nodded. "The neighbour was waiting, and he shot both of them and then himself. Kelly survived. Darcy didn't."

A tear rolled down my cheek as I thought of what Oliver had lost. No wonder he never talked about his past. How did a man get over losing a child like that? He didn't. That was the answer. Not ever. I wiped my face with my sleeve, but the tears kept coming as Emmy continued.

"Oliver gave up trial work straight away. He said no amount of money, or fame, or glory was worth that pain. That's how he ended up doing all my corporate shit. Carter was his first trial in six years, and he was on the right side this time. Carter needed to go down. It's been tough on Oliver, but you've helped him through it."

"I've barely done anything. If I'd known..."

"It was better that you didn't. Hardly anybody knows—it all got hushed up to prevent copycat attacks, and we managed to keep it out of the media. And Oliver doesn't need kid gloves. He just needs someone who cares about him to come home to at the end of the day. But you see why he struggles with commitment now?"

"He never wants to get into another Kelly situation."

"Guilt wouldn't let him get rid of her. And he hates the pain of losing someone he cares for if something goes wrong."

"So what should I do now? How can I help him?"

"Nothing but what you have been doing. Either he'll see the light and change, or he won't. I don't think pushing him will help matters. It's taken him a long time to get this far."

The sound of footsteps in the hallway made me turn my head, and Oliver walked in, looking tired.

"Steffie? Why are you crying?"

"Uh... I..."

"I told her about Carter," Emmy interrupted. "It's been an emotional time for everyone."

I managed a shrug. "Hormones."

That excuse always seemed to work with men.

Oliver put an arm around my shoulders and pulled me against him. "It's over. We all need to forget Carter now."

"I know. I'll try."

"Do you want to go home? Or stay here for a while?"

"I don't mind. Whatever you want."

He turned to Emmy. "Is Bradley still wreaking havoc?"

"Bradley's clearing up the ballroom. I've banned him from shopping until he's finished."

Oliver kissed me softly on the lips, and I caught

Emmy's smile from the corner of my eye. Not her usual cunning smile, either. A genuinely happy one. Someone should have framed that picture for posterity.

Then Oliver took my hand. "Shall we borrow the movie room for one of those old black and whites you love so much?"

"Are you going to fall asleep?"

"Probably."

I ran a finger over the furrows between his eyes. "You need to."

"Then let's go."

Oliver passed out almost immediately, stretched lengthways on the plush velvet sofa in the screening room as the opening credits rolled. I took his shoes off and found a blanket, then curled up next to him, our fingers intertwined.

I might have loved old movies, but I barely watched that one. Emmy's news had rocked me to my core, and although she said to act normal, how could I when everything had changed? Before, I'd assumed Oliver suffered from a wandering eye and my only job would be to tame him, but the truth was so much worse.

Tragic.

A lost daughter and a man who'd never managed to find himself again. Would he ever?

All I could do was stick around to help him search.

CHAPTER 35

AS THE FURORE surrounding Carter died down, I could get on with my life once more. Not so for Oliver, who still had to prosecute the man responsible for disaster number three as well as sort out the last of my Landon mess.

"Everything's dropped, so you're free to leave the state again," he said one evening over dinner. "Landon Bishop won't be so lucky, though. He'll do jail time."

"Thank you." Doing naughty things with a lawyer sure came in useful sometimes. "But I don't want to leave Richmond anymore."

"Glad to hear it, princess."

I took Emmy's advice and acted normal, or as normal as I could now I knew what I knew. I was determined not to turn into a Kelly, someone who relied on Oliver for cash and couldn't stand on her own two feet. And that meant I needed to get a second job.

"Rhodium?" Imogen suggested. "I could speak to Louis."

I recalled what Dan had said about Louis, and I didn't want to cause Oliver any more stress. "No, not Rhodium. I might ask Giovanni if he has any openings."

"I don't think Il Tramonto gets celebrities."

"I don't care about that. In fact, it's probably easier

that way."

"Plus it's right underneath Oliver's apartment."

"I can't deny that's an added bonus."

And when I broached the subject with Giovanni on our next coaching session, he was only too happy to give me two waitressing shifts a week, with the possibility of more if an opening came up. I loved the whole team there, and the extra money sure would come in useful, so I couldn't have been happier.

Even more so when I broke the news to Oliver as we snuggled on the sofa one evening.

"I know you'll do a good job there, Steffie."

"Giovanni's a wonderful manager, and I've learned a lot."

"If you have to work late, feel free to stay here."

"You don't mind?"

"It's your room, princess. But I might not be around. I've been sleeping at the office on the nights we're not together."

"Is it the new trial?"

"It's tougher than the other one. When the defendant's got a legal team of piranhas as well as being one himself, I can't leave anything to chance."

"Can I help in any way? Bring you coffee? Or lunch?"

"I have an assistant for all that."

I rubbed my foot along his thigh under the table and lowered my lashes.

"Do you need me to sign anything in your office?"

Despite his obvious tiredness, I got a smile. "I'm sure I can rustle up some papers."

"Tomorrow?"

"Any day you like."

So from that day onwards, we added lunchtime sex into the mix. Once a week, I'd stop by Oliver's office with some sort of excuse, and we'd do dirty things over his desk. The day I hid underneath while he joined a conference call was particularly entertaining. I have no idea how he kept his face straight as I licked the head of his cock. Sheer willpower, it must have been.

And every day I spent with him, I loved him a little more, and every night we spent apart, the ache in my heart grew. Emmy said he might never change, and I began to think she was right.

Don't get me wrong—Oliver could be sweet, like on the day we celebrated my birthday. I thought he'd forgotten, seeing as he hadn't mentioned it, but I guess I shouldn't have been surprised that he didn't, seeing as he had a memory like an elephant and punched the date into his elevator every day.

I turned up at his place at six o'clock, expecting to chat with Bridget for a few minutes then curl up with a movie, but I found Oliver in the kitchen instead.

"What are you doing here so early?"

He opened his arms wide, and I stepped into them.

"Taking you out."

"Like out, out?"

"Happy birthday, princess."

I looked down at myself in the jeans and tank I'd flung on before I dashed out of my apartment. I never spent much time in clothes when I stayed with Oliver, so it didn't usually matter what I wore. But with Oliver in a freaking tuxedo, I began to panic.

"I'll need to go home again and change. I'm sure I've got something that'll fit."

At least, I hoped so. I'd put on a couple of pounds

recently, what with Bridget's cooking and leftovers from Il Tramonto. I started mentally cataloguing my wardrobe.

"No, you won't. Bradley brought over a selection of gowns, and they're in your room."

Oh, this was too much. I didn't think I'd have much of a birthday celebration this year. Imogen had offered to take me out for cocktails, but she'd understood when I said I'd rather have a quiet night in with Oliver. And Mom had wanted me to go back to Georgia, but I couldn't face the travelling. But Oliver planning something? That was something I hadn't expected.

So much so that I sniffled by accident, and Oliver wiped away the tear that ran down my cheek.

"What's wrong?"

"Nothing. Nothing at all."

He kissed the path the tear had taken. "You've got a funny way of showing it." His fingers twined in mine as he led me towards my bedroom. "But you need to change or we'll be late."

"Where are we going?"

"It's a surprise."

To be honest, we could have gone to the dingiest bar in town and I'd have been happy because I was with Oliver, but when I saw the dresses, I knew that wasn't what he had planned.

A figure-hugging black bodycon, a dusky pink empire-line, or an asymmetric red number with a floaty hem. Which one should I pick?

Oliver settled back in the armchair by the window. "Come on, I want a show."

Fine, I'd give him a show. I connected my phone to the small stereo next to the television and selected something slow. I used to have a client who wanted to jerk off while I stripped, so I'd had a bit of practice at this over the years.

The music started, and I turned my back on Oliver and swayed in time. A low groan came from behind me.

"What? You said you wanted a show?"

"I wasn't thinking straight. I never do when I'm around you. We've only got half an hour before we need to leave."

I undid the top button on my jeans and rubbed a hand over one breast.

"Well, you'd better hurry up and come, then."

Shit, shit, shit. Twenty-five minutes later, I hopped around the room trying to zip up the black dress while Oliver dashed into the bathroom to sponge the white stain off the front of his pants. Why did a man in a suit have to be such a turn-on?

"Darn it! This won't do up!"

Oliver appeared in the doorway with a cloth in his hand. "You think you've got problems? I look as if I've wet myself."

"I need to go on a diet."

"Believe me, you're beautiful as you are. Fuck it. I need to change these pants."

Five minutes later, I'd stuffed myself into the empire-line and pinned my hair to the side in a hurried attempt at style, just as Oliver came back in a seemingly identical tux. How many of those did he own?

"Ready to go?"

I reached for my lipstick. "Two seconds... Right, done."

"Not quite." He closed the gap between us and drew a small box from his pocket. "You need accessories."

In the mirror, I watched as he fastened a silver necklace onto me, the heart-shaped pendant nestling in my throat. From the way it sparkled, I didn't mind betting those were real diamonds. Holy hell!

He pressed a kiss to the side of my neck. "Happy birthday, Miss Amor."

Another tear escaped, threatening my mascara. "You're too darn sweet, Mr. Rhodes."

"Not many people would say that."

"I know better."

He handed me the wrap that matched my dress. "Shh. Don't tell anyone."

Technically, this was my first date with Oliver. Despite exploring every inch of each other's bodies over the last few months, we'd never been out anywhere, save for the occasional visit to Riverley.

"Are you sure this is safe?" I asked him as we rode downstairs in the elevator.

"Trial's over; Carter's dead. And I bet Morty Granville won't put in a complaint."

I snuggled against Oliver, relishing the feel of his arm around my waist, his fingers hovering over my ass, hidden under the wrap.

"Then let's enjoy ourselves."

As first dates went, Oliver certainly delivered the goods. A limo waited for us outside his building, and as it swept into the night, he poured us each a glass of champagne.

"Cheers."

He clinked his glass against mine.

I wanted to say "to us," but I didn't dare. "Cheers," I whispered back.

We watched the city flit by for twenty minutes, and then the car slowed. I craned my head to see where we were.

"The ballet?"

"It's the opening night of *Gone with the Wind*. I thought you'd like it."

Opening night? Wow.

"You're totally right."

All around us, couples glided along the red carpet, resplendent in evening wear and diamonds. Yes, I'd been to formal events with Rubies clients, but never anything as grand as this, and I'd always tried to hide in the shadows. Oliver seemed quite at home. He chatted easily with politicians and captains of industry, one arm around my waist keeping me grounded while I got bedazzled by all the opulence.

Then we went into the auditorium and took our seats, front and centre. How did he get those tickets? I forgot to ask as I smiled and cried my way through the performance, leaving Oliver's handkerchief blackened and streaky with the remains of my mascara.

"I'm not sure whether you enjoyed that or not," he said as we walked back to the car.

"I loved it! Thank you for the best birthday ever."

"It's not over yet."

"It isn't?"

He gave me his wolfish grin, the one that meant he was planning something, and usually something dirty.

"I've booked the private dining room at Rhodium. We never did test out that new buzzer."

Chapter 36

AFTER MY BIRTHDAY treat from Oliver, I thought he might take me out again, but so far, we'd spent two more evenings in his apartment, and he hadn't suggested venturing further afield.

Sometimes, this patience thing really sucked.

And just to put more of a downer on the week, my mom called.

"You haven't forgotten what's happening next weekend, Pippi, have you?"

The weeks and months had melded into one recently. I worked at Java Monday through Thursday morning, and then all day Fridays and Sunday evenings I went to Il Tramonto. The only exceptions to my schedule were my lunchtimes and nights with Oliver, which were burned into my brain, and the occasional Saturday night out with Imogen, although we'd both been too tired for those recently.

"Er, what *is* happening?"

"It's Chester's sixtieth birthday. We're having that big party, remember?"

"Oh, yes. Of course."

I'd completely forgotten. Mom had started planning it over a year ago, but since I hadn't been home much, I'd avoided the constant discussions about party food and guest lists.

"You are coming, aren't you?" Her voice shook a little, and I heard the worry in her tone. "You didn't even come home for your own birthday, and I thought..."

I crossed my fingers even though she couldn't see me.

"Of course I'm coming. The date's been blocked out in my schedule for months. I've just been tired lately, and my head's a bit fuzzy this morning."

"Tired? Are you looking after yourself?"

"I've had a busy week at work, but the overtime money's great. And I can't wait to come home and see you and Chester."

Hopefully, she couldn't hear the deceit in my voice. Mom didn't need to know about the man keeping me awake at night in more ways than one, or the real reason I was avoiding Georgia.

"That's wonderful! I'll air out your room and make sure the sheets are fresh. We've got a full house, and it'll be lovely to have everyone in one place. Will you stay all week?"

"Uh, I hadn't really thought about that."

"Oh, say you will? We hardly ever see you anymore."

A week? A week of keeping my head down and avoiding gossip and Randy Bose. He'd undoubtedly be angry that I'd run back to Richmond after the obscene suggestion he made on my last visit to Hartscross, and I didn't suppose Darly was thrilled about me leaving the salon without notice either. But Mom was right—I couldn't make my family suffer for my mistakes, and I needed to spend some time with Mason too.

"Okay, a week. But I can't afford to take any longer

than that off work."

"You're still waitressing?"

"At the moment. The tips are good."

"I should hope so. And you can put all that practice to good use and help serve up the food at the party."

I tuned Mom out as she started listing the menu choices and mentally rehearsed what I'd say to Oliver. I knew we'd agreed at the beginning there would be nothing serious between us, but things had changed, for me at least. Now, the thought of a week without him made my heart plummet.

"Do you need a ride to the airport?" Oliver asked after dinner the next night when I told him about my trip back to Georgia.

"Thanks for the offer, but I'm going by bus."

He shook his head. "The bus takes, what, ten hours? I'll book you a flight."

"I'm still tight on money right now. Besides, I'm used to the bus. I've taken it plenty of times before."

"I'll buy you the plane ticket."

"Honestly, I'd rather pay my own way."

I didn't want to turn into a Kelly, expecting him to fork out for everything.

Oliver slid his chair back then motioned me to come over. When I reached him, he hitched my skirt up and pulled me forwards to straddle his lap. His hardness rubbed against my nub and made me squirm.

"Princess, if you're not here, I'll have to go a week without coming inside you, and if you fly rather than taking the bus, that gives me six extra hours to fuck you senseless beforehand. So I'm buying you a ticket, and I'm doing it for purely selfish reasons. Do you understand?"

I nodded, feeling my panties getting damper.

"I'll ask again. Do you need a ride to the airport?"

"Yes, please."

"Is the right answer."

Well, Oliver kept his promise, and I staggered to the gate with two minutes to spare, dragging a hastily packed suitcase. I hadn't even had time to comb my hair.

A smartly dressed attendant gave me a condescending look as I thrust my ticket at her, and then her eyes widened.

"You're flying first class?" She sounded surprised, and quite frankly, so was I.

"I am?"

She checked the ticket again and plastered on a smile. "Yes, you are. Turn left when you get on the plane."

First class? Oliver had booked me a first-class ticket? The flight would only take an hour, for goodness' sake. I was damn glad I'd sucked and swallowed this morning.

"Champagne, ma'am?"

The cute male flight attendant beamed at me. Obviously, he'd read the memo about customer courtesy.

I longed for a glass of bubbly, but I needed all my faculties to deal with my mother, who'd promised to pick me up at the other end. If I couldn't think straight, I'd get roped into making tiny penguins out of boiled eggs, black olives, and toothpicks like I did the last time.

"Do you have orange juice instead?"

"Of course. With or without pulp?"

I gorged on canapés for twenty minutes then took a nap for the rest of the flight. I'd been exhausted lately, and being woken at five by a horny Oliver hadn't helped. But I still couldn't stop smiling. The man certainly knew how to use it.

Not that I could tell Mom any of that when she flung her arms around me in the arrivals hall.

"Right on time, Pippi! You must be doing well on tips if you didn't take the bus."

"Something like that."

"I've put you down for napkin folding and hanging paper garlands. We've got no time to waste."

"But the party isn't until tomorrow."

"Some of the guests are staying over tonight, and there's always something we forget."

Like the time she forgot roast beef for the main course at her own birthday bash a few years back. She'd prepared all the trimmings, the decorations, and the party games, then suddenly remembered the meat. One of our neighbours had dashed out and shot a cow. Hartscross was that sort of place.

Back at the house, Chester was grumbling in the hallway.

"That boy's disappeared again."

"Mason?" I asked.

"Who else? I told him to stay put, and the moment I turned my back, he upped and left."

"I'll track him down."

I'd bet my favourite lip gloss Mason was at Reggie's, and the walk to his house and back would get me out of the house for at least half an hour.

"Don't take too long," Mom chirped. "We need to blow up balloons and finish frosting the cookies."

Mason was indeed at Reggie's, and I found both of them out on the back porch drinking beer without a care in the world.

"Chester's gonna go mental if he catches y'all doing that."

"So? What's new?"

"It's his birthday. Can't you at least try to stay on his good side for a couple of days?"

"Pop only worries about appearances. As long as I stay out of his hair, he don't care."

"Won't you just come home for the weekend? For me? I could do with some company."

Mason sighed and stubbed out the cigarette he shouldn't have been smoking.

"Since it's you, Stef. Nobody else in that house gives a shit about me."

"That's not true."

"Yeah, it is. Pop spends most of his time working or hanging out with his buddies. Mom's happy as long as Pop's happy, and everybody thinks they've got a perfect life. Screw reality."

Much as I hated to admit it, Mason did have a point. That was my family in a nutshell. I sank down on the swing seat beside him.

"Maybe we could just have one more beer before we go back."

"Now you're talking."

Mason and Reggie caught me up on the happenings in Hartscross, and I heard that Darly had bigger problems than me leaving the salon—her fiancé had run off with a podiatrist from the next town. At least that took some of the heat off me, gossip-wise. Then I glanced at my watch and found half an hour had flown by.

"We need to get back. I'm surprised Mom hasn't called yet."

Mason pulled out his phone. "Eight missed calls. It's on silent."

And I realised I'd forgotten to turn mine on again after I got off the airplane.

Even though we should have hurried, we ambled back through the streets, neither of us particularly wanting to get to our destination. Mason kicked at a stone on the sidewalk before sighing.

"You here for long, Stef?"

"A week. Why?"

"I've missed you being around. What's the big city like?"

"Richmond's got its good points and its bad points."

"I think I'm gonna move there. The city, I mean. Maybe New York or Atlanta. Ain't nothing to do around here, and I don't wanna spend the rest of my life workin' at the feed store."

"Mom's not gonna be happy about that."

"It's my life, not hers."

Mom saw us through the window as we walked up the drive, and by the time we reached the front door, she'd opened it with a list of tasks already pouring from her mouth.

"What took you so long? Mason, you need to help your daddy edge the path. Pippi, I need a hand setting the tables." She handed me a scrawled diagram. "That's where everybody's sitting. Write a name on each place card and stick those little silver flowers in the corner."

I turned the paper around until I saw where I was sitting, and immediately wished I hadn't.

"Mom, you've put me next to Randy Bose again."

"Yes, he's still single."

"But I'm not looking for a boyfriend."

She patted me on the hand. "Nonsense. Every young princess needs their prince."

Princess? I nearly choked. "I sort of already have one."

Okay, so Oliver still had a way to go, but he already held my heart in his hands.

"A man? What, in the city?"

"Yes."

She stared at me. "Well, why didn't you say something? You could have brought him with you for us all to meet."

The thought of Oliver sitting down to dinner with Auntie Ethel and Uncle Chip made me snort, but I turned it into a cough.

"It's not that type of relationship, Mom."

"If a man doesn't want to meet his girl's family, then it's not serious. You should give Randy some consideration. At least he's making the effort to come."

"I wish he wouldn't," I muttered.

"What was that, Pippi?"

"Never mind."

The child in me wanted to run to the bus station and jump on the first bus back to Richmond. Or, in fact, anywhere. As well as the prospect of Randy to deal with, Uncle Clovis was slouched in an armchair, snoring loud enough to trigger an earthquake warning, and Mom had informed me I'd be helping her make crab mousse in the morning. I'd never loved seafood, and the thought of scooping out crab guts turned my stomach.

But the adult in me sat out on the porch swing with Mason for one last beer while the sun went down, then trailed up the stairs to my room.

I couldn't resist checking my phone before I went to bed, just in case Oliver had sent me a message, but there was nothing. Not that I'd truly been expecting to hear from him.

Still, I couldn't resist typing out a couple of lines myself.

Stef: I can't believe you bought me a first-class ticket! You didn't need to do that, but thank you. Hope work's going okay. Can we get together next Friday?

So bland, when what I really wanted to say was *I miss you like crazy and I'll fall asleep dreaming of you. Xx.* But Oliver would most likely run for California if I wrote that.

Instead, I closed my eyes in the darkness and slipped my hands into my panties, and then Oliver came and I did too.

A soft knock at the door woke me up, and I glanced at the clock on my nightstand. Eight thirty, and I bet Mom was freaking about the crab mousse. But at least she always brought me coffee, and boy did I need the caffeine this morning. Visions of Oliver had kept me awake for half the night.

"Come in."

The door clicked open, and Randy sauntered through into my bedroom as if he had every right to be there.

"Randy? What the heck are you doing here? Get out!"

But the little toad didn't. He closed the door behind him and sat on the bed instead. Arrogant. Smug. Both things I'd once accused Oliver of being, but now I knew there was a world of difference between the two men.

"Your mom told me to wake you."

I gathered the comforter around myself like a shield. "I'm awake, so get the hell away."

"I can see that." Randy reached out and stroked one pudgy finger down my cheek, leaving a trail of slime in its wake. "But I wanted a little word."

Chapter 37

"JUST GET OUT of my room!"

I tried to stay calm, but my voice rose to a screech and gave away my panic.

"Oh, Stefanie. You disappeared in such a hurry last time you were here, but I knew you'd be back. Lucky for you, I'm a patient man."

Randy reached out again, and I smacked his hand away.

"Don't touch me."

He laughed. Well, it was more of a cackle. "You won't be doing that tonight. Tonight, Stefanie, or tomorrow your whole family will know your sordid little secret."

"I can't. I won't. I've got a boyfriend."

"Sure you do. Yet you still came here alone." He stood up. "Tonight."

The second the door clicked behind him, I flew out of bed and locked it. Now what? I couldn't tell my family Randy had threatened me without revealing my past, so that wasn't an option. I leaned my head against the window, looking out over the backyard. Chester's old Ford lay rusting beyond the twisted apple tree, same as it had for the past decade. Nothing ever changed in Hartscross. And it probably never would. It was me who'd changed, and this place didn't feel like home anymore.

I turned to my suitcase and stuffed my clothes back inside, leaving a pair of jeans and a T-shirt out to wear. I needed to get out of there. Mom would be furious, but better that than hurt if she found out the truth.

Once I'd tugged a pair of socks on, I crept next door to Mason's room, praying he hadn't broken his lifetime habit of sleeping in later than me.

Luckily, he was still dead to the world.

"Mason?" I shook him gently.

"What? What time is it?"

"That doesn't matter. Can you call Reggie? I need a ride to the bus station."

I'd have to sneak out while Mom was distracted in the kitchen. She'd be upset when she realised I'd gone, but not as upset as I'd be if Randy got his way.

Mason sat up, rubbing sleep from his eyes. "You want to start at the beginning?"

"Not really. Please, could you just call him?"

"You're leaving?"

"I have to."

"Well, I can get him to drive you to the bus station, but it won't help."

"Why not?"

"You didn't hear about the strike? The whole bus network's in chaos."

No, I didn't hear. Since I'd flown, I hadn't looked up the bus timetable or anything else. I rubbed my temples, trying to counteract my blossoming headache. How could I get home? And by home, I meant Richmond, because that was where I belonged now. My fragile finances wouldn't run to another plane ticket, but maybe I could change the one I had?

"I need to make a phone call."

"You still want me to ask Reggie?"

"Not yet, but I might need a ride to the airport later instead."

Back in my room, I pulled the ticket out of the envelope Oliver had given me, but apart from the airline name and the flight times, there wasn't anything useful on it. No phone number and no information on switching flights. In desperation, I picked up the phone anyway.

One ring, two. Please, let him answer.

"Steffie?"

"Oh, thank goodness."

"What's wrong?"

I so hadn't thought this through.

"Uh, I need to get back to Richmond and the buses aren't running. Can I exchange this plane ticket?"

"Why do you want to come back? You only just left."

Why did Oliver have to ask so many questions? Damn him and his lawyerliness. Was that even a word?

"I don't want to talk about it."

"Steffie, you're worrying me. Did something happen?"

I sniffled and snatched a tissue from the box on the nightstand. "Nothing important."

"You're crying and trying to flee the state. Now, tell me what's wrong."

The whole sorry story came tumbling out, from the first time Randy threatened me to his words this morning.

"So you told this asshole you've got a man, and he still thinks he can fuck you?"

"I won't let him, I promise. But I need to get out of here. Help me, please? I promise I'll never ask for another thing."

Oliver's voice softened. "Give me a couple of hours, princess, and I'll sort it out. Just sit tight. Can you do that?"

"I have to get out of here."

"Do you trust me?"

"Yes."

"Then wait. I'll fix everything."

Sit tight, Oliver said. An hour came and went as Mason dragged his ass out of bed and helped with the crab mousse. Every so often, Randy would meander into the kitchen to help Mom with something and give me a sickening smile.

"Such a nice young man, isn't he?" she said every time.

"He's an asshole," Mason muttered under his breath.

At least someone else in this house shared my opinion of him.

Another hour ticked by as I polished silverware, and Oliver still hadn't called me back. I began to obsess over it, checking my phone every thirty seconds. When fifteen more minutes passed, I gave in and called him again, but all I got was his voicemail. I didn't leave a message. What could I say without sounding even more pathetic than I did already?

Beside me, Mason dropped another fork onto the table. "I hate Mom's parties. Who cares if the cutlery's shiny?"

"Mom does." I checked my watch again, then the phone. Nothing. "Mason, would you do me a favour?"

"Does it involve illegal substances? 'Cos I don't know nothin' about those, I swear."

Oh, Mason. "Can you keep close to me this evening?"

"You're staying now?"

"It looks that way."

"Any particular reason?"

"I don't want to be alone with Randy."

Mason fisted a knife in his hand, and his eyes flashed. "Did he do something to you?"

"No." Not yet, anyway. "He just creeps me out, that's all."

"Yeah, I'll stick around. I can't stand the guy either."

Mom flitted into the dining room. "Pippi, I need you to be on door duty. Guests will be arriving soon, and I'm up to my arms in cake batter."

"Sure, Mom."

I conjured up a smile as I showed neighbour after neighbour into the lounge. Each time I opened the door, I got an, "About time you came back to help your mom again," or an, "I thought you'd left town for good." Between the snide comments disparaging life in the city and Randy circling in the background like an overweight vulture, I reminisced about Bradley's jail party. Even handcuff Twister with no underwear would have been less awkward than this.

"Are there many more people left to come?" I asked Mom.

"I don't think so. You can help serve food in a minute. Oh, there's the doorbell again."

What if I opened the door, let whoever it was in, and kept walking? Out of the driveway, out of town, out of Georgia. Honestly, what was stopping me?

"Afternoon, princess."

What the actual hell? "Oliver? What are you doing here?"

He shrugged, hands stuffed in his pants pockets. "Trying to talk myself out of killing some kid named Randy."

"But...but... All I asked for was help with an airplane ticket."

"I know, but I'm not letting that little fucker get away with threatening you."

A tear popped out as I stepped forwards into his arms. He wrapped me up and kissed my hair, and for the first time in months, I began to think things might turn out all right.

Then I heard my mom's voice behind me. "Pippi? Who's this?"

"Uh, this is Oliver. He's..."

Well, this was awkward. What did I introduce him as? A friend? A date? I could hardly explain he was the guy I fucked three times a week by arrangement, could I?

Oliver let me go and kissed Mom on both cheeks. Her blush said he had the same effect on her as he did on me.

"I'm Stefanie's boyfriend. I thought I wouldn't be able to make it, but my schedule cleared at the last minute."

She beamed at him. "Oh, isn't that just wonderful? We'll have to set an extra place at the table."

As we walked inside, Oliver raised an eyebrow. "Pippi?"

"It's a childhood nickname. Pippi Longstocking,

from the books."

He rubbed the back of my thigh. "Long stockings? I like that idea."

With Oliver's arrival, Randy got bumped off to the third table in the kitchen. No doubt the devious asshole would be furious his plans had been thwarted, but I breathed a welcome sigh of relief. I was safe. With Mason on the other side of me, the only wandering hands I was in danger of feeling were Oliver's, and I had no complaints about that. I inched my chair close so our thighs touched under the table, and every time he moved against me, the flames in my belly flared a little higher.

Mom beamed at him as she passed the vegetables. "So, Oliver, how long have you known Stef?"

"The best part of a year."

"Stefanie! Why didn't you say anything before?"

"Uh, I..."

Chester cut in. "How old are you, boy?"

"Thirty-five."

"Don't you think that's a bit old for our Stef? What are you, some kind of sugar daddy?"

Mom elbowed him. "Don't say things like that. Can't you see the way he looks at her? It's so romantic."

"You need to think of the practicalities, Maxine."

"Oliver's not a sugar daddy, Chester. I have two jobs, and I earn my own money."

That got Oliver a sharp look. "So you don't look after her? Do you have a job?"

"I'm a partner in a law firm."

Chester nodded. "Oh, one of those. Outrageous fees, those lawyers charge, and for what? There's nothing like a good, honest day's hard work in the great outdoors."

"He's always like this," I whispered to Oliver. "You won't win."

"I always win," he whispered back, squeezing my hand before facing Chester again. "I hear you about the outdoors, sir. I grew up on a ranch in Colorado…"

Throughout dinner, Oliver surprised me with tales of his childhood and teenage years, how he'd learned to ride horses before he could walk and later how he'd put himself through college on his own dollar. I'd thought he'd be totally out of place with my family, but by the time dessert came, he'd won Chester over and Mom practically swooned at his feet. And me? I had even more respect for the man I'd fallen in love with. Randy, on the other hand, was stuck with Great Aunt Margaret in the kitchen. I could hear her educating him on the merits of different brands of denture fixative from here, which only made me smile wider.

"It's so wonderful you've found each other." Mom dabbed at her eyes with a napkin. "And you'll be staying for lunch tomorrow as well, Oliver?"

"I guess I can find a local hotel."

Mom chortled. "There're no hotels in Hartscross, and the guest house is full of our relatives already. You'll just have to bunk in with Stefanie." She gave him a wink. "I'm sure you're used to that."

His hand tightened on my thigh under the table. "That's very kind."

Oliver was going to stay with me overnight? Suddenly, this weekend had turned from a nightmare into a sweet, sweet dream. The thought of him wrapped around me as I slept made my heart sing.

I longed to go to bed right away, but as usual, Mom had other plans for me.

"Pippi, can you and Oliver help to clear the table? Mason, the empty glasses need to be collected up and washed."

If Oliver minded being put to work, he didn't show it as he carried dirty dishes out to the kitchen. Uncle Mike got the task of washing up and looked far from thrilled. The guests moved into the lounge again as Chester brought out the whisky and birthday cake, and I was glad to be out of the spotlight. Randy was nowhere to be seen, and with any luck, Oliver and I could sneak off without anybody noticing.

"Could you take this trash out?" Mom asked.

"Sure."

The cool air outside gave a welcome respite. Oliver's presence had made me hot and sweaty, not least the way he kept brushing against me, and the slight bulge in his pants told me I wasn't the only one looking for escape. I lifted the lid off the trash can and threw the bag inside. Not long now.

"Think you're so clever, don't you?" Randy's voice came out of the darkness, and he stepped forwards into the light from the kitchen window.

"What are you talking about?"

"Getting some guy down here from Richmond to act as a cock-blocker."

Randy advanced slowly, and I backed away until I hit the wooden siding of the house.

"You can't keep blackmailing me."

"Wanna bet?"

As he pressed against me, I felt the hard evidence of what he wanted and retched to the side. He wrinkled his nose.

"Don't play so innocent. We both know you're not."

I tried to think of a retort, but I didn't have to. Oliver appeared from the shadows and tore Randy away from me. The sharp *crack* of his head against the siding echoed into the night, and I hoped his skull hadn't damaged the wood.

"If you ever threaten my girlfriend again, I'll make you sorry you ever breathed. Does the name Tiffany Smales mean anything to you?"

"I don't know what you're talking about."

Randy's voice came out weak, a far cry from his usual arrogance. Probably because Oliver had one forearm pressed against Randy's neck while his body pinned the arrogant little shit to the wall.

"Then I'll remind you, shall I? Tiffany was the other girl who said no, right before you raped her. Your father may have made the charges go away, but I bet the whole of Hartscross would love to hear about the fifty thousand dollars he paid her to leave town."

"That's bullshit."

"Really? It didn't sound like it when I spoke to Tiffany earlier, you sick motherfucker." Oliver glared at Randy in the moonlight. "I'll bring a private prosecution if I have to, and I'll enjoy every second of it."

"You can't do that."

"Try me."

"Your girlfriend's a hooker, you know that?"

Oliver leaned harder against Randy's neck. "I know what she was, and I know what she isn't now. I also know that if I hear those words come out your mouth again, you'll regret it." Oliver stood back, giving Randy space to move. "Come within a hundred yards of Stefanie, and I'll make your life the misery it deserves to be. Got it?"

Randy didn't answer, just bolted around the side of the house into the darkness. A few seconds later, a car started and tyres squealed as he shot out of the driveway.

I sagged into Oliver's arms. "I can't believe you did that. Is it true? He raped a girl?"

"I believe so."

"How did you find out?"

"You've got Dan, Mack, and Emmy to thank for that one. That's why it took me longer than I hoped to get here earlier. They were digging up dirt."

"I owe all of them so much. And you."

"You can repay me by smiling, princess. I hate to see you sad."

"You want to go upstairs and make me smile?"

"No, I want to kiss you first, then take you upstairs and make you come."

I grinned, and Oliver grinned back. And then he kissed me.

Chapter 38

"SO THIS IS your room?"

Oliver stepped inside and looked around, and I felt a little embarrassed by my collection of cuddly toys.

"It hasn't changed much since I was a child."

He picked up a toy tiara from the shelf above my desk and placed it on my head. "Princess."

I couldn't help giggling as I twirled around. "That makes you Prince Charming."

"I don't know about the charming part. I only came here so I could get into your panties."

He didn't, and we both knew it, but it was easier to pretend than dwell on the real reason. I reached for his belt buckle.

"Then tear my panties off, prince."

When I uttered those words, I expected Oliver to act quickly, but he surprised me again by taking things slow and gentle, carefully removing each item of clothing then running his tongue over the skin underneath. When he finally pulled my underwear off with his teeth, I was squirming under his fingers.

And he still wore his suit, which struck me as unfair. "Hey, I want you naked as well."

"Then undress me."

Both of us were panting by the time I gave him the same treatment, and we fell back on the bed in a tangle of limbs. Oliver nipped at my earlobes as he slid inside me, sending tingles all over my body. The plastic tiara lost its grip on my hair and tumbled off the side of the bed. I made a grab for it and missed.

"Leave it, princess. I'll buy you a real one."

"I don't want a tiara. I only want you."

And that night, I had him. Twice. Then he curled up behind me, arms and legs wrapped around my body as he caressed my breasts. That bedroom held all my hopes and dreams from over the years, from my ninth-grade spelling bee certificate to the flute I couldn't play, and tonight I made another wish on the silver star that hung above the window. *Please let this man be mine.*

I drifted off to sleep, and for the first time when I woke up in the morning, Oliver hadn't left me alone. I studied his face as I rested my head on his shoulder, his jaw relaxed as he breathed steadily. The most beautiful sight in the world. I shifted slightly and felt another male phenomenon on my hip—the glorious morning hardness of his cock.

Before I could stop myself, I'd peeled the covers back and straddled him, easing his cock into me until it was buried to the root. A slow smile spread across my lips as his eyes flickered open.

"Good morning, Oliver."

He groaned. "I'm still dreaming."

"Dream away."

I flexed my hips and began to move, relishing the tension that built inside me as Oliver's hands gripped my ass and urged me to go faster. As ever with that man, it didn't take long for me to see stars, and he soon found his release as well. My muscles gave out and I slumped over his chest, loving the feel of him still inside.

He captured my lips with his. “That’s the best wake-up I’ve ever had.”

I almost told him I’d offer it daily, but I stopped myself at the last second. Baby steps. Oliver staying with me overnight was a big deal, and I didn’t want to jinx it.

“Sure beats coffee.”

“When do we need to get up?”

I checked the time. Six o’clock. “We’re safe for another hour. If you don’t want to stay for lunch, we can make an excuse.”

“I’ll stay. Reckon your stepfather got most of the interrogation out of the way yesterday.”

“Chester’s worse than Mom about asking questions. I’m surprised he didn’t request your medical history and latest tax return.” I snuggled into him. “But it was nice to find out more about Oliver Rhodes. You’ve never mentioned your childhood before.”

Oliver sighed, and the way his eyes shuttered told me I’d said the wrong thing. Dammit.

“I left out the parts about my mother leaving when I was six, my father being an alcoholic, and the beatings he gave me right up until I left home.”

Oh. Shit.

“I’m so sorry.”

“Don’t be. It’s done now, and I’m never going back to Colorado.”

“Do you ever see any of your family?” I whispered.

“I chose a new family, and they all live in Richmond.”

He didn’t elaborate, leaving me with a single burning question: was I one of them? And the subject wasn't open for further discussion, as he made crystal clear with his next words.

"Enough about the past. If we've got an hour left, I can think of a much better way to use it than talking." And with that, he rolled us both, hooked one of my knees over his arm, and thrust deep once more.

Oliver the boy was quickly forgotten. He was all man now.

Oliver had fetched his overnight bag from his rental car the night before, and I watched in fascination as he pulled a pair of jeans out of it.

"I thought you said you didn't own anything but suits."

"Bradley bought them last week. He said I should relax more."

The pants were distressed to within an inch of their life, and the soft denim hugged Oliver's butt cheeks as I added Bradley to my list of people to thank when I got back. Next, Oliver produced a navy-blue cashmere crew-neck sweater and pulled it on. I'd always adored him in a suit, but my girly bits liked this new, casual Oliver just as much.

"What do you think?" he asked, standing a little stiffly.

"I think I want to tear you out of those clothes."

He still wore his ridiculously expensive watch, and now he glanced at it.

"Do you think we have time?"

I sighed. "No."

Mom was already flapping by the time we got

downstairs. "I need to make tea for all the guests and I've got a list for the store. And I have to stop in and see Muriel on the way with cookies because she broke her hip last week."

"I'll make the tea."

The last thing I wanted to do was get stuck at Muriel's. She'd talk for hours about her cats, and I'd never get away.

"You need to warm the teapot first."

"I know, Mom."

We'd had this conversation many, many times over the years.

"And remind Uncle Frank to take his medication."

"I will."

Oliver chuckled as Mom disappeared out the door, and I slumped onto a stool.

"Don't laugh. This is my life."

"She means well. I get Bridget and her constant lectures about my health. This week's smoothies are elderflower, chia seed, and beetroot."

My nose wrinkled all of its own accord. Normally, I liked Bridget's smoothies, even if I sometimes pretended otherwise, but beetroot?

"Yuck."

"See, tea's not so bad. Although I'd prefer coffee. Do you have that?"

By a minor miracle, we'd managed to make drinks for everyone, give Uncle Frank his arthritis pills, and make pancake batter by the time Mom walked back through the door.

"I couldn't find the maple syrup... Mom, what's wrong?"

She took one look at me and burst into tears.

"Maxine?" Chester was at her side in an instant. "What's happened?"

She pointed at me, but no words came out.

Chester eased her down onto a chair. "Maxine, you need to tell me what's wrong."

With shaking fingers, she drew a folded piece of paper from her pocket and handed it to him. "Darly saw this in a magazine last week. It's all around town. The shame of it. The shame."

I leaned over Chester's shoulder to read, but I didn't need to. The pictures were enough. Some trashy magazine spread on the Carter trial, with Oliver's picture front and centre, handsome as sin. And my photo, one taken as I rushed away from my day in court, captioned *The call girl who slept with a killer*.

Oliver grabbed me as my knees buckled, holding me tightly against him. Cold horror flooded my veins. After all the effort we'd made to keep this secret from Mom, she'd found out anyway.

Chester scanned the article, then turned on me. "Is this true?"

What could I do but nod?

He fixed his gaze on Oliver. "And you? You're paying for her 'services'?"

"No, I am not," Oliver snapped.

"I don't believe you." Chester stabbed Oliver's picture with his finger. "You obviously know what she's been up to, and no man would want her otherwise. She's damaged goods."

"This is your daughter we're speaking about."

"Ain't none of my DNA in that girl. She's someone else's mistake."

Mom burst into tears, but when I reached for her,

she shrank away.

"I'm sorry," I whispered.

"Maxine brought you up right—you didn't want for nothing. Then you go and sell yourself like a cheap slut. You're sick up here." Chester tapped his head. "No man's ever gonna want you as a wife."

Oliver squared up to him. "You have no idea what you're talking about. Stefanie may have made mistakes in her past, but she's got a pure heart, and you'll never find a girl sweeter. And someday she'll make a man a wonderful wife."

A man?

Chester guffawed in his face, his twisted sneer so far from the man who'd brought me up I barely recognised him. "What, you're gonna marry her, then?"

I held my breath.

"That's a big question to ask a man you've known less than a day."

A tear rolled down my cheek as my heart shattered.

"So your answer's no. You just use Stefanie to get your kicks. I can't say I blame you, and if I was thirty years younger, I might have had me some fun as well."

Mom ran to the sink and threw up, and I almost joined her. How could Chester say something so disgusting? Only Oliver's arm around my waist kept me steady.

And now he pulled me backwards. "Steffie, we're leaving."

"That's it—run back to your city of shame. You're not welcome here anymore."

I stumbled up the stairs behind Oliver, and he grabbed both of our bags. Mason meandered into the hallway, rubbing his eyes.

"What's going on?"

"Ask your father," Oliver told him.

"Huh?"

"I'll call you later, okay?"

I couldn't deal with Mason's questions, not now.

My feet barely touched the floor as Oliver half carried me out to his rental car, and I blinked back tears. Tears at the broken relationship with my mom, tears over Chester's cruelty, tears about Oliver's non-answer, tears that I'd never see my childhood home again. Because I knew I couldn't go back there. Everything was tainted.

Oliver shoved the car into gear and sped off, making Randy's exit last night look sedate.

"Now what?" I whispered.

"I don't know."

CHAPTER 39

ON MONDAY MORNING, I rolled over and groaned as my head pounded with a force that would make a Jedi weep. I wanted to believe the events of yesterday had just been a horrible dream, but when I saw my little case parked on the other side of the bed, I knew they weren't.

And to cap it all, Oliver hadn't stayed with me last night. No, we were back to separate rooms again.

We'd flown back from Georgia, on Emmy's private jet, no less. On any other day that would have held me in awe, but yesterday, I barely had the energy to raise an eyebrow. The argument with Mom and Chester had left me drained. Oliver simply held me, my cheek resting on his chest as his heartbeat soothed my troubled mind.

He'd left his Porsche at the airport, hastily parked near one of the hangars, and he helped me into the passenger seat before driving us back to his penthouse.

"I'm sorry if I made things worse," he whispered as we rode up in the elevator.

"Don't worry. Things couldn't have got any worse than Randy."

Oh, how little I knew.

Oliver gave me a shot of whisky, kissed me softly, then tucked me under the covers before he promptly pulled another disappearing act. I longed for his arms around me all night, but he didn't offer and I was too scared to ask.

In the morning, when I stumbled into the kitchen in search of a glass of water and some painkillers, he was already sitting at the counter, contemplating a cup of coffee as if it held the answers to life.

"Are you okay?" I asked him.

"Shouldn't that be my question?"

"I've been better."

His chest rattled with a sigh. "Steffie, I've been thinking about yesterday."

"Do we have to talk about it? I just want to forget it ever happened." I opened the drawer by the refrigerator, closed it again. "Is there any aspirin?"

He rose and fetched a packet from the cupboard over the microwave, then poured me a glass of mineral water.

"Headache?"

"Head, body, soul. I feel like I've been hit by a car."

I slumped onto the stool opposite him, the night of turbulent sleep having done nothing to take the edge off my exhaustion.

"Steffie, we need to talk."

Something in his tone made me look up. "What about?" A little quake in my voice gave away my fear.

"This. This...thing between us. Everything I said yesterday was true. You're sweet and you're pure, and someday you *will* make a man a wonderful wife."

Oliver wouldn't meet my eyes, and with a sinking heart, I knew where he was going.

"But not you? Right?"

"That was never the arrangement. And no matter

how much other shit your stepfather spouted yesterday, he was right about one thing—I use you to get my kicks, and that's got to stop."

"But I don't mind that. I mean, I want to be here."

"You deserve a man who gives you all of him, and that's not me."

"I'd rather have what you give me than all of any other man."

Oliver reached out and ran his fingers down my cheek. "That's because you've never looked for the right man. It's selfish of me to keep you."

"I freely give myself."

"It's wrong."

Tears bubbled up in the corners of my eyes. "So that's it? Over?"

"I need to think about my life and the way I live it. You need to do the same. I see in your eyes what you want from me, and right now, I can't give you that."

"Will you ever be able to?"

His voice dropped, so quiet I could barely hear him. "I don't know."

The tears kept coming, unstoppable, my soul searching for an escape. This was the ugly side of love. The side they didn't show you in the old black-and-white movies. The side that made me want to spend the rest of my life alone so love could never, ever touch me again.

"I'll pack my things."

"Do you want me to drive you home?"

Home? Where was home? Nowhere felt like home anymore.

"Could you call me a cab?"

"It'll be waiting."

I shoved a few clothes out of the closet into my case, but more outfits had migrated there over the weeks and they wouldn't all fit. I left the evening dresses behind. What use would I have for those now? And the fancy bath bubbles Oliver bought me, and the nice underwear? I no longer cared.

Oliver appeared in the doorway, his eyes haunted. "If there's anything you need—money, help with a job, anything—you only have to ask."

I wanted to scream at him: "You! I need you!" But my pride wouldn't let me.

"I'll be fine."

"I don't want you to feel like you're on your own."

"Well, you're not doing a very good fucking job of it, are you?"

"I'm sorry."

I marched past him, dragging my case behind me, and the final insult came as I punched my birthday into the elevator. Asshole.

I ignored the friendly goodbye from the concierge as I marched across the marble lobby to the doors and the black limo idling at the kerb beyond them. Oh, Oliver, at least you knew how to dump a girl in style.

The elevator in my apartment building sported a big red Out of Order sign—again—so I hauled the case up the stairs—*bump, bump, bump*—and by the time I jabbed my key into the lock, I was a sweaty mess. I flung the door open, then immediately wished I hadn't.

"Uh, hi," Imogen said from her position bent over the sofa. The guy pounding into her from behind froze mid-thrust. "I thought you weren't back until Friday?"

"My family threw me out, then Oliver dumped me. But you carry on. I'll just tiptoe past to my room."

And die. I'd just lie on the bed and die. Of a broken heart, of embarrassment—take your pick.

Five minutes later, Imogen appeared.

"I'm so sorry—" I began, but she waved a hand.

"Don't worry about it. You actually got me out of a tight spot—I couldn't remember that guy's name, but when he fled out the door, it meant I didn't have to."

Despite everything, I had to giggle.

Imogen dropped down onto the bed beside me. "Now, what happened? Tell Auntie Imogen all about it."

CHAPTER 40

AS I'D EXPECTED to be away for the whole week, I wasn't rostered on at Java or Il Tramonto, which gave me a few days to hibernate. I never wanted to see daylight again. In fact, after I'd watched all the Twilight movies in their entirety, I was seriously considering a new career as a vampire.

Imogen tried her best to cheer me up. On Tuesday, in between stuffing me full of chocolate and pouring me glasses of wine, she brought me a tiny voodoo doll with Oliver's face stuck on it and a box of dressmaker's pins.

"I made the doll myself. Impressed?"

"Very."

"You should stake him through the heart, right where it hurts."

But I couldn't.

"I think it hurt Oliver too, the split. But he didn't know what else to do."

"Stop making excuses for him. He behaved like the world's biggest asshole."

Yes, I knew that, but a tiny part of my heart would never be able to let him go.

I considered handing in my notice at Il Tramonto, but I needed the money. In the end, I decided to come clean with Giovanni, who'd proven to be a friend as well as a boss.

"I kind of had a thing with Oliver, and now it's ended. I don't know how that'll affect me working with you."

Oliver wouldn't have me fired, of that I was sure, but what if he came in to eat while I was there?

"He ended it? Or you did?"

"Him. I never would have."

"Then he is *uno stronzo*," Giovanni declared. "We will spit in his dinner."

"No, you can't do that."

"Oh yes, we can. And you will carry on working here. Oliver rarely eats in, and if he does try to book a table, I'll tell him there are none available."

"But he owns the restaurant."

"You think I care about that? He can't break your heart and expect there to be no consequences. I'll see you on Friday."

So it looked as if I still had a job. And a friend, which was the most important thing.

"You still look like garbage," Imogen helpfully told me on Wednesday after she got back from Java. "You're run down. We should go for a spa day or something."

"I'm okay. It's just all the shocks in one week. And I don't have the money for a spa day."

"How about I do your nails?"

I tried to smile. "I won't say no to that."

We settled on tiny flowers, and Imogen set to work. A white base to start with, then the leaves, and finally the petals and yellow centres. I'd just begun to regret drinking so much coffee, because I couldn't pee until my nails dried, when the doorbell rang.

Please, don't let it be for me. I couldn't face Oliver, and although Dan had tried to call me yesterday, I'd sent her to voicemail. And I hadn't listened to that, either. I needed to heal, not deal with constant reminders of my past. In time, hopefully I'd feel up to speaking to Dan again, maybe even Emmy. But not this week.

"It's for you," Imogen announced.

Oh no.

"Who?"

"Not who. What." She carried a box in and set it on the table. "A courier brought this."

"Can you open it?"

There was no return address on the package and no indication of who sent it. All I could do was watch as Imogen tore it open to reveal a plastic box of chocolate éclairs and a selection of smoothies.

"There's a card too." She passed it over. "It's from Bridget."

I read her note.

Stefanie,

I hope you're not feeling too terrible after what happened. Sometimes that boy has no sense whatsoever. If there's anything I can do, please call me.

Bridget.

She'd noted her number at the bottom, and my eyes prickled reading it. We'd gotten off to a rocky start, but over the past couple of months, when Bridget saw I wasn't turning out like Kelly, she'd been nothing but nice to me. And it seemed she didn't approve of what Oliver had done either.

"Aw, sweet," Imogen said. "Can I have an éclair?"

"Sure. If Bridget made them, they'll taste amazing."

Except I wasn't hungry today. My appetite had deserted me, which I supposed was a good thing seeing as I could do with losing two or three pounds. Okay, five or six pounds.

Imogen picked one of the smoothies out of the box. "Whoops. Can't drink that one."

"What's wrong with it?" I recognised the bottle. "Those ones are delicious."

"You haven't been drinking them, have you?"

"Well, yes. Why?"

"They've got maca in them. See, it says here on the label. That screws with your hormones and messes up your contraceptives."

We stared at each other for a few seconds, both having the same thought.

My slightly thickened waistline. Breasts that had been more tender than normal. I'd put that down to extra attention from Oliver. But...

"No, I can't be. I've still been having periods."

Light ones, and not entirely at the times I'd expect them, when I thought about it, but I definitely hadn't imagined the mess.

"Sometimes that can happen. My friend Maria bled every month, then she thought she had gastroenteritis and a baby popped out."

"I haven't felt sick or anything."

"Women don't always. We should do a test, just to be on the safe side." She grabbed her keys. "I'll go to the drugstore."

While I waited for Imogen to come back, I paced the tiny lounge, trying not to touch my nails to the furniture. No, being pregnant was impossible. I couldn't be. I mean, I didn't *feel* pregnant. Surely I'd get, I don't know, maternal or something?

Imogen burst back in ten minutes later, waving a paper bag.

"I got it. You need to go pee."

I gingerly tested my nails. Yup, they were dry enough now, thank goodness. Not that I wanted to pee anymore. I'd have held it forever if it meant avoiding the damn test.

I must have hesitated too long, because Imogen gave me a shove. "Go, go. The sooner you do the test, the sooner you'll know."

"That's what I'm afraid of."

I took a deep breath as I peed on the stupid stick. It had to be negative, right? This was just a precaution. I shoved it onto the counter face-down, washed my hands, and then walked out of the bathroom.

"Well?" Imogen put her hands on her hips.

"I can't look."

She marched inside and picked up the stick of doom. "What is it? One stripe for no, two for yes?"

"Apparently so."

She studied the test for a second. "Shit, honey. You're having his baby."

I snatched it from her. "You're joking." And it wasn't funny. "Tell me you're joking?"

Only she wasn't. The two stripes were clear as the blue sky in summer. I sank down onto the closed toilet lid and screwed my eyes shut, hoping the tiny stripes would disappear if I wished hard enough.

"What the hell am I supposed to do?"

Shoot myself? Jump off a bridge? Run into the path of oncoming traffic? Perhaps not that last one, seeing as it was what had gotten me into this mess in the first place.

Imogen, ever the practical one, crouched beside me and took my hands. "We need to get you a doctor's appointment and go from there."

I listened, numb, as she called the hospital, thanking my lucky stars that Oliver was a good employer and I had health insurance through Il Tramonto. I knew nothing about children, apart from being one myself. How could I be a mother? I had no idea where to start.

The only thing I knew was that I didn't want to turn into Kelly.

Imogen hung up. "Monday afternoon. It's the soonest I could get."

"I drank beer on Friday. And Oliver gave me whisky on Sunday." I collapsed on the sofa and buried my head in my hands. "I'm a terrible mother, and I haven't even had the baby yet."

"You'll keep the baby?"

"I have to."

Termination for the sake of convenience didn't sit well with my conscience. And it wasn't just me now. There was a little piece of Oliver growing in my tummy, and I couldn't get rid of it like an unwanted mistake.

"Shouldn't you discuss this with Oliver?"

Well, obviously I had to tell him, but how? He'd go nuts. I'd tried so hard not to be like Kelly, only to fail in the most spectacular way. I hated the thought of putting him through unplanned fatherhood for a second time.

“I need to think about what to say to him. Can I get used to the idea myself first? Get the hospital appointment over with?”

“Of course. You’re the most important person in all this. You and the baby.” She lifted my feet up onto the sofa. “You need to relax. Take it easy.”

“Are you kidding? How can I relax?”

Right then, I bordered on hysterical.

“Well, I can’t offer you a glass of wine. Uh, a movie?”

A movie? Right. Because that would cure everything.

Chapter 41

CLARK GABLE AND Humphrey Bogart did help a little, and by Friday, I felt well enough for my shift at Il Tramonto.

"You really think this is a good idea?" Imogen's expression said she definitely didn't.

"I don't want to let Giovanni down, and besides, I need the money. I can't not work for the next... Hell, I don't even know how pregnant I am."

"They'll tell you that at the hospital on Monday."

Terrific. I couldn't wait.

"It's okay, Oliver's not here," Giovanni told me the second I walked into Il Tramonto. "He hasn't been home all week. The concierge has been watching."

Giovanni was a sweetheart to keep a lookout for me. But that meant Oliver was most likely working around the clock, and that couldn't be good for him.

"At least you can't spit in his dinner."

My boss tapped his head. "I haven't forgotten."

I tried to change the subject, desperate to focus on something other than Oliver. "You said we'd go over the new marketing plan today?"

"*Sì, sì*. Let's go through to my office."

Giovanni's good humour and the rest of the staff treating me normally helped to calm my frayed nerves. Even better, a couple of big tippers dined in the evening, and I came home feeling vaguely positive for the first time all week. Maybe I could do this alone? Or mostly alone, because Imogen had already claimed the position of Fairy Godmother and started picking out baby names.

But I still needed to tell Oliver about the baby. Every time I considered talking to him, my pulse raced out of control, so I had the idea of writing a letter. I could put down everything I needed to say without the risk of getting flustered and forgetting half of it. But on Saturday morning, I went through half a notepad of wadded-up attempts and got no further with the actual words.

I needed to let Oliver know I didn't want anything from him, but if he did want to see the baby, or be involved, I'd encourage that. Because losing my daddy at an early age had taught me one thing—there was no substitute for a real father's love. Chester had proven that over the weekend.

Then on Saturday afternoon came the moment I'd been dreading. A phone call. From Oliver.

I stared at the screen as the phone vibrated on the table, the theme song from *Gone with the Wind* breaking the silence in the apartment. But I didn't answer it. I couldn't. I hadn't got things straight in my own head yet, and what if he said something that hurt me more? Not that he'd do it on purpose, but sometimes he just didn't think. He didn't leave a voicemail either, so at least there wasn't that temptation.

If he had, I'd probably have listened to it over and over, no matter what he said, because I missed the smooth sound of his voice. I missed everything about him.

On Sunday at Il Tramonto, I kept glancing towards the ceiling as if I could see through twenty floors into the apartment above.

"Is Oliver home?" I asked Giovanni.

"I'm not sure. He came back yesterday, but the regular night concierge called in sick, so I don't know if Oliver went out again."

"He did," one of the waitresses chipped in. "But, uh, it's not good news."

My stomach dropped so fast the poor baby must have thought it was on an express elevator.

"What happened?"

She popped through to the break room and rummaged in the stack of newspapers and magazines that lived on the table there, then came back with a copy of *The Richmond Times*.

"I saw this earlier. Sorry, but I guess you should know."

A write-up from last night's charity gala at the Black Diamond Hotel filled the society section, photos of the great and good splashed across each page. I recognised Dan and Ethan looking at each other like they were the only people in the room and caught a fleeting glance of Emmy as she turned away from the camera. Then I saw Oliver. Only he wasn't alone.

A blonde girl stood next to him as he smiled for the camera, her talons grasping his arm and a glass of champagne in each of their hands.

He'd gone on a date?

While I sat on the sofa crying into my pyjamas and trying not to eat another cookie, Oliver had gone on a date?

The caption underneath certainly seemed to think so: *Star lawyer Oliver Rhodes and his date for the evening.*

Giovanni snatched the paper from my hands and threw it onto the table. “The man is even more of a pig than we thought.”

The chef picked it up and glanced at the photo. “I’ll get laxatives to go in his dinner. He won’t know what hit him.”

If I saw him anytime soon, *I’d* hit him. How could he?

I mean, technically he hadn’t done anything wrong. He’d ended things with me before he took another woman out, but it still hurt so, so badly. Even more so because in all the months we’d spent together, he’d never taken me to a fancy dinner like that.

“To think I considered the man a friend,” Giovanni said. “It just goes to show that you can work with someone for years but never truly know them. I always imagined Oliver had more morals than that.”

The waitress put her arm around me. “You poor thing. Is there anything we can do?”

I shook my head.

“I know we shouldn’t drink on duty, but would a glass of wine help?” a second waitress asked.

“No, I can’t have wine.”

She gave me a strange look.

“Uh, I made a pact with my bestie that we’d cut out alcohol for a month, and I don’t want to break it.”

“I think she’d understand.”

Giovanni pushed a chair under my bottom, and I sat down.

"Wine is not the answer," he said. "We should find Stef a hot date. Make Oliver jealous."

"I don't want to go on a date either. Besides, I don't know anyone hotter than Oliver."

The first waitress grinned. "My brother knows a model."

"Please, no dates."

Unless they were with a pint of chocolate ice cream and Marlon Brando.

"Do you want to go home?" Giovanni asked. "We'll manage this evening."

"No, I just want to work. If I let this affect me, I'll never move on."

"You have the right spirit, *tesoro*. We'll help you get through this. All of us."

At least I had friends. What was life without friends?

CHAPTER 42

IMOGEN THREATENED TO scratch Oliver's eyes out when I told her how he'd spent his Saturday night.

"Honestly, the man's an idiot. If that's how he behaves, you're better off without him."

"It still hurts."

She gave me a hug. "Of course it does, sweetie. But that'll fade. One day, you'll meet someone else and Oliver won't matter anymore."

And that day would be never. Chester may have put it bluntly, but he was right. I was damaged goods. And in a few months, I'd have a baby in tow.

No, I'd be doing life alone from now on, and I mumbled as much to Imogen.

"We'll see about that, but right now, we need to get to the hospital. Are you ready?"

I'd worn a simple jersey dress to Java that morning so I wouldn't have to change. Even the little things seemed like far too much effort at the moment.

"As ready as I'll ever be."

The hospital lay a short cab ride away, and Imogen held my hand the whole way there. I appreciated her support—indeed, I couldn't have done this without her—but I couldn't help wishing it were Oliver beside me. People said having a baby was the most exciting time of your life, but all I felt was a sense of dread.

And never more so than when the nurse helped me onto the bed and asked me to put my feet in the stirrups.

"Let's see what's going on here, shall we?"

"What's going to happen?"

"The doctor will give you a pelvic exam and take blood and urine samples. Then, if he thinks it's appropriate, we'll give you an ultrasound. You might get to see your baby today. Exciting, huh?"

I guessed it kind of was, and terrifying at the same time.

Five minutes later, an older man in a white coat came in, smiling, with an easy manner and a gentle voice. I'm sure he did his best to make me feel at ease as he asked me questions and talked me through the process, but it didn't work.

"When was your last period?"

"I've been bleeding every month, and I was on the pill. Honestly, I don't even know how I'm pregnant."

"Oh, that happens more often than you might imagine. Often a small amount of cervical erosion can make you think you're having a period."

"Cervical erosion? Like my cervix is going to wear away?"

"I doubt it's anything to worry about. A little inflammation's common in pregnant women. All those hormonal changes."

He slid two fingers inside me, and I cringed. My embarrassment only grew as he inserted a speculum and peered in with a flashlight.

But he nodded. "Yes, nothing to worry about. Have you experienced any discomfort?"

Not until now, no.

"I've been fine. I didn't even realise I was pregnant, and I, uh, I've been drinking alcohol. Will that have hurt the baby?"

"How much?"

"Maybe a couple of glasses of wine a week? And a shot of whisky last Sunday. I'd had a bad day."

"A drop like that won't have done any damage, but you need to avoid it from now on."

"I will. I definitely will."

Then we got on to my medical history, and I teared up when he asked me about my family. Mom and Dad had been healthy, but thinking of them hurt.

"And the father's family?"

"I don't know much about them."

"It would be helpful if we could find out. Whether there have been any genetic abnormalities, that kind of thing."

"I'm not really on speaking terms with the father right now. We broke up."

Not that we'd been entirely together in the first place.

The doctor patted my hand in a kindly gesture, one that made me ache all the more. "I'm sorry to hear that. But lots of young ladies in your position pass through my doors, and it's perfectly possible to do this alone. Now, shall we take a look at this baby?"

I appreciated his words, even if they felt hollow. "Okay, go on."

The nurse squirted cold gel onto my stomach and pressed on my full bladder, but a few seconds later, I forgot all about the discomfort and watched, fascinated, as a tiny grey dot appeared on the screen.

"About eleven weeks," the doctor said.

Eleven weeks? I'd been carrying a baby for eleven weeks without noticing?

I thought back to one night last month when I'd lain in bed with Oliver. He'd been in a sweet mood as he covered my entire body with soft kisses. Some of those would have gone right over the tiny form growing inside me, and a lump came to my throat as I realised that even for a short time, the baby *had* felt its father's love. Would it ever again?

"Do you know whether it's a boy or a girl?"

The doctor chuckled. "We won't find that out for at least five more weeks. You'll need to come back for another scan at sixteen to twenty weeks, and we should be able to tell you then. Would you like a picture?"

"Yes, please."

Twenty minutes later, I walked out to the waiting room in a daze.

"How'd it go?" Imogen asked.

"There's definitely a baby in there."

She patted my stomach. "We already knew that. But is everything okay?"

I held up a paper bag. "I have vitamins. And my blood pressure's a bit high. The doctor says I need to relax." I couldn't help laughing at that idea.

"You can put your feet up for the rest of the day, and I'll cook dinner." She took my hand. "Let's get you home."

We'd almost made it to the parking lot when a woman's voice behind us called my name.

"Stef? Is that you?"

What were the chances of Dan believing it was my evil twin? I turned to see her and Caleb hurrying towards us, and then she crushed me in a hug. Instinct took over as I arched my back away to protect the baby, and I managed to extricate us both without any damage.

"Hi, how are you?"

And why was she at the damn hospital, of all places?

"I'm fine, but Caleb's picked up an ear infection." He stood by her side watching me, quiet as ever. "Drops should clear it up. Are you okay?"

Dan glanced up at the door we'd just come out of, but thankfully it was a general entrance and didn't give much away.

As usual, Imogen saved me. "Oh, Stef's fine, but I got a UTI and she came to keep me company." She held up my hand with the paper bag. "I've got antibiotics now. Well, we'd better go before I need to pee again."

Dan waved the car keys in her hand. "No problem. I'll give you a ride home, and we can talk on the way."

"We'll be fine in a cab," Imogen said.

"Nonsense, I insist. It's no trouble."

Caleb piped up. "They just left the hospital. They don't want to end up back in it again."

She rolled her eyes. "Kids, eh? I promise to watch the road."

I climbed into the back beside Imogen and made sure I fastened my seat belt securely as Dan started the engine. I'd heard a lot about her driving and none of it was good, but at least we were in a big SUV. That had to count for something safety-wise, right?

Dan pulled up to the exit, looked right and left, then floored it into the path of an oncoming truck. My knuckles turned white as I gripped the door handle. How had I thought this was a good idea?

"So, how are you?" Dan asked. "We've all been worried."

I plastered on a smile and lied. "I'm fine. I mean, these things happen, right?"

"Breakups are never easy on anyone."

I couldn't help myself. I had to ask. "How's Oliver?"

"Oliver's a fucking idiot."

Imogen couldn't help herself either. "Stef saw him in the paper with that girl. What an asshole."

"What girl?"

"At some gala on Saturday night. A blonde."

Dan laughed. "Oh, her. Oliver wasn't with her."

Really? "It sure looked like he was."

"The paparazzi twist everything. She recognised him from the news and came over to flirt, and Oliver made a half-hearted attempt at flirting back. Then Emmy told the girl he had VD, the girl threw a glass of wine over him, and he left alone."

"Emmy did that?"

"She thinks Oliver's being an asshole as well. From the sound of it, you had an awful weekend with your parents, and he only added to the problem."

"He told you about it?"

"Not the details, but we pried the basics out of him. He spent the week moping around Riverley, but after the VD incident he went back home."

"I don't suppose any of this is easy for him either."

"Stop defending him. You're as bad as each other. Everyone knows he's madly in love with you, but he won't admit it, not to us and least of all to himself."

My heart stuttered. "You really think so?"

She reached back to squeeze my hand, but as her other one was tucking hair behind her ear, the car lurched into oncoming traffic. Like a pro, Caleb leaned across and jerked the wheel back again.

"Thanks, sweetie." She grinned at him, and he rolled his eyes in the mirror. That kid would go far. "So, what was I saying? Oh, yeah, about Oliver. He's crazy about you. Hang in there, honey."

I didn't have much choice, did I? What had Emmy said all those months ago? That Oliver would change or he wouldn't, and it was out of my control.

She'd been totally right.

I didn't know whether to feel better or worse as Dan deposited Imogen and me in front of the apartment. Imogen let out a long breath and took a couple of shaky steps.

"How did we survive that ride? It's a miracle. I need a drink." She glanced at my stomach. "Of juice. Let's drink juice."

Chapter 43

"HOW ARE YOU feeling?" Imogen asked as we hung up our aprons the next day.

The shift at Java had only been six hours, but it seemed like twice as long.

"Tired. At least I know why I keep needing to sleep now."

"Let's go home. You can spend the afternoon on the sofa. But I don't suppose you've got a few minutes to help with my business plan first?"

"I'd be happy to. It'll be good to have something to take my mind off...you know. Are you getting any closer to taking the plunge?"

"Every time I think that, something goes wrong. I found a lovely little storefront, and then someone offered more rent than me and I lost it. It's difficult to find something in my price range in the right area."

"It's out there."

"I know, but I'm tired too. Tired of looking, tired of coffee, just tired."

"Maybe we both need that spa day? I'd offer to do your nails, but art wasn't my strong point in high school. I painted a portrait of Marilyn Monroe once, and the teacher thought it was a polar bear."

Imogen poured us both drinks, then we settled onto the sofa and tweaked her cash projections. She was right—finding the perfect location would be key, somewhere with reasonable rent but in a good enough area that the clientele had disposable income.

"I can look on the internet if you like? I've got more spare time than you at the moment."

"Are you sure you don't mind? I need all the help I can get. If this ever takes off and I can afford a store manager, you've got the job."

"I need to work out a plan for my own life once the baby comes. How I'm going to work, where I'm going to live."

Imogen's eyes widened. "Live? What's wrong with here?"

"You didn't sign up for a crying baby when you offered me the room."

"So? I didn't sign up for a new bestie either, but I got one. And if your baby daddy doesn't come to his senses and take you back where you belong, you're staying right here. I'll help with all the stuff." She wrinkled her nose. "Except diapers. I'm not sure about changing diapers."

"I can do that bit. Remember Timmy?" I'd told her the whole story now.

She hooted with laughter. "Who'd have thought it? Catering to weird fetishes may have given you a head start in life after all. Let's sit down and write you a business plan too. We can call it Yummy Mummy, Inc."

"Yummy Mummy? You've been watching too many British TV shows. And besides, I don't feel yummy. Right now I feel more scummy."

"In six months, that'll all have changed. You'll see."

She laid a blank sheet of paper in front of me, and over the next hour, we wrote a list. It ran longer than I thought—seven sides—but getting everything out of my head helped. And with six months to prepare for the birth, I had time to hunt down secondhand furniture and clothes and learn everything I could about bringing up a child.

Imogen was right. Between us, we could do this, not that I had much of a choice.

Chapter 44

IMOGEN WENT TO view a possible location for her nail bar the next day after our shift at Java. I'd offered to go with her, but she said she didn't want me getting more tired than I already was.

"I'll do the first visits myself. Then if it's good, you can come with me."

"I am..." I covered my mouth in a yawn. "Kinda exhausted."

She patted my barely existent bump. "Sleep. You need it."

I dragged my heels as I walked home, thinking. Maybe I could ask Imogen to paint the crib when I bought it? The baby could do with some colour in its life. But which colour? Would it be a boy or a girl? I was torn as to which one I preferred. A girl would mean dressing up and sparkles, but a mini Oliver would be so darn cute.

I choked at the thought, because I wanted grown-up Oliver too, and I couldn't push the idea out of my mind. And I was so busy wondering whether I could get Oliver 2.0 a tiny suit and tie, I didn't notice Oliver 1.0 sitting in the hallway until I tripped over his feet.

Heck! I came dangerously close to falling, but I slammed a hand onto the wall to save myself. Pain shot along my arm and brought tears to my eyes.

Oliver scrambled to his feet and steadied me. "Fuck! Steffie, are you okay?"

"That's not a good question to ask me right now."

He stepped sideways, and the dim light from the overhead bulb illuminated his face. I didn't need to ask how he was doing. He'd aged ten years in two weeks. Lines criss-crossed his forehead, he hadn't shaved for days, and his hair was crying out for a cut.

In fact, he probably looked something like me—apart from the beard, obviously.

"I know."

"Then why ask it?"

"I mean, I *know*. About the baby."

My knees buckled. Oliver lowered me to the floor, then sank down at my side.

"How? How do you know?"

"Dan told me."

"But I didn't tell Dan."

"Dan's an investigator. Whatever you said to her yesterday, she didn't believe you, so when she got home, she had Mack hack into the hospital database."

"That's... That's..."

Unethical. Invasive. Rude.

Oliver held up his hands. "Look, I don't condone it, but it happened and she told me."

"I'm so sorry." Of all the ways for him to find out, this was the worst. "I wanted to tell you, but I didn't know how. Honestly, I only just found out myself. It's okay, though. Me and Imogen have worked everything out and we're gonna manage. You don't need to be involved at all. Unless you want to be. I mean, if you do, then that's great, but I'd never expect anything from you, because it's not like this was planned and..."

Oliver laid a finger against my lips. "Steffie, please. Stop talking."

"I get it. You're freaked out. I understand how you feel."

He leaned his head back against the wall. "Yesterday I was freaked out. I didn't eat and I didn't sleep. Today I went out and bought an SUV with a car seat."

I stared at him. "You mean you want to help with the baby?"

"I want to be a father." He closed his eyes. "Again. I want to be a father again. I had a daughter."

I took one of his hands in both of mine. "I know."

His eyes popped open. "You do? How?"

"Emmy told me. And I desperately didn't want to be like Kelly. I didn't want you to feel trapped."

"You're nothing like Kelly. And you've never made me feel trapped. But I've been stupid. Stupid for thinking I can live without you when I can't."

"You want to see me again?"

He pulled me onto his lap, and I forgot about the pain in my arm. Forgot everything except the man in front of me. "I want to do more than see you. I want to hear you, touch you, taste you." He pressed his lips to mine. "Princess, I love you."

Tears flooded my cheeks, but this time they were happy ones. "I love you too. I have for a long time." I burrowed against him, seeking his strength. "But I'm so scared. I don't know how to be a mom."

Oliver stroked my hair, and I wished I'd had the energy to wash it that morning. "You'll make a great mom." He took a deep breath then slowly exhaled. "I know how to be a father, but I don't know how to be a husband."

I stared up at him, and he wiped away my tears with his thumb. Did he just say "husband"? My heart stopped beating, I swear, and a little bud of guilt began to blossom in my chest. Was he only saying this because of the baby?

"After I bought the car, I went to the jewellers..." He fumbled in his pants pocket and held up a ring. "And I bought this. Fuck it. I don't know how to do this."

"Oliver, do you want me to wear the ring?"

He nodded.

"And marry you?"

He nodded again.

"Are you doing this just because I'm pregnant? Because we can still be together without the piece of paper."

"You don't want to be my wife?"

Oh hell, now he looked devastated.

"Of course I do. More than anything..." I waved my hand in front of my face because I couldn't speak properly anymore.

"Princess, I want you to have my name, my baby, and the other side of my bed. I want to give you the world, but I'll start with a ring."

"Then put it on me."

He grabbed my hand and slid the slim band over my knuckles. White gold? Platinum? It didn't matter. It could have been tinfoil and I'd still have been his. But even so, there was no mistaking the diamond sparkling in the middle.

For five minutes, ten, we sat on the grubby concrete floor in the hallway, holding each other. Nothing else mattered. I had the only man I'd ever truly wanted, and in six months I'd have his baby as well.

Then a screech pierced the air. "You guys! Are you back together?" Imogen barrelled down the hallway towards us. "Or do I need to kick him where it hurts?"

Oliver helped me to my feet and settled his hand over my belly. "We're together."

"Thank goodness for that. So, when's the wedding?"

Oliver and I looked at each other. "Uh, we haven't decided on that," I said.

"I was kidding!" She caught sight of the sparkler and squealed again. "You mean you're really getting married?"

Oliver shrugged—a careless gesture, but I'd come to understand he did it when he was nervous as well.

"We are."

She pointed at her chest. "You're looking at your number one bridesmaid right here. How about dark pink for the dresses? That always looks classy. Church or civil ceremony? Are you going with a theme?"

"At the moment, I'm thinking a quickie in Vegas looks like a good plan," Oliver muttered.

Imogen totally ignored him. "I'll start planning the bachelorette party right away. I'm excellent at these things. And can you do me a favour and make sure at least one of the groomsmen is single?"

"Have you met Bradley yet?" Oliver asked.

"No. Who's Bradley?"

"He likes parties too. I have a feeling you'll be best friends."

"Is he single?"

"No, and he's gay, but don't let that stop you."

"Come in and give me his number. I'll make coffee, and we can start planning this shindig."

Oliver picked me up and walked off along the landing, Imogen's cries trailing behind him.

"Hey! Where are you going?"

He kissed me on the nose. "I'm taking my beautiful wife-to-be home where she belongs." He dropped his voice. "Then I'm going to make love to her for the rest of the afternoon. The evening too. Anything else can wait until tomorrow."

Bridget took one look at us when we walked in the door to Oliver's apartment and took off her apron. "You won't be needing me again today." She grasped my hand on her way out and held it up so she could see the ring better. "Congratulations, dear. I'm glad he's finally seen the light."

The instant the door closed behind her, Oliver's lips found mine, and when he pushed me back against the kitchen island, he was already hard. "I need you, princess. Here or the bedroom. Your choice."

"I choose...both."

He grinned, and the darkness that shrouded him earlier had disappeared. "Good answer, Mrs. Almost-Rhodes."

He lifted me onto the cool marble counter and inched my dress up my thighs. But he didn't stop there. He raised it to my breasts and gazed at my stomach. "Our baby's in there." His voice held the awe I felt.

"For the next six months."

"You're three months along?"

"Eleven weeks. I can't believe I didn't notice."

"It doesn't matter. Six months is plenty of time to

set up the nursery, and we already have Bridget. But we need to go to antenatal classes and find you the best obstetrician."

We. I loved the sound of that. This having-a-baby thing had just gotten a whole lot easier. And I'd have a family again, albeit a small one. That was all I needed.

Well, not quite all. The pulse between my thighs reminded me of an altogether more urgent requirement.

"Mr. Rhodes, will you stop talking? I need your cock inside me. Now."

"Nothing would give me greater pleasure, princess."

EPILOGUE

"JUST ONE LAST finishing touch."

Bradley carried the vase of orchids past the waiting area and set it on the corner of the reception desk.

"There, it's perfect."

And it was. From the white-and-silver nail stations and the funky lighting to the quiet music and the private treatment room at the rear, Imogen's new nail bar, Nailed It, was everything we'd imagined. Better still, the schedule was full for the next month. Imogen and Lisa, the new nail technician Dan had poached from somewhere, would be rushed off their feet. Not me, though. Oliver had insisted I have a very comfortable chair to go with my little desk in the back office, and with Il Tramonto right next door, I wouldn't go hungry either.

In fact, the whole venture was a scheme cooked up by Giovanni and Oliver, assisted by Bradley and revealed in his typically over-the-top style.

"I've got a surprise for you," Oliver had told me over breakfast one morning last month.

"Nothing's ever going to beat the Audi."

He'd bought it for me the week before, a top-of-the-range bright-red SUV with leather upholstery and every possible option. He'd screwed me on the hood too, my legs wrapped around his waist as he explained in detail why having stiff suspension was so important.

"You'll need to reserve judgement on that."

He'd blindfolded me then, and I thought it was part of some kinky sex game until the elevator stopped in the lobby and Bradley threw confetti all over us.

"What the..." I tore the blindfold off.

"You said you and Imogen needed a retail unit."

"But... But..."

"When I bought the building, this place was a jewellery store, but the tenant retired a few months later. Since it was only small, I never wanted the hassle of renting it out again, so we just put a false wall over the front and used it for storage. Giovanni thought it might work as a nail salon."

Bradley grabbed my hand and dragged me inside. "We'll need to rewire and totally refurbish, but that shouldn't take long. I've got catalogues and paint samples, and a rep from one of the big salon supply companies is meeting us here tomorrow afternoon."

Imogen had been equally stunned when I broke the news to her, and I didn't even get jealous when she threw her arms around Oliver and kissed him on the lips.

"Thank you, thank you!" She danced around and did a little wiggle, then paused. "Uh, how much is the rent?"

Oliver shrugged. "I don't care about the rent. Just make sure Steffie takes it easy."

Imogen insisted she'd start paying Oliver when the business made a profit, and I promised to take breaks whenever I got tired. I'd help Imogen with paperwork in the mornings and carry on giving Giovanni a hand with marketing a couple of days a week.

Not quite the career I'd planned for, but over the past few months my goals had changed, and now I couldn't think of a better way to spend my weekdays.

The evenings, of course, belonged to Oliver.

Two weeks after the salon's official opening, I curled up on the sofa with Oliver, a smoothie that looked far better than it tasted, and a copy of *The Richmond Times*. Oliver had made the front page again.

"It's over," I murmured. "It's finally over."

Oliver rested his hand on my six-month baby bump and nuzzled my neck.

"No, it's only just beginning."

The former front-runner for the position of Commonwealth Attorney, Jay Skinner, today found out what it was like to be on the other side of the dock when he was sentenced to life in prison for the murder of public defender Lyle Rogers, plus the attempted murders of Ethan "the Ghost" White and an unidentified woman.

Skinner was transferred last night to notorious supermax prison Redding's Gap, where he will serve his sentence with no possibility of parole.

In a bizarre twist, the State Attorney General banned anybody from the Commonwealth Attorney's office from prosecuting in order to avoid possible leniency, and defence star Oliver Rhodes switched sides to fulfil the brief.

"It was a victory for justice," Mr. Rhodes said outside court today. When asked if he would be

throwing his hat into the ring for the top job, Mr. Rhodes replied, "No. I prefer to be able to pick and choose my cases. I'll only fight for those people I believe in."

We won't be seeing Mr. Rhodes in court for a few months, however. He'll be taking a well-deserved break with his family while he celebrates his latest win.

"Hey, did you feel her move?" Oliver asked.

"Yup." Every damn minute, it seemed like. Our little girl was a kicker, and I still had three more months to get through. "Perhaps we should sign her up for soccer lessons."

"Just don't tell Bradley—he'll arrive with a set of goalposts for the nursery."

We hadn't even told him we were having a girl, because neither of us wanted to wake up the next morning to an entirely pink apartment. Oliver had gone quiet after we found out the sex, and I'd worried he was still grieving for his lost daughter, but a day later, he asked if I'd mind having a picture of Darcy on the wall. Of course I didn't. She'd been a huge part of his life, and I wanted him to remember her even as he moved on. She'd been so damn cute—dark hair and chubby cheeks and Oliver's brown eyes.

Our child would have a lot to live up to.

"My lips are sealed," I said.

"Not later they won't be."

He was totally right. Oliver was always right, but I'd given up being annoyed by that.

"And now that your case is over, we can stay in bed all day tomorrow."

He gave me a cunning grin. “True. But we also need to make some decisions. Where do you want to go on vacation? And when do you want to get married?”

Oliver had left the wedding plans up to me, and I’d been agonising for weeks. Did I want a quick wedding before the baby came or something fancy afterwards? Summer or winter? Chapel, hotel, beach, garden, museum, boat? Imogen and Bradley wanted the party of the century, but I just wanted Oliver.

“I have no idea. Really. My head’s so full of nail designs and Il Tramonto’s new menu right now.”

“What do you think of Florida for a short break?”

“Florida?”

“Ethan’s playing a live gig there in two weeks.”

“His first since he got arrested?”

“Yes, and it’s sold out. He and Dan have rented a villa on the beach, and they’re taking Caleb to Disney World afterwards. Dan asked if we wanted to join them for a few days.”

A chance to laze in the sun with Oliver wearing something other than a suit?

“I’d love that.”

“And the wedding?”

“I’m thinking something small. Just a handful of friends.”

“What about your family?”

Oliver had already said he didn’t want to invite any of his relatives, and from the rare comments he made about his childhood, I couldn’t blame him. But my family? Mason had taken to calling every couple of days, from Reggie’s phone to start with since Chester had stayed furious for weeks. But three days ago, Mom had phoned me and apologised for their behaviour even though I didn't think my stepfather was at all sorry. The conversation had been stilted, awkward, but it was a start, and she'd said she looked forward to meeting her grandchild.

"I'll invite them, but I'm not sure if they'll come. We've got a lot of bridges to mend."

"Chester's the one who broke them, not you."

"I know, but... I miss my mom."

"Then we'll postpone the wedding until you two are in a good place."

"You don't mind?"

"Princess, as long as I've got you in my bed every night, I'm a happy man." He paused for a moment. "It's what I wished for, you know."

"Wished for?"

"On my birthday when I blew out those stupid candles Bradley bought. I wished that I wouldn't go through the rest of my life alone. And then I nearly screwed it up."

"You won't get rid of me that easily, Mr. Almost-Amor."

"Damn right, or I'll have to get those scarves out again."

We thought we'd gotten away with it. Or rather, without it—a celebration after the second trial, I mean. Bradley went quiet for almost a week, but then Dan emailed a photo of a giant dartboard with a life-sized cutout of Jay Skinner pinned to it.

Dan: Party at Riverley tonight. 7 p.m. and we've got non-alcoholic cocktails. Don't be late.

Oliver read over my shoulder. "Today would be a good day to elope to Europe."

"We can't. Not when they've gone to all that trouble."

Oliver grimaced. "Two hours, then I'm faking an emergency at work. An urgent debriefing. You can help with that."

"Sure. Perhaps we could do it on the balcony off the library?"

He hugged me close and kissed my hair. Hair I no longer felt the need to fidget with. Being with Oliver left me in a perpetual state of bliss, and besides, he found other uses for my mouth and hands.

"Two hours, Mrs. Almost-Rhodes."

At Riverley, it turned out Bridget had been helping with the cocktails. The moment we stepped through the door, she walked over with a tray and a huge smile.

"Stefanie! Lovely to see you. I'd hug you if it weren't for the tray. And your bump. Here, have a drink. We're calling this one Skinner's Surprise."

Heaven help us—she'd caught Bradley-itis. I took a glass filled with ice and mint sprigs and some kind of orange liquid.

"What's in it?"

"Grapefruit, lemon juice, sugar syrup, soda water, carrot, and just a pinch of chilli powder."

Oliver snorted and quickly turned it into a cough, but Bridget didn't let him off lightly.

"You should try it too. It's not fair on Stefanie to be the only one not drinking."

"Yes, Oliver. You definitely need to try this."

He took a sip and tried not to grimace as his eyes watered. "It's certainly got a kick to it."

I was trying to think of a tactful way to pour the concoction into the nearest plant pot when Emmy rolled up. Like, literally, on a pair of roller skates.

"What's with the wheels?" Oliver asked.

"We've got a roller derby rink set up out back. The Toxic Tigers versus Satan's Sweethearts. Bradley named the teams, by the way, not me."

"This I've got to see," Oliver muttered.

"You'll have to fight the other men for a front-row seat. But I need to borrow Stef for a few minutes first. Do you mind?"

She didn't wait for an answer, just waved an arm towards a corridor off the hallway. I followed. Nobody questioned Emmy.

In the music room, she leaned over and sniffed my glass. "Is that part of a drinking game? Truth or dare?"

"Uh, I was hoping to find a sink to pour it down."

She grabbed the glass and tossed the contents out of the window. "There. Sorted."

Those poor flowers. "What do you want to speak to me about?"

"I need a favour."

"Okay."

There wasn't much else I could say. Firstly, Emmy and her friends had done so many favours for me I'd spend the rest of my life repaying them, and secondly, she still scared me.

"I've got a friend coming to stay soon. Roxy. She's been at school in London since last September, but she's just finished her medical degree, and she's coming to the US for a short break. Or it might turn into a longer break. She doesn't actually know that last part yet, so if you could keep it quiet, I'd be grateful."

Good grief. "How does that involve me? Does she need someone to show her around?"

"More than that; she needs a friend. She used to be in the same line of work as you, except not voluntarily."

"You mean…" I couldn't even say the words.

"Roxy was trafficked. We're looking after her, but she's still painfully shy, and she needs to learn how to have fun. Will you help?"

"Of course. When's she arriving?"

"Next week. And…" Emmy fell silent.

"What?"

"A little social engineering may be required."

"Huh?"

"There's a guy she likes. He likes her too, except he's too dumb to do anything about it."

The words "like Oliver" hung in the air between us. She didn't need to say them.

"Sure, I can help with that too."

Emmy grinned, a cross between happy and cunning. Oh, sugar honey iced tea, what had I gotten myself into?

"Perfect," she said. "Enjoy the party. I've left the balcony doors unlocked for you."

WHAT'S NEXT?

Have you tried my Blackwood Security series? You can read the beginning of Stefanie's story in book nine, White Hot.

White Hot

When private investigator Daniela di Grassi is given a new case, the evidence is so compelling that even her client himself thinks he did it. Ethan White was one of the world's top music producers, at least until last week, when his spectacular fall from grace began with the discovery of a mutilated college student in his bed.

A dead girl nobody cares about, cops with one agenda, and a prosecutor with another—nothing about this case is simple. And when Dan digs deeper into the mystery, the conflicting clues aren't the only thing she finds intriguing. Ethan's got his own secrets too.

As the worlds of black and white collide, who will come out on top?

White Hot is the ninth book in the Blackwood Security series but can be read as a standalone - no cliffhanger!

Find out more here: www.elise-noble.com/white

The next story in the Blackwood Elements series will be Platinum, Roxy and Gideon's story.

Platinum

After a run-in with her new boss costs junior doctor Roksana Bartosz her job, her friend Sofia has the perfect solution—a short break in Virginia to take her mind off the problem. Little does she know that Sofia and Emmy Black are intent on playing matchmaker in the craziest way possible.

Gideon Renard avoids relationships, especially with girls as fragile as Roxy. Taking a new job in Washington, DC seems like the perfect way to put space between them. But his friends have other ideas, and in between hunting down three missing assassins, resisting the temptation to strangle his ex, and fighting the demons of his past, he has a big decision to make. Can he walk away from Roxy for the second time?

Find out more here: www.elise-noble.com/platinum

If you enjoyed Rhodium, please consider leaving a review.

For an author, every review is incredibly important. Not only do they make us feel warm and fuzzy inside, readers consider them when making their decision whether or not to buy a book. Even a line saying you enjoyed the book or what your favourite part was helps a lot.

Want to stalk me?

For updates on my new releases, giveaways, and other random stuff, you can sign up for my newsletter on my website:
www.elise-noble.com

Facebook:
www.facebook.com/EliseNobleAuthor

Twitter: @EliseANoble

Instagram: @elise_noble

I also have a group on Facebook for my fans to hang out. They love the characters from my Blackwood and Trouble books almost as much as I do, and they're the first to find out about my new stories as well as throwing in their own ideas that sometimes make it into print!

And if you'd like to read my books for FREE, you can also find details of how to join my review team.

Would you like to join Team Blackwood?

www.elise-noble.com/team-blackwood

End of Book Stuff

Oh, Oliver, you filthy git... Emmy would never have a boring lawyer, would she? Oliver first appeared in Forever Black, defending Emmy from accusations of murdering her husband, and back then, I never realised what a big part he'd play in the Blackwood story. Or how bad he would be.

But after White Hot, I decided Stefanie and Oliver both deserved a second chance at love, and it also gave me the opportunity to rinse my brain out and stuff all the grubby scenes festering in my head into one story. And now I'm a bit *hides face* because he turned out dirtier than I ever expected. I've banned my mum from reading the book.

As always, huge thanks to my beta reading team—Renata, Harka, Jeff, Helen, Lina, Musi, Quenby, Stacia, David, Jessica, and Nikita. Thanks to Abi for such a pretty cover (I love the colours in this one!), thanks to Amanda and Nikki for editing, and thanks to John for proof reading. You guys rock!

Other books by Elise Noble

The Blackwood Security Series

Pitch Black
Into the Black
Forever Black
Gold Rush
Gray is my Heart
Neon (novella)
Out of the Blue
Ultraviolet
Red Alert
White Hot
The Scarlet Affair (2018)
Quicksilver (TBA)

The Blackwood Elements Series

Oxygen
Lithium
Carbon
Rhodium
Platinum (TBA)
Nickel (TBA)

The Blackwood UK Series

Joker in the Pack
Cherry on Top (novella)

Roses are Dead
Shallow Graves (2018)
Indigo Rain (TBA)

The Electi Series
Cursed (2018)
Spooked (2018)
Possessed (TBA)

The Trouble Series
Trouble in Paradise
Nothing but Trouble
24 Hours of Trouble

Standalone
Life
For the Love of Animals (A Blackwood Prequel) (2018)
A Very Happy Christmas
Twisted

Printed in Great Britain
by Amazon

56857269R00218